THE
AIR
RAID
KILLER

THE
AIR
RAID
KILLER

THE FIRST CASE OF MAX HELLER, DRESDEN DETECTIVE

FRANK GOLDAMMER

TRANSLATED BY STEVE ANDERSON

Text copyright © 2016 by Frank Goldammer & dtv Verlagsgesellschaft mbH & Co. KG, Munich
Translation copyright © 2018 by Steve Anderson

Previously published as *Der Angstmann* by dtv Verlagsgesellschaft mbH & Co. KG, Munich in Germany in 2016. Translated from German by Steve Anderson. First published in English by AmazonCrossing in 2018.

Published by AmazonCrossing, Seattle

www.apub.com

Amazon, the Amazon logo, and AmazonCrossing are trademarks of Amazon.com, Inc., or its affiliates.

ISBN-13: 9781503900578 (hardcover)
ISBN-10: 1503900576 (hardcover)
ISBN-13: 9781503900653 (paperback)
ISBN-10: 1503900657 (paperback)

Cover design by Damon Freeman

Printed in the United States of America

First edition

THE
AIR
RAID
KILLER

TRANSLATOR'S NOTE

As the winter of 1944–45 set in, the German city of Dresden suffered mounting stress and strain. Masses of desperate refugees from the east overwhelmed local authorities, rations grew scarcer, and the mighty and vengeful Soviet Red Army advanced ever closer. As 1945 began, many still clung to the hope that the grand old city would be spared the worst. After all, Dresden was a baroque and rococo wonder with a long cultural and artistic history representing all that had once been admired in Germany. The city remained largely undefended, its military significance questionable. Many air raid warnings had sounded, to be sure, yet no serious Allied bombings had ever come.

That would all change in February, when over 1,200 British and American bombers dropped more than 3,900 tons of high explosives and incendiary bombs on the city, unleashing a vicious and unrelenting firestorm that obliterated much of the historic city center and killed an estimated 22,000 to 25,000 men, women, and children in macabre fashion over four raids between February 13 and 15.

In the weeks leading up to this fateful and tragic event, as February grew nearer and the despairing people huddled in cellar shelters at night when the air raid warnings sounded, a deranged evildoer could have wreaked havoc on those darkened and abandoned streets of Dresden's blacked-out neighborhoods. Such an ominous specter would be fueled by increasingly frantic rumors, fears, and delusions. So would arise the one they called the "Fright Man" . . .

PART ONE

November 30, 1944: Afternoon

Max Heller had trouble pulling himself up. His six-foot frame barely fit in the BMW sidecar, but a military motorcycle was the only vehicle available. He winced as he freed his right leg and planted both feet on the cobblestones. A freezing drizzle had set in on the ride over, and he wiped his face, then shook his head in disapproval. Instead of driving him all the way up to the building, Strampe had dropped him off at the gate. Heller took this as a show of contempt. The young SS sergeant clearly didn't like him.

Heller stood facing the Dresden Rowing Club building. He turned up the collar of his long overcoat and buried his fists deep in the pockets. And there he stood. The moisture collected in his short, gradually graying hair since he'd forgotten his leather flat cap, and he drew his shoulders up against the cold. He wasn't sure where he was supposed to go.

The Elbe River was a dreary sight, all gray and faded on this last afternoon of November. A few trees stood along the bank, leafless and darkened from the damp. Upstream, Heller could see the barrels of dummy flak guns. The clouds hung low, shrouding the slopes of the opposite bank in a foggy haze. Soon it would be dark. He sniffled. Then a figure emerged from the shadowy backdrop of damp plaster walls.

"Herr Detective Inspector?" asked the uniformed cop, walking toward Heller. He thrust his right arm into the air. "Heil Hitler!"

Heller was forced to wrench his hand from his pocket. He returned the salute without a word.

The cop stepped to the side and bowed, letting Heller go first. "It's in the old boathouse," he said.

It was less than fifty yards away, yet the cold had crept into Heller's bones, and he struggled on his right foot. He took every step with caution, feeling the cop growing impatient.

Once at the boathouse, Heller halted to let the cop go first.

The cop didn't move. "You go ahead. She's in the far back of the workshop."

Heller stared at the man, then entered the structure. It was little more than a shed attached to the large garage where the boats were kept along with long oars and other equipment. He smelled brackish water, oil, and worn metal.

"Right through there," the cop told him.

"You could just go first," Heller said, annoyed. There was a light on, though the bulb was weak and dim. It was depressing, like everything these days.

"No one else here?" Heller asked. "No photographer?"

"No one yet, Herr Detective Inspector, but we requested the works."

Heller nodded. All they could do was try. "Was anyone at the scene? Anyone touch the body?"

"No, Herr—" The cop ran into Heller, who'd stopped abruptly.

The door to the workshop was wide open, and nothing could've prepared Heller for what he saw in there.

"Who found her?" Heller asked, his voice straining.

"Two boys. We have them over in the clubhouse."

"So no one's entered the room?" Heller made himself stop staring at the corpse and scanned the floor for clues. Something must have been left behind among all this dust and oil. The blood had congealed. A pool of it had formed rifts, like a dried-up mud puddle.

"I'll need light in here, plenty of it, and the photographer."

"We'd have to black out the windows."

"Then get it done."

The cop nodded and disappeared. Heller studied the woman. She was sitting, her wrists bound to the workbench with strong rope, her arms spread wide as if nailed to a cross. Her blouse and undershirt had been torn open, her skirt as well. A length of the same rope was used to bind her legs. Her lower areas were fully exposed, her underwear and long stockings pulled down to her ankles. Her head hung forward, down to her chest, and Heller could only see the back of her neck. He wiped at his face again.

The rain was coming down harder, hammering the tin roof and gurgling down the gutters and downspouts. Heller crouched to see if the woman was gagged. He couldn't tell, not with the room so dim, and he couldn't risk touching the light switch. He left her face in the dark.

Soon he heard engine noises and male voices. He straightened up and stuffed his hands in his overcoat pockets. Oldenbusch from forensics came in, a wooden tripod under one arm and a large brown case in the opposite hand. No one followed him, so they spared themselves the Hitler salute.

"Give it here, Werner." Heller went to grab the case, but Oldenbusch shook his head. He was thirty years old, short and sturdy and somewhat pudgy.

"You do your thing, Max, I do mine," he said. "A horrible sight—I already heard."

Heller nodded. "Such suffering."

"Suffering all over these days."

Heller didn't comment. It was best to avoid conversations like this.

"Try and capture every detail. All the clothing. But first, scan the floor for any clues. I think I saw a footprint. I'm guessing there might be fingerprints on the workbench, on the light switch as well. Might be someone's hair on her clothes. Where'd that rope come from? And I'm not sure, but is that a sickle over there?" Heller pointed to a dark crescent underneath the workbench.

Oldenbusch gave him a reassuring nod. "Got it. I know what to do. I need to get a spotlight. Flashes are scarce too. Everything's scarce. At first, Klepp couldn't even understand why I needed to be here."

Heller gave the forensics man a wary look. "Did he say why?"

Oldenbusch grunted, which he seemed to think said it all. He headed back outside. Heller followed him.

"This'll take me a while," Oldenbusch said. "Remember Friedrich, that young new forensics man? He also got called up last week."

Heller hadn't even met him. "I'm going to go talk to these boys. If you need me, I'll be over in the clubhouse," he said, and pointed his chin toward the building.

The two boys sat at a table, looking well behaved. They hadn't touched their tea. Both were wearing overcoats, under which Heller could make out collar insignia for the Hitler Youth.

As he approached, the boys leaped up and thrust their arms out. "Heil Hitler!"

They couldn't be more than twelve and had never known any other way. He returned the Hitler salute properly this time. He was always careful with children—they were often the most eager informers.

"Sit down," Heller said. He sat with them. "What were you two doing in that boathouse?"

"Playing, Herr Chief Inspector," they said without missing a beat.

"Your names?"

"Merker, Gustav."

"Trautmann, Alwin."

"You two broke in."

"We didn't, Herr Chief Inspector! The door was open."

Heller looked at the adjoining table. There lay two wooden dummy rifles.

"It's Detective Inspector, by the way. Do your parents know where you are?"

Both shook their heads.

"Tell me what you were doing and what you saw. Leave nothing out. You first, Gustav." Heller noticed movement out the window. Klepp's car was pulling into the courtyard.

"We were playing. We come here a lot. We live over on Gneisi—on Gneisenaustrasse. The door was open a crack, so we went in because it was cold and there could be a spy hiding in there. We saw the body soon after." This didn't seem to bother Gustav, but Alwin winced.

"Did you see anyone running away? Hear screaming?" This part was more routine than anything. The woman had been dead for hours when they found her.

"No one was there."

"Did you touch anything? The door? The light switch? The body?"

Gustav and Alwin shook their heads. "No, Herr Detective, not a thing!"

"Then how did you open the door?"

"I pushed it open with my weapon," Gustav said.

Heller nodded. "All right. You two go on home, and take the quickest way. You're not lying about your names, are you? You know that means prison."

Both furiously shook their heads.

"Good. Then go!"

Gustav stood up. But Alwin didn't move. "It was the Fright Man, wasn't it?" he said.

Heller looked up. "The Fright Man?"

"Mother says the Fright Man roams the streets."

"Tell me about him."

"He captures little kids!" Alwin was dead serious, his chin quivering. Heller stood. "Look. Go home. There's enough fright to go around as it is—no need to bring the bogeyman into it."

"You think he'll go after us now, because we found that woman?"

Heller grabbed Alwin by the shoulder. "Go back to your mother. If this really was the Fright Man, he's got far more to worry about than a couple of boys like you."

"Fright Man," Heller muttered under his breath as he crossed the courtyard back to the crime scene. What was he supposed to make of that? No one was the same during wartime. But who would tie up a woman and do such awful things to her without bothering to conceal the crime? The killer could've easily tossed the body into the river, then hosed off the floor. There was even a sink and hose in the boathouse.

SS Obersturmbannführer Rudolf Klepp came up to Heller just as he was heading back into the boathouse. The man was nearly as tall as Heller but weighed a good deal more and was a few years younger. He was Heller's new superior, but he'd never even been a policeman, having trained to be a butcher before his career in the SS.

"What a mess," Klepp said. Heller didn't reply. Men with SS skull badges on their caps should be able to stand a sight like this. "I'm going back to headquarters. Keep tidying things up here. Not much worth keeping, I'm guessing."

Heller felt the rain soaking into his hair and the shoulders of his overcoat, running down the back of his neck. He hadn't had to deal with Klepp much until now. Klepp was with the Waffen-SS—the SS's own armed forces—and had been transferred home from Poland. His position with the Dresden Police was likely a reward. There had been certain rumors about things that happened in Poland. Heller wasn't sure how much of them to believe, especially with a war on.

"I'd like to have an autopsy done on the body," he told Klepp.

Klepp waved a hand. "You do what you have to. A final report by tomorrow should work." He nodded goodbye and rushed over to his car. His driver, who'd been standing still in the rain, flung the door open.

"A final report?" Heller asked, but the driver had already shut the door.

Heller watched the car drive away, then went back into the boathouse.

Oldenbusch looked like he'd been waiting for him. "Come on in." He pointed to a broom against the wall near Heller. "The killer must have swept the floor. I haven't been able to detect a single footprint."

Heller studied the broomstick. Fine streaks of pale dust had settled on it. He reached for it, but Oldenbusch cleared his throat.

"It still needs to be checked for fingerprints," Oldenbusch said, and got right to the point, just as he'd done for years now. "The killer forced his way in—through that metal door over there that leads out to the Elbe. Simply pried it open. No sign of burglar's tools. The rain's already washed away any clues outside. As for the victim, no papers, nothing, not on the clothes either. She's not wearing a star, looks Aryan. Klepp thinks"—Oldenbusch glanced up with a start, making sure Klepp was no longer present—"he thinks she's Silesian German, but for me the clothing doesn't fit someone from southwestern Poland."

Heller pointed to the dead woman's feet. "Those are hospital stockings."

Oldenbusch pursed his lips. "From Gerhard Wagner Hospital?"

"It is in the area."

"The sickle is clean, by the way. The murder weapon must have been different—a really sharp knife, from the looks of it. I've taken dozens of photos, and I'll get them developed today."

"Klepp's talking about a final report already."

Oldenbusch gave Heller a sympathetic glance. "He told me it was a random act, committed by someone passing through."

Heller stared at Oldenbusch for a few seconds, then said, "Let's have her taken over to the medical examiner."

Oldenbusch shook his head. "They're all at the front. Dr. Kassner got his marching orders last week."

Heller snorted. Not even those once declared "indispensable to the home front" were exempt anymore, apparently. At some point, they'd even send *him* to the front.

"It can't continue like this," Heller said. "It's all going down the drain." He immediately regretted his emotional outburst. "No killer just passing through would bother covering up his tracks so thoroughly. He must've washed up somehow—no one can carry out a crime like this without getting blood on himself. You're telling me he simply rushed out the door wearing the same clothes?"

Oldenbusch frowned. "It would be easy enough to throw on an overcoat. Or he could've washed off in that sink. No fingerprints there, though."

"All I mean is, he knew what he was doing—had it all planned out. The location, the crime, his exit."

"Yet he just leaves the body."

Heller drew a breath between clenched teeth. This part was really bothering him.

"You carry on here," he said. "I'll go find out where we can take her."

November 30, 1944: Evening

Heller was completely soaked from his walk to Gerhard Wagner Hospital. Once inside the doctor's waiting room, he removed his overcoat to dry it out on the radiator. It had been tough for him to track down any kind of specialist. The hospital was overcrowded, the staff overworked. Severe illnesses were increasing, wounded men from the front came in daily, undernourished refugees had to be treated, and a plague of lice was going around. Eventually Heller was shown into the doctor's office and left to wait for nearly an hour. It was now dark outside. He pushed up the sleeve of his jacket, checked his watch again. Then the door opened.

Heller stood yet the doctor strode right by him to his chair, pulled his white coat tight, sat down, and with a curt gesture instructed Heller to sit back down. Dr. Alfred Schorrer leaned back in his chair. He was in his late forties like Heller, maybe a little older. His hair was clipped short, military-style. His mustache was trimmed down to little more than a silvery veil. His eyes were gray, flashing bright and sharp.

"You're correct in your assumption, unfortunately. It was indeed one of our nurses. Klara Bellmann. She hadn't been here long. Maybe three months. She was working in the women's clinic." Dr. Schorrer propped his elbows on the armrests of his chair and placed his fingertips together. "I'm afraid she must have endured terrible suffering before the Lord took mercy on her. None of her wounds appear to have been fatal. Her heart is unscathed. There is a stab to the lungs, but usually this only results in the particular lung filling with blood. A very slow death by asphyxiation. Happens often enough at the front. You fought on the front lines?"

Heller cleared his throat. "Yes. In the last war."

Schorrer perked up. "I was there too. Fifth Guard Grenadiers. And you?"

"Hundred and First Grenadiers." It was all he was going to say about it.

Schorrer seemed to sense this and got back on topic. "Laceration wounds to the abdominal wall always involve a great deal of pain, and there were deep cuts to the arms and legs as well. She must have screamed, unless she lost consciousness quickly. Her death occurred from either shock or blood loss. The latter seems more likely." He tapped his fingertips together.

Heller wanted to rub the back of his neck but didn't want to look uneasy before the doctor's commanding presence. Heller wasn't feeling too well; he was getting chills, and his shoulders chafed under his suit. He could tell he wasn't going to sleep well tonight.

"Do the results show if she was inebriated, unconscious, numbed in some way? Wouldn't she have put up a fight? She certainly wouldn't have entered that boathouse willingly."

Schorrer leaned forward and looked at a document. "A blood sample has been taken. Any other questions?"

"You help manage this hospital? I was told you're a pathologist."

"That I am. But current times require special measures, so they expanded my duties beyond the pathology clinic." Schorrer shrugged. "Now, Herr Detective Inspector, I have much to do."

Heller got the message and stood. "Thank you very much for your help on such short notice. Could I come back for more advice if necessary?"

"Any time. I live on the grounds. They freed up two rooms for me in the nursing school."

Schorrer stood. They faced each other to say goodbye, each man hesitating.

"Heil Hitler," Heller said. He raised his arm yet didn't extend it fully before letting it drop.

Dr. Schorrer did the same, and for a moment they searched each other's eyes.

Out in the waiting room, Schorrer's secretary gave Heller his overcoat back, now dry and pleasantly warm. He thanked her and left.

Out in the corridor it smelled of dinnertime, of bread and broth. Heller hadn't eaten since his meager lunch of a few potatoes and salted turnips. The staff, indifferent, kept going about their work. He had to get out of the way a couple of times, pressing himself to the wall as carts of food and beds rolled by.

He didn't wait for the elevator, opting for the stairs instead.

"Tell me," he asked a nurse rushing by on the ground floor, "where can I find the personnel department?"

"The administration building is just over there, but everyone's left by now." The nurse pointed at the building.

"Thanks."

"You're welcome." The nurse headed up the stairs.

Heller felt a twinge of guilt and turned around. "Heil Hitler," he added.

The nurse paused and turned to look at him. Then she continued up the stairs.

"What's wrong with you?" Karin asked as she took Heller's overcoat. She placed it on a hanger and brought it into the kitchen, where she hung it next to the oven. Then his wife came back out into the hallway. Heller had sat down on a little bench and was wearily pulling off his shoes. Karin frowned. "Your cap?"

"Forgot it at the office." He slipped his right shoe off with a jerk, which made him grimace.

"What am I going to do with you? Last thing we need is you catching cold."

Heller didn't like it when she got like this, but she was right, and he was annoyed with himself. He decided not to tell her he was getting the chills.

Karin sat next to him. "So. What's going on?"

"A woman was murdered near here, fifteen minutes by foot. A hideous crime. Really ghastly. Someone had . . . sliced her open."

"A robbery?"

"No, this had nothing to do with robbery, Karin. This was the work of a madman."

"Is there anything you're able to do?"

Heller snorted. "No staff, no gas, no flashbulbs, no time. Klepp thinks it was just someone passing through."

"Then he's an idiot."

Heller placed a hand on her forearm and gently squeezed. She shouldn't talk so loudly near the door and the hallway.

"It's true, though," Karin whispered.

"What's there to eat?" Heller said.

"Stew—potatoes and turnips." Karin got up, and Heller followed her into the kitchen. "I stood in line for four hours at Kiebels because people said there was fat, but I was too far back."

"Anything else happen?"

"Nothing," Karin said without looking at him.

This was both good and bad. It meant they hadn't gotten one of those so-called hero letters, stating that one of their boys had fallen for the Führer, Volk, and Vaterland. It also meant there was still no mail from the front. For months now, the letters they'd written had all come back marked "Return to Sender, Await Further Correspondence."

They sat at the dinner table in silence, hearing only the gentle clanking of spoons on soup plates. The radio stayed off. Heller liked classical music—Handel and Vivaldi—yet he couldn't listen to the inane babble between the music, always the same old clichés.

Karin finished first, having put far less on her plate. She carefully set down her spoon so it didn't make noise. "Today, Frau Lehmann was saying that they're on the advance again in Russia."

Heller finished eating, tipping the plate to spoon up the last of the broth. He set his spoon down carefully too. "People are claiming the most ridiculous things. If they really were making progress in Russia, it would make headlines on the front page." He stood to go into the living room. He'd read the newspaper, now down to just a few small pages and nearly half-filled with death notices. Karin would clean up and join him soon. And there they would sit, in candlelight, waiting to find out whether the air raid siren would sound tonight. Only when they were certain the English weren't coming would they go to bed. Heller turned to Karin from the kitchen doorway. "Has Frau Lehmann ever mentioned something called the 'Fright Man'?"

Karin was clearing the dishes. She paused in thought before shaking her head. "The Fright Man? No."

Heller was annoyed with himself for bringing it up, just like he'd gotten annoyed with himself for calling after that nurse with a much too loud "Heil Hitler." He read in the newspaper about yet another "heroic battle." The heroic battles were everywhere, just another of so many empty slogans. Everyone knew—everyone had to know—just how little worth news like this had. None, to be exact. And yet people craved reading it, searching for the tiniest clue as to what was actually going on. In the war he'd fought in, they too had fought heroic battles. They had lain in the mud so heroically, cowering as shells landed all around them, their faces pressed into the mud.

"What's that mean anyway—the Fright Man?"

Heller started; he hadn't heard Karin coming. "The woman today. Well, two boys found her, and one of them was really terrified by it. He asked me if it had been the Fright Man. That's all I know."

Karin moved the candles to the coffee table, turned off the overhead light, then sat on the sofa and threw a blanket over her legs.

"You said they sliced her open." She paused. "Who could do such a thing?"

Heller gave her a contemplative look. "I don't know. This is no normal murder. Definitely not robbery. This is something different, I can feel it."

"Listen, Max," Karin whispered, her face barely visible just beyond the candlelight. "Don't you go getting too involved, especially if this Klepp doesn't want you to."

"It's a murder, and I have a job to do."

"This wouldn't be the first time you did more than necessary."

"I only ever did what was necessary."

"But right now—"

"Right now is exactly the time not to start throwing the rules out the window, to go losing any common decency we have left."

"Don't interrupt me! I'm just concerned, Max. You might wind up the only decent one left among all these maniacs."

"What are you trying to say? I'm supposed to behave like a maniac too?"

Karin shook her head, annoyed. "Don't act dumb. You know what I mean."

The warning siren sounded at 10:03 p.m., the full alarm siren a few minutes later. Heller, who'd dozed off in the armchair, stood and fetched his overcoat from the kitchen. Then they grabbed the suitcase they'd packed weeks ago and had already carried down to the cellar twenty times now.

In the stairway, they joined their neighbors and the renters from the top floor. All mumbled greetings and went down into the cellar. No one joked anymore or dared claim that Dresden was going to be spared. Not since the seventh of October, when bombs had fallen for the first time. It hadn't been a lot of bombers. A few buildings had collapsed, and there were several dozen dead. Yet those few bombs had been enough to destroy all illusions.

Down in the cellar, each person sat in their customary spot. All light came from a single bulb. They'd have to wait until the all-clear siren sounded. No one spoke a single word. Heller knew why. He was the reason. He was a policeman, and the regime had strongly advised all police to join the SS or its security service, the SD. No one had dared trust him from that point on, just as he no longer dared trust any of them.

December 1, 1944: Early Morning

"I'm sorry, Herr Detective Inspector, but Nurse Klara moved out of the nurses' quarters. Unfortunately, no one noted her new address." The middle-aged woman, her hair parted and braided into a severe wreath, flipped once more through the three whole pages making up Klara Bellmann's file. She ran a finger along the lines of text only to look diligent, Heller saw. Her gray skirt and white blouse, buttoned to her neck, gave off a strong odor of mothballs. Dark rings showed under her eyes. She clearly hadn't slept well in months. Behind her, three other women banged away at their typewriters. "She came from Berlin, twelve weeks ago. I could call the nurses' quarters or her department?"

"Thank you, Frau Schmitt, I'll find my way over there instead." Heller took his cap from the table and stood. "Maybe Nurse Klara simply didn't report her current residence?" he said. "Or maybe the record got misfiled?" He deliberately phrased this in an unfavorable way.

"Well," Frau Schmitt snapped, "it's certainly not my fault if Frau Bellmann didn't do her duty to notify authorities."

The other three women kept their heads lowered, not daring to make a sound. With that, Heller left the office.

"Are you here about Klara Bellmann?" a young woman asked him out in the hallway. She wore a nurse's uniform and seemed to have been waiting for him.

Heller studied the young woman. She didn't have a hint of local Saxon dialect, no accent at all. He noticed something else too. "Aren't you that nurse from yesterday evening?"

"You here about Nurse Klara or not?"

Heller straightened; he wasn't used to this kind of disrespectful tone. "I'm Detective Inspector Heller. And, yes, I was trying to find out where Nurse Klara lived, but no one can tell me. You knew Frau Bellmann?"

The nurse nodded. "We'd become friends. I know where she was living."

Heller took out his notebook and pencil, then licked the lead tip. "Tell me your name and address, please."

"Rita Stein. Klara was living with relatives a few days ago—name is Schurig, 17 Jägerstrasse."

Heller wrote fast. "When was the last time you saw Frau Bellmann?"

"The evening before last, when our shift ended."

"She have anything planned? Make any kind of remark? Maybe shared a sense that someone was following her?" Heller studied Nurse Rita. She didn't seem as young as she'd looked at first glance. He took her to be older than thirty. He could see dark hair under her cap, her eyes were bright and didn't look tired, and there was something about her that intrigued him.

Rita shook her head. "No, nothing."

"Why didn't she keep living here at the nurses' quarters like you?"

"Because they need every room they can find, and they're urging anyone who can get accommodation elsewhere to take it."

"Jägerstrasse is way over in Albertstadt, though. Did she come by streetcar?"

"She came by bicycle. It was a men's bike, a Diamant, silver. She bought it off some woman who didn't need it anymore."

The rest was clear enough. The crime scene would've been on Klara Bellmann's way home, since the shortest way to Albertstadt from the hospital was over Albert Bridge. It was entirely possible that the murderer had been stalking her for several days.

"We didn't find a bicycle," Heller said.

"So it was a robbery?"

"I'm fairly certain the killer wasn't after the bike. Why did she leave Berlin?"

"She'd been bombed out and lost everything there. All her possessions. Even the hospital where she was working was destroyed. She had relatives here, so she left."

Heller paused. "So why would she bother living in the nurses' quarters first?"

"Well, I can only venture a guess . . ." Rita drew back a little, as if suddenly realizing whom she was speaking to.

"Feel free to let me in on it," Heller prodded.

"All right, fine. She was married to a man who wasn't exactly pure racially. They got divorced in '38. Her relatives wanted to be sure it was true, so they demanded she get new divorce records from Berlin since all her documents were lost in an air raid." Rita snapped her mouth shut, as if frightened that her knowledge might lead Heller to jump to conclusions.

"How did you two become friends?"

"Is that important? Like always, you find things in common. You share the same worries."

Heller shut his notebook and stuffed it and the pencil into his overcoat pocket.

"Thank you very much. I'll go and visit the Schurigs later. First, though, I need to see Schorrer again."

"Dr. Schorrer? I'm supposed to go to his office too. He apparently wants me to work in one of his departments."

"That's a compliment to your work."

"Is it? I don't even know him."

Rita headed for the stairway at a fast pace.

Heller followed her down the stairs at a distance and only caught up with her once they were in front of the building. They walked in silence past the buildings leading to Schorrer's office.

Heller stopped. "Wait," he blurted out, "that men's bike was yours, wasn't it?"

Rita kept going, yet her pace slowed. She stopped when they reached the front door.

"My husband is an artillery staff sergeant in Africa. I haven't heard from him in nearly two years. He's considered missing."

"That doesn't necessarily mean anything," Heller said. He didn't bother adding the usual encouraging smile.

Rita looked him in the eye. "I'm not going to fool myself."

Dr. Schorrer's conduct had made it clear that he thought Heller was wasting his time. Still, Heller insisted on seeing Klara Bellmann again.

Her body lay on the dissecting table, eyes closed. Her head was untouched, but long, deep slash wounds covered her body from the neck down. The lamp's bright light revealed every horrible detail. A sickly sweet odor filled the air.

Heller scrutinized everything. The smallest detail, even a chipped fingernail, could hold meaning. "He didn't violate her?"

Schorrer stood watching with his hands clasped behind his back. "I'm certainly not a medical examiner, yet I can say with reasonable certainty that this did not occur."

"And you see no signs of anything cannibalistic?"

Schorrer shook his head as if insulted by the question. "Herr Detective Inspector, the hospital is overflowing with patients. This is a horrific act, without a doubt, but do you really require my presence here any longer?"

"It's likely the killer had some need to make the victim suffer. He reveled in her pain, in her fright. I'm wondering whether the crime was aimed at Klara Bellmann—if the killer was venting his rage specifically on her."

Schorrer thrust his hands into the pockets of his lab coat. "I'm not a psychologist. I'm a doctor. I attempt to heal the sick and patch up the wounded. At the front, I did nothing else for years. I stopped wondering about motives a long time ago. And I've seen so many opened bodies that I could not tell the difference between an Aryan, Russian, or Jewish body. Here I can't plan more than a few days ahead, and we're lacking everything. Soon constant shortages won't be the rule—soon it will be having nothing at all. We're hurtling toward our own destruction, with our eyes wide open. So this deceased woman is just one among so many. Her killer as well."

"But you do understand what I'm trying to accomplish?" Heller asked in a gentle yet firm voice.

Schorrer nodded. "Of course. It's very clear to me. What you're doing involves rules and laws that need to be obeyed. All for the sake of order. God help us if our beloved order perishes. Now will you excuse me?"

Schorrer didn't wait for an answer. He simply left. The swinging door banged back and forth in his wake.

Dr. Schorrer had been transferred to head a hospital clinic for good reason, Heller figured. His experience at the front undoubtedly made him the right man to help steer this hospital through tough times. Yet that didn't make him a detective.

Heller waited a moment before going over to the dissecting table. He carefully studied the deceased woman's right hand. He found rubber gloves on a shelf and pulled them on. He cautiously raised her hand and turned her palm upward. She had several abrasions on her palms and wrists, the type someone would get falling from a bicycle and landing on their hands. They looked fresh. Heller leaned across the table, lifted the other hand, and found the same scrape wounds. She must have been riding that Diamant bike and either fallen or gotten knocked over. The bicycle might still be lying near the crime scene, along the Elbe. Normally, he would've already had someone out searching for it, just as he would have someone out talking to the Schurig family. But all that would have to wait.

He leaned over the dead body again so he could see her face. He inspected it thoroughly and cautiously opened the mouth. He started. She was missing her tongue. How could Schorrer overlook this? Heller now wondered whether the doctor had given her any more than a few minutes of his attention. Heller pulled out his notebook, fumbled to find the right page with rubber gloves on, and wrote down his observations.

Next, he held the deceased woman's chin and forehead with both hands and turned her head back and forth in the light. He saw something in one of her nostrils and grabbed long, narrow forceps from the dissecting instruments. He used the forceps to remove a fine white thread, barely two millimeters long and as thin as a hair. Both ends looked frayed. He had no idea what that could mean. He fished out a little paper baggie from his pocket and dropped the fine thread inside. Then he pressed the baggie inside his notebook.

When he left the dissecting room, he found two nurses waiting for him. "What should we do with her?" one asked. "Should we let burial services have her, or her relatives?"

"She needs to remain here. And please tell me where I can find a phone."

"Down the hall, to the left."

Heller nodded and started off in search of the phone. He needed to call for a driver. As he headed down the hallway, his heels clacking on the cold polished floor, it suddenly occurred to him that neither he nor Schorrer had used the Hitler salute.

A driver wasn't available, of course, so Heller had to take the no. 3 streetcar and then the 9 to reach Jägerstrasse, which was no picnic. The cars were packed, the air was thick, and many people were coughing. All the world was on the move, and everyone had handcarts and backpacks. Among them were refugees going around begging, ragged and dejected, far from the transit camps at the main train station. The locals eyed them with suspicion.

Fallen leaves covered the damp cobblestones on the Jägerstrasse, making it slippery. Heller pressed on gingerly, step by step, keeping an eye on his feet. He turned for the entrance to the building numbered 17.

"Who you looking for?" an elderly woman shouted down from the fourth floor.

"The Schurigs," he shouted back.

"Not home. Been out since this morning. Should I pass a message?"

"I'll wait, thanks," Heller said.

"You're not really going to stand down there the whole time, are you?" the woman said, her voice resonating with a slight horror. "If you're here for that new girl, she's gone too."

Heller stepped back so he didn't have to crane his neck so much. "What new girl?"

"I'm sure you know better than me. This used to be an upstanding neighborhood!" The woman slammed the window shut.

Heller wasn't about to wait now. He entered the building and climbed the three and a half flights of stairs before reaching a door with "Werker" on the nameplate.

"Not opening this door," squealed a woman from inside. "I'm calling the police!"

Heller stood so close to the door his forehead nearly touched it. "Frau Werker? I am the police."

"You are?"

"I'll show you my ID—feel free to take a peek through the mail slot." He held his ID before the narrow flap. Sure enough, the chain came down and the door opened. Heller stepped into the large entryway and was amazed at the size of the place. At least four large rooms, not including the kitchen and bathroom. Frau Werker was a gray-haired lady, about sixty.

"May I use your telephone?" Heller asked. "It's urgent."

Frau Werker nodded. Heller had himself connected to police headquarters on Schiessgasse and again requested a driver from the motor pool. This time he was in luck—they'd found one. "Have him wait out front," Heller instructed, then hung up.

A large portrait of Hitler adorned the wall in the entryway. All around it were photos of a man in uniform, the largest with a black mourning ribbon in one corner.

Heller asked, "What can you tell me about Frau Bellmann?"

"She was married to a Jew and came from Berlin, bombed out apparently, but who knows if it's true? Only been living here two days and already had a man visiting. Can you even imagine? If my husband only knew. Such low standards!"

Heller could smell coffee, the real stuff. He hadn't had any for months. Frau Werker surely noticed him sniffing away, since she quickly positioned herself between him and the kitchen as if frightened he might confiscate the good stuff.

"Could you describe the man who came visiting?"

She waved aside the notion. "He came in the dark, so no. Wait, listen. Here they come." She rushed to the door and flung it open. "Waltraud, the police are here for you!" she shouted down the stairs.

"For us?" Frau Schurig replied with disbelief.

Heller pushed past Frau Werker to the stairway and went down the steps. Herr and Frau Schurig were entering their apartment with the day's booty. Their tin milk can glug-glugged and their baskets were full, though it was just potatoes. The sight made him wonder yet again if he wouldn't have been better off spending his time standing in line for food instead of chasing after a killer who'd likely escaped the city. He was hoping he wouldn't regret this, but not for his own sake. It was for Karin, who did nothing day and night but hit the shops hoping to find something, anything, with their ration coupons.

"Are you here because of Klara?" asked Herr Schurig, a little gray man the same age as the Werker woman. Breathing heavily from all the carrying, he pulled a handkerchief from his pocket and wiped his forehead.

Heller entered their apartment without asking and closed the door behind him. "I'm sorry to have to tell you that Klara is dead. She was murdered. So I'll have to ask you a few questions."

"Murdered?" Frau Schurig said. She was a haggard woman with hard facial features.

"Did Frau Bellmann have any visitors? Any men come by?"

"She'd only been living with us a few days," said Frau Schurig.

Heller raised his chin and gave Frau Schurig a stern look.

"No. We didn't know of any visitors."

"She was very reserved," added her husband.

"Did she mention anything along those lines? She have anything planned? Was she expecting to meet anyone?"

The Schurigs glanced at each other. The husband shrugged. "Well, she did seem to be interested in those ads in the newspaper—you know, from marriage seekers. Maybe she got mixed up with some kind of swindler."

"A murderer, you mean," Heller added. "Did she mark up the ads?"

"No, definitely not. We would've noticed that."

"Where are the newspapers?"

Frau Schurig nodded at their oven.

"Which paper do you read?"

"*Dresdner Zeitung.*"

Heller took out his notebook and wrote, "Check ads."

"So did she come home from her shift the day she disappeared?"

"No, she never returned from work."

"Frau Werker thinks she saw an unfamiliar man out on the street."

Frau Schurig shook her head. "She also talks to her late husband, that one."

"I'll need to take a look at Klara's things."

The Schurigs showed Heller to Klara's room. It had just enough space for a bed and a wardrobe. Heller opened it, reaching into compartments and pulling out drawers, but only found a few articles of clothing and a small bundle of documents: registration forms for Berlin and Dresden, confirmation that she'd been bombed out of her home, a certificate for emergency vocational training, and a copy of her divorce document. Her ex-husband was named Daniel Kohn.

Heller wrote that down.

"Do you know who initiated the divorce? Was Frau Bellmann forced into it?"

Herr Schurig shrugged. "We don't know."

"What's your relationship to her?"

"She's the daughter of a cousin. Or was she a second cousin?" Frau Schurig looked to her husband for the answer, but he didn't know either.

"So she didn't say anything? No suggestion she was being followed, that someone was lurking around? Any reason at all that could've made her move here from the nurses' quarters?"

The Schurigs just stared at him, clueless. They obviously weren't very interested.

"I'm leaving you a telephone number. If something occurs to you, ask for Detective Inspector Heller."

"Well, there is one thing," Frau Schurig said. "It's about her ration cards. We get to keep hers, right? I mean, no one's going to take them from us, are they?"

Heller took a deep breath. "No, you go ahead and keep them."

Heller waited outside the building for several minutes before the driver rode up on a BMW motorcycle. It was Strampe again. The SS sergeant stopped, didn't salute, and glared through his goggles at Heller, who climbed into the sidecar.

"All right, where to?" Strampe asked, his tone brazen.

Heller was already freezing in the cold, wet air and would've preferred to head home, since he was gradually becoming aware of how pointless his endeavor was. He was also none too pleased with how this kid kept speaking to him. But then he recalled what Karin had said about acting stupid. So he restrained himself.

"To the hospital," he said.

"Weren't you just there? Waste of gas."

Strampe drove off, shooting into the first curve far too fast. Heller slid down into the sidecar as much as his long legs would allow, pulled his cap down over his forehead, and held it there. Strampe nearly lost control of the bike turning into Bautzner Strasse, almost defiantly so, and could only steer it fully back on track once the road straightened. People along the street jumped out of the way, shaking their heads.

Heller rode hunkered down in the sidecar as they roared on, watching people scurry away with bags and packs in hand because they must have believed the rumor that today there was lard at the butcher's, red beets at the grocer's, coal briquettes at the fuel seller's. The war didn't interest them in the least—they only wanted food and a warm oven, nothing more. Long gone was the euphoria of those first few years, that firm belief in Adolf. And somewhere among them was someone who attacked a woman, tied her up, gagged her, and sliced open her still-living body without even trying to conceal the act. Had the killer intended for her to be found like that?

Heller tapped Strampe on the leg, and he bent sideways a little without slowing.

"Go to Gneisenaustrasse first!" Heller shouted into the wind, and Strampe sat upright again without any indication he'd heard him.

Yet Strampe did go to Gneisenaustrasse, where Heller struggled to get out of the sidecar. "You drive on back. I'm walking from here."

Strampe tapped at his left wrist. "Off duty at five!" he said, and revved the engine as he sped off.

Heller took out his notebook and searched for the boy's name and address. Alwin Trautmann lived in building 4, where the front entry door had been left open. Heller checked the nameplates in the foyer. He had to go up to the fifth floor.

A hardy-looking woman with ashen skin and a head scarf answered on the first ring.

"Frau Trautmann? I'm a police detective, Heller. Is your boy here? Alwin?"

"In his bedroom. He won't dare go outside after yesterday."

"Were you the one who told him about the Fright Man?"

Frau Trautmann shook her head. "The children started telling themselves that story."

Heller nodded. "Has Alwin told you anything else?"

"No, he's gone quiet, like when he's getting sick."

"I'd like to see him."

Alwin's mother gestured toward a door. Heller went inside. Alwin was sitting on a chair and peering out the window. His wooden dummy rifle was on his lap. Heller stood next to him and peered out with him.

"What are you looking for?"

"Keeping watch for Yankee bombers."

"Spotted any yet?"

Alwin shook his head, still looking at the sky.

"Were you able to sleep last night?"

The boy didn't answer.

"What's bothering you? Was it seeing that woman? Or the Fright Man, maybe?"

Silence.

"Who told you about him? The other boys?"

Alwin nodded.

"What does he do?"

Alwin whispered something, and Heller had to lean down to hear.

"He creeps around after the air raid sirens. And if you don't make it into the air raid shelter in time, he comes and snatches you up and makes you die like that woman."

Heller straightened back up and placed a hand on the boy's shoulder. "That's hogwash, Alwin. I'm a policeman. I know. What happened to that woman is something else entirely. But you will need to help me find the murderer."

"Help? How?" Alwin eyed him anxiously.

"By telling me some things you know. Are you boys at that boathouse a lot?"

"Sometimes."

"And you've never seen anyone lurking around? A man? Anyone at all?"

The boy shook his head. "We never tried going inside before."

"Did you ever see a bicycle there? Say, a woman on a bike, in the days leading up to it?"

Alwin shook his head.

"And that door in back, had it been open like that long? Or did you boys go inside that day because you just discovered it had been pried open?"

"It was that day, like you said—Gustav, he spotted it so we went in."

Something else was eating at Alwin. Heller could tell.

"You can hear him sometimes, though," the boy whispered.

"Who?"

"Him! He creeps through the night, and sometimes he laughs and giggles or howls at the moon."

Heller tensed. "Enough of that now, boy."

"But I heard him, I really did. Mother too. Isn't that right, Mother?"

Heller looked over to the doorway, where Alwin's mother stood. She gave them a hapless shrug, as if she wasn't sure she could still trust her own mind.

December 1, 1944: Midday

The hospital grounds acted like a giant funnel. People poured in from all sides, plunging through the gates, gathering before building entrances, filling every space and path in between. Ambulances arrived from the center of town, bringing sick people writhing with coughing fits, most looking as if they'd just endured a long journey marked by utter deprivation. The National Socialist People's Welfare served hot soup and tea from large pots while Red Cross workers rushed around writing down names and symptoms, separating out the most severe cases. Disputes flared up about who should be allowed in first.

Heller fought his way through the throngs, heading for the nurses' quarters, and was more than relieved to finally get inside with the door shut behind him. Calm prevailed here. Only a few footsteps sounded now and then. Heller was crossing the entry hall to the first-floor mezzanine when he spotted a nurse heading up to her room.

"Excuse me!" he called to her.

The nurse hesitated but came over. Heller showed her his police ID. "Did you know Klara Bellmann?"

"The one from Berlin? I didn't really know her very well. Is it true she was murdered?"

Heller nodded. "Do you know anyone who was good friends with her? Apart from Nurse Rita?"

"You could ask the gals on the fourth floor, or there's also the building caretaker who lives in the cellar—he's been here the longest." The nurse curtsied and darted off.

Heller pursed his lips as he considered the options, then took the stairs to the cellar.

Down in the cellar, he saw signs pointing to the air raid shelters. On the walls hung fire buckets filled with water and sand. Neat stacks of blankets were everywhere, with fire swatters, gas masks, and goggles close at hand. He knocked on a door labeled "Boiler Room / Workshop." No one answered, and he heard nothing. But he wasn't about to get discouraged, having dealt with building caretakers many times before. He pounded on the door again, much harder this time.

An older man in work overalls finally opened the door.

"Yes?"

"Heller, detective. And you are?"

"Glöckner."

"You're the caretaker?"

"Air raid warden, boiler man, caretaker, you name it."

"May I come in?" Heller asked, and Glöckner stepped aside. Heller made him lead the way, noting the man's limp as he followed him through a workshop to another door, which opened to a comfortably furnished living room.

Heller looked around. "Real nice and warm."

"Better small than none at all! My wife isn't here, otherwise I would offer you tea." Glöckner seemed eager.

"You've heard about the death of Nurse Bellmann?"

"Yes. They say she was horribly mutilated."

They all knew about it, to Heller's dismay. "Did you know Nurse Klara or any acquaintances, friends, or people who were close to her?"

"No, I only knew her in passing. Pretty little thing. They say she was messing around with some private here on leave. And supposedly she was making eyes at one of the doctors."

Glöckner might not know her, but he certainly knew the rumors.

"They say she was expecting—from that private—but she got rid of it."

Heller heard a soft patter and turned around. A German shepherd came out of the kitchen. Through the open door Heller spied various foods on the kitchen counter that he hadn't seen for a long time, among them a whole stack of chocolate bars.

"I named him Zeus," Glöckner said with pride. "Zeus, sit!" The dog sat, staring at Heller and panting loudly—it was too hot for him in here.

"Plenty of lowlifes around the building at night, and the girls get all kinds of wild ideas. But no one gets by Zeus. Zeus, Heil!" The dog raised its right front paw. Glöckner smiled.

"So no one ever came here inquiring about her? Never any other issues or talk involving her?"

"Well, the two of us did have a little spat."

"About what?"

"She, with her Berlin mouth, thought she could get the best of me. She got these ideas in her head that the heating wasn't hot enough, that the water was brown. I quickly cured her of that notion. I reported her and complained about her behavior, which took care of things. She was out the door by that point anyhow."

"You know of any girls showing envy or jealousy? Any enemies, feuds?"

"Sure, there might have been, but my knowledge only runs so deep. She got along with that other Berliner."

"Who?"

"The Stein girl."

"Rita Stein is from Berlin?"

"That's what I heard. But been here awhile."

Heller took out his notebook and made a note.

"And your wife, what's she do?"

"She works here, as head nurse. She was the one who got me this job seven years ago. But that's not something everyone needs to know, do they?" Glöckner winked.

"You looking for me?" asked Rita Stein. Heller had taken the stairs up to the fourth floor and waited in the hallway.

"I need to question some of the nurses about Frau Bellmann, if possible."

"You won't find out anything. Most are so young; Klara had no use for them."

"Did Frau Bellmann have a certain reputation?"

Rita's eyes narrowed.

"It does have to do with my trying to solve her murder." The fact that he even had to remind her of this was only further proof of her arrogance.

Rita didn't answer.

"Her tongue was cut out," Heller added. "Did you know that?"

Rita turned and waved him into her room. "Come in. Have a seat."

Heller sat down at the table. The room had two beds at odd angles. Two lockers separated them, and another wall had a sideboard and small stove. The bulky radiator under the window rattled away as if full of pebbles. A joyless room.

"What do you want to know?" she said.

"It's crucial that I learn about any contacts Frau Bellmann had. That includes who she was socializing with, what kind of reputation she had, whether she was considered easy, whether some envied her, and whether her divorced husband was still in contact with her."

Rita was sitting across from him but made it a point to look past him, out the window. "He's a Jew. He's not allowed to leave his own city or to have contact with anyone. He might not even be in Berlin anymore. The way I hear it, most Berlin Jews were taken to Warsaw."

"I'm hearing about her and some private as well as a doctor."

"What? What kind of blabbermouth went and told you that?"

"They're saying things about her over in the Schurigs' building too."

Rita placed her hands flat on the table and stared at Heller. "These are uncertain times; you know that. People cross your path and disappear forever. You take what you can. Klara, she'd been through plenty. She wasn't thinking about the future, only about the here and now. But that doesn't concern you, and it's got nothing to do with this."

"Why did you two get along so well? Because you're a Berliner too?"

Rita's eyes narrowed again. "Who told you that? Yes, I was born in Berlin and lived there until I was ten. Then my parents moved us to Dresden because my father found a job here. I was friends with Klara because I liked her. Such things do happen, you know."

"All right, all right." Heller sighed and stood up. He wasn't going to learn much more from Rita Stein today. "I won't keep you any longer." He nodded goodbye, put on his cap, and left the room.

"So it has to be that Jew! This Kohn." Klepp leaned back in his chair, eyeing Heller.

Heller held his stare, despite sitting across from a man who used to slaughter for a living. "What about his motive?"

"His motive? Isn't it clear? It's revenge for divorce."

"Don't you think he'd have far greater concerns than making his way here from Berlin just to hunt down Klara Bellmann and take his revenge?" Heller tried not to sound too sarcastic. Klepp had made it his mission to support the local Gestapo with every means at his disposal—together they were rounding up the last of the Jews, removing them from the few Jewish homes left, and sending them to the temporary camp in Hellerau or directly to the concentration camps at Theresienstadt or Buchenwald.

Klepp placed his fingertips together like Schorrer had, only his fingers were much fatter than the doctor's. "It's exactly what he'd do. He had nothing more to lose. I saw far worse in Poland, believe me. Revenge is the only thing keeping some Jews alive. The Bellmann girl had her divorce documents sent from Berlin. So that put him on her trail. Who knows who he knows in the registrar's office? The Jews, they've infiltrated all our best institutions! So he comes here and kills her. Who else would do such a thing?"

Heller stared at his superior. Obersturmbannführer Klepp could not be this dim-witted. Clever and brazen, sure, but not dumb.

"What about now?" Heller said. "Where has he gone?"

Klepp waved his hand. "Gone's what he is, taken off, headed underground. They'll smoke him out somewhere."

"Still, have you been able to confirm where Kohn was at the time of the crime?" Of course Klepp couldn't have.

"That's completely irrelevant now. Because we really have our hands full. Nieland, that weakling of a mayor, summoned me today. Gauleiter Mutschmann has been complaining to him about conditions near the train station being unsustainable. The refugee camps are bursting at the seams. Camp number one is a particular thorn in his side. It's supposed to be just a transit camp, but it's been overflowing for some time. None of those people want to move on. They feel safe here, they're getting food, they're waiting for relatives. It's causing theft, assault, rape, and surely there's more than enough subversive elements for you there, Herr Detective Inspector—possibly spies or even Jews on the run."

"Hold on. You're taking me off the case?" Heller sat upright in his chair. This could not be happening. It was absurd and defied all sanity.

"Heller, we're at war. People are dying every second, and no one can do a thing about it. What's important are the living! Why bother with one Jew? Together with the Gestapo, I'm planning a big raid for that whole part of town—homes, cellars, attics, hovels, lavatories. You'll see. We'll find that bastard somewhere along the way."

"I can't work like this," Heller complained to his wife that evening. "That Klepp, he's just incredible."

Karin didn't respond. She stood at the sink, washing the dishes with only water.

"Today, Frau Zinsendorfer, know what she said?" Karin said without looking up. "She said they heard howling outside, night before last. Like a wolf."

Heller stared at Karin.

She glanced over her shoulder at him. "But then dogs howl in the night too, and fright always plays a part."

"Are you afraid, Karin?"

She set aside the last plate, dried her hands, and leaned back against the cupboard. She was getting thinner, her housedress hanging off her, the belt around her waist as tight as it could go, her skin dry. All her worry about their two sons was branded on her face. To Heller she was still beautiful. Even now he could see that twenty-year-old he'd met all those years ago on a summer retreat in the spa town of Bad Schandau. When he saw her for the first time, she had just stepped off the Elbe River steamboat, and in the village square a brass band was playing "In the Prater the Trees Bloom Again." She had her blonde hair tied up high, and the wind was blowing golden strands into her face and they were catching in the corners of her mouth. She'd pushed them off her face, laughing, and looked right at him.

"Yes, I am afraid. Afraid of being alone," she said. She wouldn't look at him.

Heller rushed over and took her hands in his. "You are not alone. You're not."

Karin looked up, just as she'd done when they were married—in church, like she'd wanted. Her eyes had glistened with so much joy and emotion back then. Now they revealed only a tiny glimmer of hope. "Promise me," she whispered.

"I promise you."

The air raid siren sounded again during the night. Down in the cellar, Heller sat across from Frau Zinsendorfer—seventy years old, gray hair tightly bound, eyebrows raised. She kept crossing herself, again and again, and was speaking to God under her breath. He tried not to listen. The siren stopped, which meant they still had to wait for the all clear. Heller tried listening for anything out in the dark night. But the cellar walls were thick, reinforced with concrete, and there were no windows. All he could hear were people breathing, then the flak guns started up somewhere in the distance, sputtering briefly before falling silent again.

December 18, 1944: Morning

Heller pulled out his handkerchief and held it over his nose and mouth as he forced his way through all the people and horses. It was unusually warm for December, and dust filled the air. His overcoat had turned gray from all the street grime swirled up by everyone's footsteps. The air stank from all the unwashed people who'd been on the run for weeks with so few clothes to change into. It smelled like rot, urine, and feces. DDT powder drifted over from the delousing stations.

The first time he went to the refugee camp, he was horrified. The people looked like beings from another world—homeless, hounded, disillusioned, filthy, reduced to their basest instincts, having to relieve themselves where they stood, prodded by constant fright and fears and the hope of eventually trading their immense troubles for lesser ones.

And yet their fellow countrymen were here too—Germans fleeing Silesia and points east, the women wearing head scarves and the men fur boots, toothless, half-starving, their faces dreary, lacking expression. Tied to their carts were old nags about to collapse, little more than walking dead.

Heller did what he could to help. He went around reassuring people, registering them, taking their questions about searching for loved ones, giving instructions on where to find water and food. He marked down the people coming from delousing, sent those with the worst illnesses to the medics and helpers from the Order of St. John charity. He tried to avoid getting sick from the ones with tuberculosis, staying clear of bodily contact and of all the dysentery and diphtheria, and tried not to let the constant misery get to him. The infants crying from hunger, the old ones with ulcers on their feet, the children with rags for shoes, the other children who'd become separated from their loved ones amid the panic and chaos, lost and forgotten, not knowing where to go and having lost all spirit from such an unspeakable loss. Every night he'd leave this world to return to a warm home, a hot meal. Every day brought a worse feeling of helplessness, since the flood of people would not subside. For every few hundred cleared for transport to a new destination, hundreds if not thousands of new refugees arrived in their place. Their speech became more and more alien, and in turn the locals' will to accept them and view them as fellow countrymen turned weaker and weaker, since they were all becoming competitors for the little food that still remained, and for housing, for clothing. The locals' own fear of not getting enough grew stronger, as did those rumors that had survived the long trek from the easternmost borders of Silesia. The Russians, the Russians, just don't let the Russians get through. The Russians devour the children, the women. They murder, they rape, and they're not humans at all but monsters bringing the Devil incarnate.

Heller knew it wasn't true. Both of his sons had told him what the Russians were like when they'd visited on their last leave home, back in the fall of '43. Most were uneducated, but not barbarians. Poor, but not criminals. What his sons did reveal to him were the acts German soldiers had committed in plain sight. There was this ditch, Klaus had explained to him in a low voice, a long ditch, barely covered over, with the shoes of women and children lying before it. Hundreds. His sons had asked him how they were supposed to act when confronted with all that. And when Heller said nothing, since he knew their dilemma all too well, Karin had advised them to keep acting in a way that would get them back home alive. And yet none of this meant Heller's chest did not tighten at the thought of what could happen when the Russians conquered the city. It made his fingers go cold and his legs stiff. Good thing he always had his duty weapon on him. That meant, at the very worst, that he always had the option of putting a quick end to things, for himself and for Karin.

There were those other rumors too. They were a strange mixture of religious apparition, of wishful thinking, of revenge fantasy—Hitler was their savior, their messiah, their faith healer. They whispered about "wonder weapons." The wonder weapons, they rejoiced, were sure to wipe all foes from the face of the earth, while there at the German border their soldiers stood tall as one, determined to halt the enemy, to send the Bolshevik wave crashing down like the surf against a steep cliff.

They were now counterattacking in the west too, in the Ardennes forest of Belgium. It was then, of all times, that a long-delayed letter from Erwin came telling them he was being transferred to the Western Front. The letter was already six weeks old, and its stamps and seals told them what a rough journey it had traveled. Not the most reliable proof that Erwin was still alive.

"Herr Heller! Herr Detective Inspector!"

Heller stopped and gazed around the refugee camp.

"Herr Detective Inspector!"

Heller saw a hand waving above dozens of heads in the distance. It was a military medic. "A call came for you. You should check in with headquarters. By telephone. Right away."

"I'm coming." Heller hurried after the medic, relieved that he could depart this place.

Heller saw a large cluster of people in front of the tenement building at the corner of Holbeinstrasse and Silbermannstrasse as the medic slowed his VW jeep to let Heller out. They were speaking to each other in whispers but hushed as Heller approached.

"Heil Hitler!" bellowed a policeman from the entryway, thrusting out his arm.

The concerned onlookers opened a path to let Heller inside the building, where he raised his arm to return the Hitler salute.

"It's up in the attic," the policeman said, then turned on his heel and headed up the stairs.

At the third floor, Heller stopped so he could give his sore right foot a break. The policeman waited in silence on the landing before continuing at a slower pace.

The policeman halted again when he reached the open door to the attic. "With your permission, I'd rather stay here—I've seen enough for today."

"That the detective inspector?" Heller heard Oldenbusch shout from up in the attic. He sounded a little distressed.

"It is. He's coming up," the policeman said.

"Max, wait, I'm coming down."

Heller grimaced. This did not bode well. Let alone that Klepp thought it necessary to call him away from the refugee camp.

Oldenbusch came clattering down the steep wooden stairs. "I want to show you something first," he said, and took Heller by the arm.

Heller shook his arm free. "Go get personal details from those residents outside," he ordered the policeman. "And let no one up here—no one!"

"They've all been up here already," Oldenbusch told Heller. "A Frau Dammke from the top floor was screaming so loud it got the whole neighborhood up here. Not that you can blame her. Now come on, Herr Detective Inspector."

Oldenbusch took Heller by the arm again and led him into Frau Dammke's apartment.

"There, see that?" Oldenbusch pointed through the open door into the living room. A plate-size brown stain had formed on the ceiling. In the middle of it hung a dark, heavy, congealed drop. "Coagulated blood. Bet you've never seen that before."

"I've seen a lot in my time, Werner."

"Yeah, yeah, I know. But that was during the war. This is man-made."

"Everything I saw was man-made."

"But that was random chance. Or fate. A shell lands two yards away, showering mud on you while the others die horribly. My father once found himself lying under four dead men. They had to pull them all off or he wouldn't have made it. But that up there—"

"Enough, Werner. I'll go take a look for myself."

Heller straightened his shoulders and went upstairs.

It was warm in the attic stairway. The sun had been shining down on the roof, heating the space like a greenhouse. The air was thick and humid and carried a tang like rotting garbage. It reeked so badly of blood that Heller didn't want to breathe in. He held the back of his hand to his nose, breathing in the grit of the street, the rare bit of soap that Karin used for his laundry.

"Prepare yourself," said Oldenbusch as he followed Heller up the stairs. "It's a woman again, quite young, at least according to her face."

Heller's head emerged into semidarkness, and he took his time climbing the final steps before entering the attic. It had wooden floorboards, and washing lines spanned its beams.

He first thought it was a curtain with all its fabric shredded. A nearly black drapery, appearing to hover between two wooden posts supporting the roof truss. A dark, sinister dragon, spreading its wings.

"Lord in Heaven," Heller blurted once he realized what he was seeing.

He recognized the arms spread out. The thin rope tight around the wrists. Tied to the posts and pulled taut, so the victim's toes just brushed the floor. Her blood had seeped down the ropes and through the floorboards. Her head lay on her left shoulder, her eyes wide open, two bright white stars amid this ominous scene. Her dark hair was down and framed her stained face.

"We found her clothes tossed into a corner. From the looks of it, she must've been a refugee. Found no papers, not one piece of info. He used a clothesline to tie her up. I was able to take five photos before running out—"

"Stop," Heller said. Oldenbusch was only giving him these details so he wouldn't feel completely powerless. This was his job. He had chosen it and wanted it even before he was drafted into the war. It was why he had studied and overcome all the odds that should have made him a tax official, an accountant, a salesman.

What all these types in their uniforms with their skull badges didn't understand was that it wasn't about status or title for him. It was about steering people in the right direction, providing them with justice, maintaining the values that constituted a good society. And the more he saw society going to the dogs and how little value human life now held, the more he would stand up for it.

This was exactly why he now forced himself to step closer to endure this horrific sight that was more than enough to rob him of sleep for nights on end. It was also why he reached out to close the woman's eyes—the least he could do for her. But he shrunk back in horror when he saw that it wasn't possible. That her eyelids had been cut out. He kept shrinking back until he stepped on Oldenbusch's foot.

"Work of a madman," Oldenbusch said, pretending not to notice Heller's sheer horror. "You think it's meant to represent something? An angel maybe?"

"Can you please keep quiet!" Heller tried to pull himself together. Compared with the overall condition of the corpse, the eyes were actually a minor thing. Yet it told him just how twisted the murderer really was.

"Werner, please go downstairs and help that cop gather everyone who's been up here. Tell them we'll be questioning witnesses."

Oldenbusch squinted at him. "You think the killer would dare try to blend in with them?"

Heller gave him a stern look. "We'll talk later, Werner."

Oldenbusch nodded and rushed down the stairs.

Heller turned back to the victim and took in the whole sight. He was trying to get accustomed enough to it that it might eventually become just one of many images he kept stowed away. Only retrieved when utterly necessary.

He noted how sharp the knife must have been. And that it seemed as if the killer brought a certain expertise. Was it the same killer? This looked somewhat different. The woman was even more mangled than the first victim. But maybe the killer had been interrupted when murdering Klara Bellmann, which would have prevented him from finishing the job. Maybe he'd succeeded this time and felt more satisfied with his work.

Heller would have preferred to lower the body. He wanted to cover her face, her nakedness. Yet how could he manage without touching her, without her hitting the floor when he loosened the rope? Suddenly a fear overtook him that the corpse could start moving, might flap its arms like an angel of death. He felt a pressure tightening his chest, as if someone was watching him from one of the attic's dark corners. He must keep his head on straight. He couldn't dare think of fleeing. Nobody else was there. No enemy, no madman, no Fright Man. This was not hell—this was an insane person murdering women. Heller forced himself to do his job. He stepped closer to the dead woman's face, searching for a white thread, for other clues. But he couldn't find anything without good light. He stuck around for a few more minutes.

That, he knew, would be enough. Then he could leave without feeling like a coward.

When the municipal undertakers reached the top floor, Heller instructed them to take the body to Dr. Schorrer. Heller was planning to go meet him.

Two of the undertakers' three workers, gaunt and ashen-faced men of indeterminate age, were wearing Jewish stars on their jackets. Heller took the third man to the side. He was stocky and starting to go bald. "Have those two been with you long?" Heller asked in a whisper.

"They were assigned to me a couple weeks ago. I've had four employees drafted."

"Do they have any experience?"

"One was a doctor. The other . . . not sure. We're doing all right. People get used to it. I had two others up until a little while ago, but they're gone now."

Gone. Heller slowly gazed up at the attic. "Up those steps is something else altogether. Take your time. And bring everything. We need to ascertain if . . . if anything's missing."

"Oh, I see." The man made a face. "Well, the Lord giveth, the Lord taketh away. You go on ahead—we'll handle it."

Heller nodded and went down the stairs, a hand on the railing. When he reached the landing, he noticed a narrow strip of dust on the inside of his hand. He took a good look around. The landing was clean. The killer had wiped it down. Heller smelled his hand, and he rubbed the fine white powder between his fingertips, yet he saw no good reason to believe that it was anything other than dust.

Down on the street he took a deep breath, relieved to be taking in this air that now felt so fresh, almost chilly.

"Is it true he peeled off all her skin?" asked a woman.

Heller ignored her, turned away, and waved Oldenbusch over.

Oldenbusch was holding a notebook. "We have fifteen people. Eight women and five children among them. That leaves two men, neither of them near the building. Others had snuck away when they realized we were checking papers."

"Would you rule out the women?"

Oldenbusch nodded but wasn't sure. "He did have to carry the victim up there, after all."

"Or she went up with him willingly."

"Why would she?"

"I believe a person will do just about anything these days to get some food."

"Even us Germans?"

"Even us, yes. So did any of the residents notice anything?"

"They're all spouting the same nonsense. They all think they heard something. Sounded like an animal."

Heller pursed his lips. These tales couldn't really be true, could they? A Fright Man? No. Impossible. There was no point looking into them. People absorbed these things like sponges and passed them on as if they'd experienced it themselves. Come tomorrow, the whole neighborhood would be claiming they'd heard the noises.

December 18, 1944: Midday

Heller ran into Rita Stein outside Dr. Schorrer's office. She looked exhausted, distracted. "Anything new?" she said without a hello.

The nurse's abrupt tone surprised him again. She fascinated him for some reason. Maybe it was her tough and matter-of-fact way of dealing with life.

"Bad news," he said.

"So it is true."

"You already heard?"

"The word's getting around. I guess it wasn't the Jew after all?"

She sounded bitter, and Heller didn't get why she was speaking to him like this. The face he made had to speak volumes.

"It says in the *Dresdner*," she said, "that the Jew Kohn had taken revenge on Klara in 'bloodthirsty fashion.'"

Heller had read that too. He'd shown the article to Karin yet neither wasted a word discussing it. Klepp's officers had found two men on their big raid, hiding in the false floor of a small apartment building. They were Jews. Klepp's men supposedly discovered blood on the men's hands and under their fingernails. But Heller never got to see their faces. He certainly didn't know if either was Daniel Kohn. All he'd been told was that they got hauled half-naked to headquarters, where Klepp's men

beat them up and took them straight to Münchner Platz for sentenc-
ing and execution, along with the building's four unfortunate residents,
who were charged with knowingly hiding the Jews.

"What can I say? My boss used to be a butcher," Heller said.

He thought he saw her face brighten a second.

"Maybe my new boss used to be a butcher too," she remarked,
keeping her voice low. "As surgeons go, it's pretty clear Dr. Schorrer has
been on the front lines awhile."

"Well, he is a pathologist, not a surgeon," Heller reminded her.

"That's true. And he is good at running things." Rita was backped-
aling now.

"I'm here to see him, about the new case."

"You hear what people are saying? There's a demon lurking around."
Rita scoffed at that, then she was all business again. "Dr. Schorrer isn't
here today, unfortunately. Dr. Reus sent him home. He's been battling
a virus for a few days now."

Heller still wanted to get back to that nearly confidential tone they'd
shared moments ago. "I get the impression you don't like him," he tried.

"He's my boss now" was all she said.

"All right, well, I'm having the corpse brought to him. I'm hoping
he'll find time to examine it as soon as he's back. Also, could he please
let me know what he finds?"

"I'll give him the message."

Klepp was looking a little harried when he received Heller in his office.
He gestured for Heller to take the chair in front of his desk, marched
past Heller, and sat down, only to stand back up. He suddenly seemed
to recall the role he was playing and clasped his hands behind his back.
Then he strutted over to the window, past the Saxony police standard
and the swastika flag, and ended his little tour by pausing face-to-face

with his Führer, who stared out into the room from the picture frame with that stern expression of his.

"It's just like I told you, Heller: there's a copycat killer!"

Klepp had said nothing of the sort. This meeting was already proving pointless, Heller realized. He never should've bothered getting his hopes up.

"So what are you going to do?" Klepp added.

Heller looked up. Was this helplessness the SS man was voicing? Klepp wasn't showing his face. He kept gazing at his Hitler portrait.

Heller took a large, deep breath.

"We need to thoroughly question witnesses so we can find out whether any strangers were frequenting the neighborhood and behaving unusually. The killer had studied the crime scene; he didn't choose the spot randomly. And there must be a reason why both homicides took place in the same area. We need to search the attic more thoroughly. The killer must have stepped in some blood or had blood all over himself. There must be fingerprints. He could've left something behind, like hair, clothing fibers. In addition, I'd keep looking into Klara Bellmann. It seems the killer's act fulfilled a certain purpose and unconsciously served as a trigger for impulses that had been well suppressed until now."

"There's nothing to look into. That first case is over with!" Klepp pivoted, his boots glistening. "We'll focus only on the case in the attic. What do you need to get the job done?"

Heller knew Klepp would never admit being wrong about the Bellmann case. The only thing Heller could do was make the best of the situation.

"Three men," Heller said. "A vehicle. Camera flashes. And we have to send for a medical examiner—a proper one." This was already pushing it.

Klepp finally turned around. Heller spotted a scratch on his face, running from his left temple down to his cheekbone.

"I'll give you one man, who'll serve as your driver. I'm assigning Oldenbusch to other matters. Between you and me? I'm only letting you work the case so people see that we're taking care of it, that things are happening. So go out and make yourself seen. Question anyone you want. Our Reich is facing the toughest times it's ever seen. In order to thrust the final dagger into our enemies' heart, all our forces must become unified. In the west, the Ardennes offensive has been under way for two days, and our forces keep advancing. But the enemy is trying to block us by attacking from the rear. They're setting off bombs, disrupting transportation lines, committing sabotage—"

"I don't understand," Heller said in a firm voice, "what any of this has to do with the case."

"You don't need to understand. You were only a common soldier in the Great War. I know what you went through—it's the only reason you're still here. But that's far beside the point. What we're dealing with here is enemy agents. What happened there in that attic, it's sabotage, you understand? It distracts and stirs up fright among the population. The more horrific the act, the greater the advantage. But we can't let ourselves be distracted. We must keep our eyes trained on the higher goal. We will clean up this mess here, but not until all our enemies are facedown in the dirt. Dismissed!"

December 18, 1944: Night

There hadn't been as many air raid sirens lately, but tonight they had to go back down into the cellar. Herr Leutholdt turned the radio dial, searching for better reception since they couldn't always rely on the sirens to sound the all-clear signal. He discovered a little music on one frequency and leaned back to listen. His wife gave him a shove, adding a quick nod in Heller's direction. Yet it never occurred to Heller that Leutholdt might be listening to an enemy broadcast, seeing as how the man had been the first in the neighborhood to join the SA back in '36.

"I should have gone to the bathroom one more time," Karin whispered to Heller.

Heller nodded. He was now watching Frau Zinsendorfer, who was making the sign of the cross more fervently than ever, rocking back and forth like mad. He'd seen something like this once before—in an insane asylum.

She was now staring back at him with a sinister look.

"It's the Devil!" she snarled at him.

"Excuse me?"

"The Devil walks among us, snatching all those souls he's been promised!" She shut her mouth and crossed herself three more times. "He's telling us that the end is nigh!"

All faces had turned to them. A dozen people.

"Don't talk nonsense!" Heller said, and turned away.

"The demons, they're crawling out from every hole, howling in the alleys at night. Haven't you heard them cackling and grunting? You don't see them climbing up the walls and peering through every crack and crevice? Clattering along the roof with their claws? Soon they'll be tearing away the roof tiles and coming inside."

"Quiet!" Heller shouted.

"You're all in league with the Devil, all of you! You and the whole gang. You're the ones who called him here. All of you!" Frau Zinsendorfer stood and made a half circle with her index finger, and everyone pulled back as if her finger were some sharp weapon. Her overcoat had opened, exposing her nightgown. She turned to point her finger at Leutholdt and hissed, "He'll take you all and peel your skin off, one after the other!"

Leutholdt shot up and balled his hands into fists, his jaw grinding away. "You sit back down and shut your dirty mouth or I'll report you for traitorous gossip harmful to the Volk and for undermining the war effort!"

Heller was about to let them both have it, but Karin beat him to it.

"Silence, both of you! Start behaving like adults. Fighting like this isn't helping anyone. We're stuck here together, and we'll just have to get through it."

It was the same voice she used to break up their sons whenever their wild playing developed into a fight. It brought Leutholdt and, unexpectedly, Frau Zinsendorfer back to reason. Embarrassed now, the two stared at the floor as if they'd lost something, then sat back down again. Everyone was trying not to look at one another.

December 19, 1944: Early Morning

"Things are going well on the Western Front," Dr. Schorrer said the next morning. He wasn't looking great—it probably would've been better for him to take a couple more days off. Yet his lab coat was in proper shape, his collar unfashionably high and stiff, and his mustache freshly trimmed, though the doctor had two or three tiny shaving cuts. His face looked sallow, with dark rings under his eyes.

He sounded more interested in Heller's opinion of the war itself than in any actual details.

Heller hesitated to respond. "I don't know the details so I couldn't really judge," he said without changing his expression. He didn't reveal that his younger son, Erwin, was likely somewhere on those very front lines, even though Schorrer's casual comment had reignited that fear.

Schorrer had turned away and was looking out the window. "I see this as our last stand," he said.

Heller couldn't allow himself to be provoked into commenting. There was no leeway for voicing one's opinion. No one could be trusted. It was even possible that Schorrer and Klepp were in contact. And Klepp was probably just waiting for that one rash comment as an excuse to get rid of him. Even if they only suspended him or put him on leave, it meant losing his food and ration coupons and being left with less to live on.

Schorrer turned, and looked him in the eye. "They'd be better off seeking an armistice in the west and throwing everything at the Russians. But what do I know?"

Heller returned the doctor's stare, showing no expression. He had to keep quiet. Schorrer's approach was far too bold even if he did mean it sincerely. The skull-badge gang was getting extremely nervous, and they had listeners everywhere. Just one word could cost a person their head.

"You never joined the SS? Or its Security Service? Not even the Nazi Party?" Schorrer wasn't really asking. It was more of a statement.

Heller withstood the man's stare. "No."

"You must be an amazingly good criminal investigator to be able to keep your job. Is there some specific reason why you refuse to join?"

Heller sat up a little in his chair. It was time to end the questioning. "This isn't what I came here to talk about. I was hoping you could help me with the second murder case. But I'm probably taking up too much of your time already, so I can find someone else." Heller was bluffing. If Schorrer didn't reply, he'd have no help at all.

"No, it's fine, Herr Detective Inspector, make yourself comfortable. I unfortunately can't offer you any coffee as I only have tea, and I'm afraid it's only wild herbs. I just thought we could talk among ourselves a little, like upstanding men. These days, it's not easy to remain upstanding, as you know. I've been finding it tough to comprehend some of the things I've seen on the Eastern Front. Naturally, I don't enjoy the same perspective as our beloved Führer. Yet I still can't quite comprehend the policy of terror that's being pursued there, along with all the rest of it. I keep a low profile, but up here . . ." He tapped his temple. "What goes on inside here, no one can control. So. Both your sons are over there?"

How did he know that?

"Well, in this case at least," Dr. Schorrer continued, "I can say that I'm lucky I don't have any children."

Heller had no interest in talking about this. But if Schorrer was suddenly going to be affable, he'd accommodate.

"Where are you from?" Heller said. "You don't sound like a local."

Schorrer ran his fingers through his flattop. "Görlitz. Such a small town, everybody knows everybody. I wanted to get out in the world. Out of a hospital and into the war. An adventure was what I was looking for then, and still am. Baptism by fire—nothing could shock me after that. I've surely been proven right there. If I could make a little confession?"

Schorrer lowered his voice. "Certain developments at the front did not escape my attention. They speak of 'tactical withdrawals' and 'straightening out the front lines.' That's all farce. This was what motivated me, among other reasons, to request my discharge from military service after five years and get transferred to the rear. I certainly can't deny my military past and don't intend to, yet here I do hope to find myself in a more favorable situation once the enemy is at the city gates, which"—he lowered his voice even more—"is sure to happen."

Then his voice grew louder again—a little too loud for Heller's taste.

"So, your victim? No more than twenty, I would say. A refugee, by the looks of the clothing. Might have gotten lost while begging. That, or someone took her with them. Probably drugged her. Or maybe she was unconscious from a blow. There's a hematoma on the back of her head, caused by a heavy object, probably a club. We can only hope her suffering didn't last long. She had a gag in her mouth. And then there's the matter of her eyes." Schorrer shook his head.

Heller shifted in his chair, wishing Schorrer had offered him some of the tea he mentioned. He asked the doctor, "How long would it have taken him to do what he did to her?"

"An hour, maybe two. It might help to ask a butcher how long it takes to skin an animal of similar size."

Heller could have done without the comparison, but it hadn't seemed to affect the doctor. "It must have occurred at night?" Heller added.

Schorrer looked down at a document. "I've put the time of death as the night of the seventeenth of December. This can't be established precisely due to the condition of the corpse. I'm assuming the killer dragged the victim up to the attic during the air raid warning, when no one was out on the street or inside their homes. Leaving the crime scene would've proven far less problematic that way."

"Did he need to carry her, or did she willingly follow him?"

Schorrer held up his hands. "That's outside my field. I could examine the skin again for any exterior wounds, but what good would it do? And she could've received any such wound on the way to Dresden, even that hematoma. You also asked for the stomach contents to be examined. Porridge, potatoes, milk, nothing that suggests any kind of lure, such as chocolate, meat, things like that."

Heller had his notebook out, jotting down the essentials, but none of it was very helpful.

"Any sexual acts?" he asked without looking up.

"Not to my knowledge."

"I'm wondering about the motive. What sort of hate must a man carry for him to do what he did?"

Schorrer pulled out a handkerchief and blew his nose. "What do you think? Do you think you could harbor such hate inside, even just a trace? I don't hate anyone. Or maybe I hate them all the same, all of us human beings. But doing something like that, it goes far beyond hate. I'm assuming there's no standard motive to fall back on."

"You think the killer could be religiously motivated?"

Schorrer laughed, though he didn't look amused. "Herr Detective Inspector, it looks like you're making me do all the work for you."

Heller slapped his notebook shut. "Not at all. I'm only trying to get my thoughts sorted and voice them out loud. The way things look, I'm pretty much on my own if I want to solve this case."

"I understand it's not just the personnel that's lacking."

A silence ensued. The clacking of a typewriter could be heard from the outer office, and Heller had to consider how much of what they were discussing had reached the secretary's ears.

"Looking at the corpse and her . . . various parts," Schorrer said, "it occurred to me that the killer might be interested in a certain visual aesthetic. Does that mean anything to you?"

Heller tried to come up with something, running his tongue over his teeth, realizing his teeth might be getting looser. "My first thought was that an angel of death was appearing before me."

"Really? That was quite levelheaded of you."

Heller nodded and stood. He apparently wasn't getting any of that tea. He figured he'd go check out the attic one more time.

Dr. Schorrer stood to walk him to the door. Once there, he put out his hand.

Heller shook it. "Thank you so much."

"If you need anything else, anything at all, don't hesitate to get in touch. And please, call me Alfred."

"Glad to, Alfred, and you can call me Max."

That afternoon, Heller sat at his desk in his office, staring at his typewriter. He had written down all the information he'd compiled. It wasn't much. Searching around the attic again, he'd been able to get a few fingerprints, which would need to be compared to all the tenement residents' prints. He'd already tried comparing the fingerprints from the Bellmann case and couldn't find any apparent similarities. This was all time-consuming work for specialists, though, not something a person just fit in when he had the time. He hadn't spotted anything else in the attic—no telltale fabric remnants, no cigarette butts, no note. Not that there wasn't a message being left here. That was what troubled Heller the most. The killer wasn't the type you'd figure out by thinking in rational terms. The only way to comprehend what drove him was, as Schorrer had already supposed, to start searching for motives that simply couldn't be grasped by sound human intellect alone. Whatever that was supposed to mean. Was the killer religiously motivated or delusional? Did he hate a specific type of woman—young, independent, emancipated? Was that the common thread? Could he even presume that both murders were committed by the same person?

A knock at the door interrupted his thoughts. "Come in!"

Oldenbusch stuck his head in the doorway and waved a brown portfolio. "Just got the photos. Made three prints of each."

Heller nodded and took the portfolio. "Where have they been sending you?"

"Security detail at Neustadt train station. Our city's becoming a massive traffic hub, I'm afraid. They have a hundred trains passing through each day. Max, the things I've seen."

"I know, Werner, believe me. Please take a photo of the woman's face back with you. Maybe someone knows her."

Oldenbusch was standing inside the room now. "At first, I thought this was just someone venting their rage. But the thing with her eyes? It's downright scary."

That annoyed Heller. He smacked his hand on the table. "Look, don't you go starting with this nonsense too."

December 19, 1944: Afternoon

"Do you know this woman?" Heller showed a man the photo of the attic murder victim.

The man was older, wearing a fur jacket and leather cap with earflaps, and he recoiled, crossing himself. "Satan!" He shook his head and ducked back into the crowd.

Heller, used to the reaction, continued through the mass of refugees who were camped out there.

He showed a dozen more people the photograph, which didn't seem so bad at first glance until they saw what had happened to the dead woman's eyelids. No one had seen or knew the woman. Heller could tell there was little point to this, yet he couldn't just sit doing nothing. He had to keep at it. In war, everything was different, out where the fighting and killing was legitimate. But that didn't apply to civilian life; the rule of law couldn't just be switched off. Even so, Heller knew all too well that the regional court at Münchner Platz was handing out executions every week. When the life of one human truly had lost any worth, why should these two unfortunate women retain any? If the offensive on the Western Front fizzled out, the Reich's last reserves would be exhausted. Germany wouldn't be able to put up any effective resistance to the Russians, let alone the Americans. By that point, he would be forced to consider how to survive at all.

"Anyone know this woman?" he kept asking as he moved through the crowd. He held up the photo to a group of four women. One covered her eyes right away in horror. "You know her? She was murdered."

The women started whispering to one another in a foreign tongue.

"Yes or no?" Heller barked.

"No," one of the women replied while another whispered something frantic and hoarse, and Heller cursed their Silesian dialect.

"Well? What are you saying? Tell me."

"The Piotrovskys, they lose girl," one said sheepishly, her accent thick.

"Who are they?" Heller asked, worried he was saddling himself with more dilemmas instead of solid leads.

"Three over there, have ox." The woman pointed them out. Heller left the women and went over to a family standing next to an ox cart. The animal was emaciated, its ribs protruding as if someone had draped a blanket over a wooden frame. A small child of indeterminate gender was lying asleep on their pile of baggage, while an old woman crouched in apathy next to one of the wooden cart wheels, just feet from the stinking pile the animal had just expelled.

Heller didn't feel like crouching down to her. "Good day. Are you Frau Piotrovsky?" He gently poked her with his toe. She looked up and tried giving a little room.

"Police detective," Heller added.

The old woman started moaning and flailing her arms with her hands clasped.

"You know this woman?" He held up the photo. The people around them recoiled, as if fearing they'd be pulled into a situation they wanted no part of.

The old woman stared as if she'd never seen a photograph before.

"She not understand!" explained a stooped man. "She go crazy, because airplanes! A terrible horror."

"You know the Piotrovskys?"

"With them also a woman, she go get water, go over one hour now!"

Heller nodded, unsure how to proceed.

"Are you looking for me?" a woman said to him.

"Heller, police detective. Are you Frau Piotrovsky?"

The emaciated woman nodded and set aside a full metal bucket. The ox raised its head, desperate for a drink. "We only wish to pause here, a little rest before continue soon. They say they tell us where to, say they send us to Bavaria."

Heller held up the photo. "You know her?"

The woman made a face. "That not Agnieszka. Is she dead?"

"The woman here is. Is your daughter missing?"

"She my niece, Agnieszka. She go run off yesterday evening. No run off, I say—when we gotta go, we go."

"How old is she?"

"Seventeen. Some man maybe offer her cigarettes and bread."

"A man? Can you describe him?"

"I never see him. Someone tell me."

"Who? Tell me. Is the person who saw him here?"

The woman looked around. "Nah."

"For God's sake." Heller stuffed the photo into an overcoat pocket. "You have a photo of Agnieszka?"

Frau Piotrovsky started rummaging around in her personal effects on the cart, under a thick blanket. She pulled out an ornate oval picture frame surrounding a family portrait. "Here," she said with pride, and Heller sighed with frustration. Agnieszka was no more than five years old in the picture.

"How tall is she? What color hair? What clothes was she wearing?"

"About tall as me, dark hair and eyes. She wear trousers under dress—black-and-white dress. Jacket blue, lined in fleece."

Heller had pulled out his notebook and was writing it all down. "Did she do that a lot, go off with someone for bread?"

"Sometimes a person gotta do it."

"Did she do it a lot?" Heller stressed again. "How often?"

"Three times, maybe, but she never go this long."

Heller flipped to the last page of his notebook, wrote down his telephone number, and tore out the page. He handed it to Frau Piotrovsky. "If Agnieszka shows up, please report to the authorities at the train station and tell them they're supposed to call me for you. Do you understand? You need to do this."

Frau Piotrovsky threw a skeptical glance at the train station. "Where these offices?"

"You see those army vehicles near the entrance with red crosses on them? Ask those medics there."

Heller paused. What he'd just said gave him an idea.

"Are you losing your mind, Heller? Is that it?" Klepp eyed him with put-on dismay. "Now you don't even bother getting your superior's approval?"

Heller stood next to the chair in front of Klepp's desk, which kept Klepp standing too so he wouldn't have to look up at Heller.

"There was no time to lose. Otherwise I wouldn't have done it."

Klepp leaned forward, propping himself on his desk, which was piled high with stacks of documents. "Just because of some Polack whore?"

"She's not a whore, and she's not Polish. She's ethnic German, and she's disappeared. It's possible she's gone off with a man who promised her food. I think it's appropriate to follow this lead. One, to find the girl, and two, to possibly—"

Klepp pushed himself away from his desk and knocked off a heap of papers in the process, scattering them all over the floor. "See there, you just said it yourself: possibly! We can't afford 'possibly' these days, now that the German Volk are closing ranks to face the final struggle. Ordering a search for this girl? Have you gone completely out of your mind? Wasting all our resources? No more, done, enough!"

Heller stood at attention like he'd learned in the military. "May I leave?"

"Not a chance," snapped Klepp. "We're just getting started. Staff Surgeon General Funke complained to me that you were questioning his army medics and taking their names before moving on to question military police. What's gotten into you? A good dressing-down is what you need."

"I was only doing my job. There remains the possibility that one of the medical corps was using his position and food rations to lure young refugee women away from camps. The killer could have gotten at his second victim this way."

"I can't believe what I'm hearing!" Klepp thundered, and Heller hoped it wasn't obvious how fast his heart was racing. "You really are crazy! Second victim? You dare to question me, to publicly embarrass me? Trying to show everyone and everybody that you're the big criminal investigator? Well, it doesn't work like that anymore, Herr Detective Inspector. You think we're not watching you, that we're not wondering why you've never joined the SS? You even snubbed the Party! What kind of a German are you, anyway? What kind of Aryan? Do you even have a clean bloodline? Do you?"

"I do." Heller hoped his superior couldn't see his hands shaking with rage. First his thoroughly unqualified boss had the audacity to launch into a foaming rant, and now here he was, trying to imitate the gestures and facial contortions of Propaganda Minister Joseph Goebbels.

"I didn't hear you, Heller!" Klepp said, the skin around the scratch on his face turning bloodred.

"I do!" Heller repeated, louder.

Klepp put on a smug face. "So you, a purebred Aryan, dare to claim that our German men would even touch such a dirty little hussy, and you even go so far as to call it your job?"

"I'm not claiming anything. I simply have to cover all eventualities." Heller hoped Klepp couldn't see how hard it was for him to remain calm. A man like Klepp was unpredictable. He had reached his position of power by acting this way, but his brain couldn't handle it.

If it hadn't been for the war, Heller would have been promoted to the same position long ago. He would have at least reached chief inspector—except for the National Socialists and their war. That was why his career hadn't progressed in more than seven years, why an idiot like Klepp got appointed as his superior. For his part, Heller was only able to remain in his job because of one thing: eight months on the front lines in Belgium in 1915, of all things, along with four verified combat missions.

Obersturmbannführer Klepp was about to launch another full-scale offensive rant when someone knocked on the door.

Klepp raised his head. "One second!" he shouted. He spoke lower to Heller: "Don't go looking at me like that. Acting cocky. I've got you in my sights! That search you ordered has just been terminated. Now go do whatever it is you do while I go see to our city's greater needs. The time is coming soon when we'll get even with elitist troublemakers like you once and for all. You'll find out what Fright Man really means!"

Fright Man? How did he know about that?

"Don't go making things miserable for us," Karin whispered to Heller that night, pressing herself against him for warmth.

Heller didn't respond. He really would like to be able to shave for once, but even with ration coupons it was getting tougher to find razor blades. He never used to go longer than three days without shaving.

And he'd really like to drink a real coffee for once. And he'd really, really like to sleep a whole night through. Yet even on those nights when the siren stayed off, he couldn't get to sleep and would just listen to the darkness.

"I can feel your heart, Max."

Karin used to say that a lot. She would lay her head on his chest, and then it was his turn. And they would listen to how each other's hearts beat, and they both loved hearing that steady throbbing. Yet even that had brought a certain wistfulness. How many more such beats would they have? Millions, hundreds of thousands, a thousand? They didn't contemplate it too much, just listened and listened, letting each other's beating heart lead them off to sleep. At this point, though, they'd stopped having good dreams. Death was too near for that, too ever-present, on the streets, in the newspapers, in conversation.

"Just hold on a little longer, Max."

"They're still advancing on the Western Front," he said.

"That won't last long," whispered Karin, "you said it yourself."

But what did he really know about it? They were always talking up new weapons, rockets, bombs, giant turbines that sucked aircraft out of the sky. Who really knew what was happening? Yet he kept that to himself and just nodded along in the darkness.

They lay like this a long while, yet his heart would not calm. The images would not leave his head. The one of that poor girl up in the attic and the one of Klepp with spittle in the corners of his mouth. It all combined into a single confused nightmare. He smelled mud and rot, heard that eternal drumbeat of artillery.

"Max!" Karin sat up, her hand on his chest. "It's all right, Max."

Heller had started awake. He'd obviously been screaming in his sleep.

And then he heard it. Howling. A wolf's howl.

"Did you hear that?" Karin breathed in his ear.

Heller raised his head to listen. "It's just dogs."

"What are you planning on doing?" she said after a while.

Heller nearly had to smile. They knew each other so well. She could tell he had something in mind.

He turned on his side, laying his head on her pillow. The tips of their noses touched. "I can't just leave things like this," he said, and gently held her cheek.

"Don't do anything that puts you in danger. People like that Klepp, they're dangerous, they're unpredictable. Max, promise me—you need to promise me you won't do anything stupid."

In times like these, such a thing was far too much to promise. "I promise you," he said anyway. "I just want to hear what people are saying—even Klepp has heard of the Fright Man."

"They're all talking about this Fright Man, about some demon. But it's not a demon, is it, Max?"

Heller fell silent. There was no point in trying to placate her. She was a smart woman, and if she was questioning him like this, it meant it had been on her mind for some time.

"It's not a demon, Karin," he said. "It's a person."

December 23, 1944: Early Morning

"You called for me, Herr Obersturmbannführer?" Heller said, taking one step into his superior's office. Four days had gone by since Klepp's fit of rage. They hadn't crossed paths since. Klepp sat at his desk looking distracted and didn't notice that Heller hadn't bothered giving the Hitler salute.

Klepp busied himself with the documents in front of him. Heller just stood there waiting for Klepp to acknowledge him. He wasn't about to clear his throat or show his impatience.

"Any progress, Heller?" Klepp eventually asked without looking up.

"None, sir. The missing girl hasn't turned up, and there haven't been any breaks in the case. Witnesses are contradicting each other, and people seem to be getting a certain pleasure out of serving up their scary tales. I've tried creating a profile of the killer's movements but don't have enough leads, unfortunately."

"What do you think the man's motive could be?" Klepp said, still not looking at him. Heller wondered if Klepp had taken a peek at a criminology textbook since he'd last seen him.

Klepp finally looked up. "Is it just a desire for killing and torturing?"

Heller shook his head. "That sounds too simple. Because that's not the way he goes about it. Killers out to torture use other methods—ones that keep their victims conscious longer, for instance. I'm going on the assumption that the young woman quickly lost consciousness. The way I see it, the killer isn't quite right in the head. He acts juvenile."

"Juvenile?"

Heller wasn't sure if Klepp simply didn't understand or wasn't able to follow. "Like how he removed his victim's eyelids. Did he want her to keep watching even when she was unconscious or even dead? That's the way a child thinks, I'd say."

"So a grown man with a childlike mind? But at that first crime scene, any possible clues in the dust had been removed with a broom, which meant the killer knew what he was doing and was considering the consequences. Doesn't that contradict his being childlike?"

"Not in the least. If a person's conditioned to perform a certain task, the behavior becomes automatic. So it's highly likely that this was standard procedure for the killer—cleaning up after the job was over."

"But leaving the victim behind?"

"Just like a child leaves his drawing out on the table so his father sees it when he comes home. Or the cat proudly offering the sparrow it killed."

Klepp gave a loud sigh. "We have a woman who claims she was hunted down in the night. She's in interrogation room 4. Go question her and verify what she says as best you can. And keep me apprised of all developments."

Klepp returned to his documents, leaving Heller to contemplate his superior's shift in attitude. Heller couldn't see any reason why Klepp was suddenly treating him like a detective to be taken seriously. He withdrew from the room and closed the door behind him.

"Frau Krumbach?" Heller asked as he sat across from the woman in interrogation room 4.

From the way she nodded, it was clear she regretted coming here. She was wearing a faded red dress. Her black overcoat hung on the chair. She sat with her legs pressed together and her hands folded in her lap, her leather bag next to her chair.

"Year of birth?"

Frau Krumbach started to answer, but her voice gave out. She cleared her throat. "April 24, 1910."

"Residence?"

"Schumannstrasse 5, fourth floor."

Heller wrote it all down. Then he set down his pencil and studied the woman. He could hardly believe she was in her midthirties. At first glance, he would've put her at fifty. He then caught himself wondering whether he too looked older than he was, and whether that held true for just about everyone these days.

"Pardon me, but I only came to give a quick statement, yet they've kept me in this room for nearly two hours. And my girls are at home, and I still haven't—"

"Just tell me what happened." Heller picked up his pencil.

She sighed. "So last night, I was on my way home from my shift at the factory."

"Which factory?"

"Seidel and Naumann, on Hamburgerstrasse 19. I get there by streetcar—"

"Line?"

"Nineteen."

"What time?"

"My shift ended at ten in the evening."

Heller gave her a stern look. "There was an air raid siren at ten that night."

"That's right, yes. The streetcar halted at Cranachstrasse. I got out. Four men stayed behind in the car to wait, but I chose to go by foot." Frau Krumbach paused so Heller could get it all down, but he wagged his pencil for her to continue. "So I was heading down Striesener Strasse, one intersection before Schumannstrasse. That's when I heard someone calling out, coming from St. Andreas Church."

"What did you do?"

"I wanted to keep on going, but then the person called out again. It sounded like a cry for help."

"Explain."

"Well, like a kind of squealing, like . . . like a child."

Heller raised his eyebrows.

"A child's voice. So I called out too. 'Hello? Who's there?' I said."

"You weren't afraid?"

"Oh, sure I was, very. But I didn't want to just go running off when there could be a child out there on its own."

"Did anyone answer back?"

"No. It was silent. Then I heard leaves rustling. And then this panting. So then I'm thinking it's wild pigs. I heard there were wild pigs in the nearby park that sometimes came out at night and destroyed people's yards. Then I really did start getting scared, and I wanted to get home quick. I searched my pocket for the front-door key and dropped it. It was really dark, and I couldn't find the key. I felt around on the ground, finally found it, and when I looked up there was someone there. I said, 'Who are you?' He didn't answer. He just stood there breathing like that."

Frau Krumbach imitated his breathing, and Heller nodded for her to go on.

"I got up and . . . and . . . I have a knife in my bag, a bread knife. Should I show it to you?" she asked sheepishly. Heller nodded, and the woman pulled out the knife and laid it on the table.

"I pulled it out of my bag. 'Back off!' I said, and that's when he started cooing."

"Like a pigeon?"

"No, it was more like he did it to amuse himself. And he took a step toward me and . . . he stank so horribly bad. I started to back up real fast and headed for the front door of the nearest building, to ring the bell. Then he started growling. It was this real rolling sound, coming from deep in his throat. And he kept sucking up his spit. Then he tried grabbing me. That's when I started shouting for help. So he ran away."

"Did you see his face? Can you describe him?"

"No, not any better than I just did. Please know that I only came here because I thought it might help."

"Do you think he could've been stalking you?"

"No, I don't think so. He hadn't seemed to notice me until I called out to him."

"Did you see if he was armed? Did he have a knife on him?"

"The streetlamps were off, and everything was blacked out. But I did notice one thing: he wasn't any taller than me, and his arms were really long, his hands nearly hanging down to his knees. Listen, do you think this is going to take much longer? I really need to relieve myself."

Heller slapped his notebook shut and stood. "Come along."

Frau Krumbach put her knife back in her bag, grabbed her overcoat, and followed Heller down the hallway.

"It might be better if you didn't go out alone anymore at night," he told her, and was practically ashamed of giving her such advice, since he suspected the woman had no other choice.

When Heller returned to his building that evening, he smelled something slightly burned. He climbed the stairs, trying to locate the source of the smell. It grew more intense the higher he climbed. The smell was very strong on the third floor. He knocked on the first door to the left.

"Frau Zinsendorfer?" he shouted at the apartment door and listened. He got down on a knee and pushed in the mail slot. Smoke and stench came billowing out. "Frau Zinsendorfer?" he shouted again and hammered on the door.

"What's wrong?" a neighbor shouted from above—Herr Leutholdt.

Heller ignored him and kept pounding on the door until the time for being considerate had passed. He proceeded to kick at the door. Finally the lock busted, and the door swung back. Heller had to hold on to the door frame a second to ease the pain in his foot. Lights were on in the hallway and kitchen.

"Frau Zinsendorfer?" Heller shouted again. He ran into the kitchen, grabbed a pot spewing smoke from the stove, and turned off the gas. On the floor lay a little knife, its blade bloodied. He heard careful footsteps coming and went back out in the hallway.

"Go back to your apartment, Herr Leutholdt."

"What's wrong with her?" Leutholdt tried to pass Heller, but Heller blocked his way with a straight arm. A staring contest ensued, which Leutholdt soon lost.

Heller heard something. He placed a finger to his lips, then pointed at the living room.

The room was clean and tidy, giving no sign the woman might be in there. But Heller was certain of it.

"Frau Zinsendorfer, it's me. And Herr Leutholdt is here too."

Heller heard light sobbing, like a child trying not to cry. He dared a glance behind the sofa, which was moved away from the wall a little. Frau Zinsendorfer was cowering behind it, squeezing her eyes shut tight.

"Turn the light on!" Heller shouted at Leutholdt. The light came on, and Frau Zinsendorfer recoiled and started smacking her face with her palms.

"No, no, no," she whimpered.

Her face was smeared with blood.

"Get something to bandage her!" Heller said, then dragged the sofa away from the wall and grabbed her by the arms.

"What have you done to yourself?" he said, hauling her onto the sofa.

"Let me go, please, it's fine. It's better when I bleed, you know, then he'll keep going, off looking for someone else."

"Now just calm down."

"She's gone mad," said Leutholdt before handing Heller a metal first aid kit. Building residents had gathered behind him. Karin pushed through the doorway along with Frau Porschke, the young woman from the ground floor. Both women saw to Frau Zinsendorfer, who'd inflicted deep cuts on her arms. She turned away, mute and weak. Her hair had fallen over her forehead.

"She needs to leave," Leutholdt said. "She's a danger to the whole building, and—"

"Herbert, will you stop talking nonsense!" Leutholdt's wife said. "She gets scared being so alone like this."

"What if she burns down the building?"

"Would you like to stay with me?" Frau Porschke asked the bewildered Frau Zinsendorfer. "I have a room free, and it's not as far down to the cellar."

Frau Zinsendorfer suddenly stopped holding back. "It's his fault!" she hissed and pointed at Heller, her eyes wild. "He brought it here. It's already inside the building. Lying in the shadows. We opened the gates, and now the Devil is here."

"If you don't keep quiet," Heller said, "I'll have to have you admitted." He could feel all their eyes fixed on him now. "It's not the Devil. It's a person, a crazy man. Do you understand?"

Frau Zinsendorfer shook her head. "You'll never catch him. He won't let himself be hanged. He was stalking me!"

Heller didn't believe it. "He was, was he?"

"He was chasing after me, darting from corner to corner, climbing up buildings, jumping over the roofs, and he found me here. He was hissing and grunting, told me I was next."

Heller knew she'd heard this from someone else. People stood in lines for hours, dragging themselves from neighborhood to neighborhood, always hoping there might be something, anything to buy, toilet paper, sugar, ersatz coffee, lard. They chatted and told themselves stories of wonder and horror. It all found fertile ground with old Frau Zinsendorfer.

Heller bent down close to her. "It's a person, Frau Zinsendorfer. He prowls around once the air raid sirens sound. All you have to do is head down to the cellar like always. Our building's front door gets locked, so nothing can happen here either. So now stop with your crazy talk or I'm taking you to a doctor."

Frau Zinsendorfer hushed. Frau Porschke said she could wait around for a while.

Heller and Karin climbed back up the stairs, arm in arm.

"God, Max, people are talking about it everywhere," Karin whispered. "They're telling each other that it's a cannibal. Everyone knows someone who's supposedly seen him. They're all calling him Fright Man now. He makes a fire and roasts flesh, they say."

Heller supposed that his inability to find the killer was partly at fault for all the talk. At this point in the war, where not even the most hard-boiled Nazi felt he could trust the newsreels anymore, where the newspapers were reduced to four little pages so thin you could see through them and only provided the type of news that left far too much room for speculation, the rumors were now running wild like a forest fire.

Upstairs in their apartment, Heller took Karin in his arms. They stood silently, leaning into each other awhile. Something else was bothering Karin.

"Tomorrow's Christmas Eve," she said, "and the boys aren't here."

Heller sighed. "They weren't here last year either."

"But at least we got letters. Our little Erwin and our Klaus. Ah, Klaus . . ." She broke into sobs and put a hand over her mouth.

Heller hugged her tight. He didn't know what to tell her. But he did know he needed to be strong for her. He needed to keep her strong, even if he had no idea where he was going to find the strength.

It took a while for Karin to calm down. She wiped at her eyes and went over to the window.

"All those refugees outside. There will be more and more. They're stealing things. How poor they must be to resort to that. Many of the children are barefoot. Max, what's going to become of us? I always want to give them something, but I never know what, and I can't go giving away what little we have. I feel so terrible about it. Is it true that the Russians have broken through in Hungary, near Lake Balaton? We're going to end up just like them, I'm telling you, having to hit the road with just a suitcase. But when it does come to that, Max, promise me this: we'll just go, and we'll never look back."

Heller held her by the shoulders. "I promise you."

December 24, 1944: Early Morning

Klepp gave Heller a weary look. "You're doing it."

"Pardon?"

"What's not to understand? You'll coordinate it. You're responsible. I can give you four men for good measure. No more. Go find things out for yourself. I don't know what to do about all the people coming here now. Supposedly typhus has broken out at Alaunplatz. They're butchering horses on the streets. Stealing each other's grub. What good are they if they'll just flee? Fight hard is what they need to do."

Klepp had balled his right hand into a fist. "Me, I've got other things to take care of. We were clearing these two Jew houses, and a Jew got away from us in the process, the bastard, damn filthy Jew. They'll be hiding out up in the Elbe Sandstones. And who knows what else is hiding out there in those mountains? And here in town we'll need to get excavating soon, start digging split trenches. Arm ourselves for the final battle. Over in Silesia—in Breslau, they're already forming Volkssturm units. The people's militia! Once it gets to that point here, you'll need to get onboard with all your frontline experience. We must hold out until the wonder weapons come. That's when the mighty German fist will smash them all to bits!" Klepp clobbered his desk with his fist.

Had Klepp been drinking? Heller couldn't be sure. He also noticed the button on Klepp's leather holster was undone. "Herr Obersturmbannführer, let me ask you again if—"

"You're doing the night shift from now on, going on patrol. Four people is what you'll get. They'll report to you starting this evening so you can start patrolling the neighborhood. Stop anyone who crosses your path in the dark, get their names. You'll get a whistle and a flashlight, help yourself to an overcoat from uniform supply. Anyone acts suspicious, don't mess around. You shoot, understood?"

"But it—"

"No wasting time being soft, not on anyone. Anyone who runs away in the dark is a suspect. That's an order, understood?"

Heller took a breath. "Understood," he said. He felt like someone was playing a joke on him. Klepp was drunk; that, or he was sick. Just a few days ago he was shouting at Heller for spinning fantasies; now he was providing him with extra men. Maybe the Christmas season had helped change his mind. Even though no one dared say it out loud, it was wholly obvious that this was to be their last Christmas under the swastika. Klepp's time atop the mountain would be over soon enough. All his purpose, his prestige, his authority—it was all slipping from his hands. The city was bursting with refugees, and supplies, even the most common items, were running low. Disease was breaking out. And where was Klepp? Clearing out the last of the Jewish houses. Absurd.

"Why are you standing there gaping like that? Dismissed!"

Heller clacked his heels together and stretched out his right arm. Klepp returned the salute in a sloppy manner, like the Führer liked to do.

Heller could certainly do with an overcoat. He did still have his, which worked well enough in the deepest of winter as long as he had two sweaters on underneath. But Karin didn't have a winter overcoat. He had no ration coupon for it, nor had Klepp written down the order, yet maybe his word would be enough.

Heller went to the upper floor, took the long hallway where he had to yield for busy police officers rushing from office to office, carrying stacks of paper, handing out telegrams.

"Herr Detective Inspector?" someone asked, sounding surprised. It was Rosswein, a younger man who'd been rejected as unfit for the military because of his curved bones. He came hobbling up to Heller. "May I help you find something?" he asked. These days Rosswein had taken to compensating for his disability with jubilant subservience, all because the Nazis hadn't sent him off to an institution like the Sonnenstein euthanasia center in Pirna as someone they liked to call "dead weight."

"Here to pick up an overcoat."

"For that you'll have to go down a floor, just take these stairs right here!" Rosswein took Heller by the arm as if escorting an old woman across the street. "Head down there, then right, and right again. Just look for the sign: 'Uniform Supply Office.'"

Heller, somewhat unnerved now, nodded and freed himself from the young man's grip. Then he heard a muffled scream, followed by dull thuds and a loud clatter like a chair tipping over.

"What's that?" asked Heller.

"Interrogation, most likely." Rosswein smiled sheepishly.

Heller went to the nearest door and pressed on the handle, but the door was locked. He pounded on it.

"What?" someone thundered back.

"Heller here, from Detectives!"

The door swung open so violently that Heller had to jump out of the way. A big man in plain clothes, sweating, the top three buttons of his shirt open, eyed Heller up and down. His hair was neatly parted, yet a strand stuck to his damp forehead. He snorted. "Yeah?"

Heller tried to look past him. He could make out a young woman. Her head was leaning against the wall, and her hands were clasped behind her back. Blood was running from her nose and off her chin.

"What's going on here?" Heller said.

"Who are you?" the man shouted back.

Heller now recognized him as one of the Gestapo.

"Detective Inspector Heller."

"From the criminal police? This has nothing to do with you!" The man slammed the door shut. Heller heard the key turn in the lock.

"There's stuff they do," Rosswein said, trying a smile, "and the stuff I do, and the stuff you do."

Exactly, thought Heller, until everyone ends up dead.

SS Sergeant Strampe had joined Heller along with three other men he didn't know. His list told him they were Elkan, Borman, and Wetzig. The three were about Heller's age, if not older, and wore regular police uniforms. Strampe wore a dark SS trench coat and carried an MP 40.

"What are you going to do with a submachine gun?" asked Heller.

Strampe stared at him, emotionless. "This is my weapon. I don't have any other."

Heller restrained from commenting. The other men were equipped with normal duty pistols just like he was. "As you all know, we're seeking a man who's presumably slain two women. I suspect that, after an air raid siren sounds, he somehow lures his victims into a specific hiding place and kills them. Up until now, he's only been active in this general area. Witnesses have been reporting strange noises—"

"Herr Detective Inspector?" One of the men had a hand up.

"Yes."

"Does this mean we're not supposed to go find an air raid shelter when a siren sounds?"

"It does." Heller checked each man's reaction. None had a problem with it, apparently. They might actually believe the story about Churchill's aunt, that the British prime minister intended to spare the city because she supposedly lived here. A smirk flashed across his face, which confused Sergeant Strampe the most.

"If you spot someone suspicious," Heller continued, "shout at them. Loud and clear. 'Halt, don't move, police!' Should the person try and get away, you can then use your firearms."

"The Obersturmbannführer says we should fire at once," Strampe said.

Heller stared him in the eyes. Men like Strampe were the real ones to fear. These young guys had never learned anything except that the Führer was always right.

"People do need to know, however, that they're not supposed to make a move. I've marked down who's to patrol which streets. Avoid taking the same route every time—mix it up. If you run into one another, be careful not to start shooting each other. If there's an incident, use your whistle. If you must shoot, aim low! Do you all understand?"

"What's the point?" Strampe asked.

Heller knew there was no answer that would satisfy the young SS man. So he punished him by not giving him one.

The city had been blacked out at night for years. The streetlights stayed off, and all the windows were sealed with blackout shades, black paper, or heavy curtains. Cars and bicycles moved along with darkened headlights, many without any light. Heller had walked these dark streets and alleys so often that he could hardly remember what the city had looked like at night during peacetime, with those high slopes along the opposite side of the Elbe twinkling and glittering, and especially at Christmas, when people put candles or festive candle arches in their windows.

Traffic was still heavy. Many were leaving the factories after their late shifts, most on foot, a lucky few on bicycles. New bicycles didn't exist. Cars were rare. Everything seemed normal, routine. But something had changed. People were walking faster, speaking in hushed tones, rarely laughing. Heller could sense a depressing stupor. He walked slowly, his shoulders high, his overcoat collar turned up, his scarf so tight around his neck it was nearly choking him. He had on long underwear and a second pair of socks. Yet he still felt the cold. He walked faster.

They weren't going to get the killer this way, Heller knew. Why had he even bothered asking Klepp for extra men? Was it so he could justify his position? So he didn't lose his job? Ration cards? No, that really had little to do with it. He simply could not allow someone to murder at will while they did nothing to catch him. What would that say about this country, this German Reich?

The shift was supposed to last until five in the morning, and Heller knew what that portended for him and his men. He was already freezing and he hadn't even been out an hour yet.

He'd already run into Borman twice. "No unusual incidents," the man had reported before their paths parted again. It was fully dark out now, and a blanket of clouds covered the moon. Heller took Fürstenstrasse, intending to walk toward the hospital before taking a left at Pfotenhauerstrasse for Gneisenaustrasse, where young Alwin lived, all the boy's fun playing war spoiled for good. Heller's pistol rested inside his right overcoat pocket, his hand around it. Feeling its grip calmed him. His left hand held a flashlight that he'd fitted with a red lens, just to be on the safe side.

January 1, 1945: Just After Midnight

Seven days and nights had already passed. Futile days, wasted nights.

Heller halted a moment. He briefly shone a light on his watch: seventeen minutes after midnight. The new year had begun, and he hadn't even noticed. The second air raid siren of the evening had sounded two and a half hours ago, yet the all clear still had not come. Maybe the all clear was only announced over the radio again—that, or there was none. Heller looked up into the starry clear sky that was so bright it was casting shadows. There was nothing up there. Their few flak guns were silent. Could they have a guardian angel? Maybe it really was Churchill's aunt. He shook his head without giving that another thought and moved on, his soles clacking on the granite sidewalk, his breath condensing into little white clouds. He'd run into Wetzig and Borman an hour ago. They apparently were patrolling together, counter to his instructions. He couldn't blame them. Those two were bravely hanging on, whereas Elkan had dropped out without a replacement, reporting himself ill. SS Sergeant Strampe, meanwhile, had gotten called away to other duties two nights ago. It was plainly obvious that he'd asked Klepp to do it.

Heller looked around. Klepp lived in this area, near Grosser Garten park—in a house taken from its owners back in '39 or '40.

Suddenly Heller spotted a man. He held his breath, stopping at the intersection of Müller-Berset and Laubestrasse. The man wasn't moving. He was leaning against the wall of a building in a strangely rigid fashion, as if lying in wait for someone.

"Hello," Heller shouted. "Who's there?"

No movement. Heller slowly stepped nearer, yet kept to the other side of the street. He was grasping his pistol tighter inside his overcoat, releasing the safety with a swipe of his thumb.

"Who's there?" Heller asked louder, yet the person didn't budge. "Answer me." He took his pistol out of his overcoat and pressed it to his side so the person wouldn't see.

"This is the police. Do not move!" Heller rushed across the street and ran up to the man. He only saw his mistake once he was halfway across: someone had left a grandfather clock standing there. His flashlight revealed the smashed wood and busted clockwork. Heller could feel the tension draining from him. He put his gun away and continued onward.

Heller hadn't even slept two hours before he heard the doorbell ring. Karin went to the door, and he heard whispering. The conversation seemed not to end. Karin was sternly talking someone out of something. He rolled over, caught between grogginess and curiosity.

"You there, Herr Detective Inspector?" the male visitor shouted into the apartment. "It's really urgent!"

"Some nerve!" Karin scolded the man.

Heller struggled to get out of bed, threw on his robe, and pulled on his slippers.

"I told him you need to get some sleep," Karin shouted to him as Heller came out.

"It's fine," Heller said. "Who are you?" he asked the man at the door.

"I'm from the hospital. You're supposed to come there, please." The messenger turned his cap in his hands, embarrassed.

"Who sent you?" Heller asked.

"The head physician, Professor Ehlig."

Heller gave the man a quizzical look.

"Please, it's really urgent. I'm supposed to get you to the hospital no matter what."

Karin's hand felt ice-cold in his. He instantly knew what she was fearing. It could be one of their sons. But at the hospital? What could that mean? Was it bad, or could it mean they were in luck somehow?

Heller didn't hesitate. "You have a vehicle?"

The messenger's look alone provided the answer—of course there was no vehicle. So Heller gently slipped his hand from Karin's and went into the bedroom to get dressed. Before he left, he took her in his arms once more. "It's not about the boys, Karin. Listen to me, don't go getting your hopes up." It was bad enough that he was getting his own hopes up.

Karin nodded. He let go of her and followed the messenger down the stairs.

It was a hurried march on foot to the hospital, and the cold could not have invigorated Heller more. The notion that one of his boys could be in Dresden had electrified him.

Seeing all the people out in front of the hospital left him speechless. They were standing in tight crowds or were camped out against the walls. There was no way through. Heavy coughing, moaning, and crying children could be heard everywhere. Heller smelled phlegm, pus, blood—a brutal stench everywhere. For a moment, he thought he'd gone back in time thirty years. Now he could see their despairing looks fixed on him. In his long overcoat, he was giving off a certain impression of authority, and it wasn't pleasant. His messenger noticed his reluctance.

"Just you wait. There's millions more on the way. East of us, in Breslau, they're already starting to hear the sounds of battle. If the Russians continue advancing like this, they'll be here in a few weeks. Then God have mercy—"

"Be quiet," Heller snapped.

They cleared a path to one of the buildings. A uniformed cop met them at the entrance. The messenger showed identification and explained who Heller was, and the cop let them inside.

The air was so foul in the hallways that it nearly took Heller's breath away. Beds were everywhere, though they still weren't enough. More sick were lying on the floor, on cots, blankets spread out. It smelled strongly of disinfecting agents, of ethyl alcohol, of urine.

Heller followed the messenger as quickly as possible, squeezing past bed frames, pressing himself to the walls to let nurses or doctors pass. They eventually reached a room with the door open. A head nurse stood next to a desk, where an exhausted-looking older man sat.

"That's the head physician," the messenger explained and cleared out.

"Are you Heller?" asked Professor Ehlig.

Heller nodded.

The professor turned to the head nurse. "As I said: only the most urgent ones, children above all. Tell the doctors this. All others should be transferred to the infirmary. Curtail the admissions procedure to only the most crucial cases. And do inform Hofmann, once again, that we are lacking everything; penicillin is most crucial. He must press them on this, in Berlin if need be, preferably in my name. Thank you."

The nurse hugged a stack of papers and squeezed by Heller to head out the door. The professor stood and took Heller by the arm.

They walked in silence to the end of the hall, stopping at the last door. The professor leaned toward Heller, to speak in full confidence.

"I'm told you're the right person to talk to. This was once one of our death rooms. But as you've seen I require all available space, so this room has been equipped with four whole beds. But in this case, I needed to make an exception." He opened the door and let Heller step inside.

A nurse was keeping watch at the side of the bed and looked up. "Pulse extremely weak, breathing like before, on resuscitator. Morphine on highest dosage. No sign of regaining consciousness."

Heller hardly heard what the nurse was saying. He stared at the bed. Someone lay there, entirely bandaged. Blood seeped through various spots. The artificial respirator panted, the mouthpiece and wide bandage over the eyes covering nearly the whole face, and only the blond hair poking out looked normal, so human and yet so disturbingly alien among all the white.

Erwin was blond.

The professor turned to Heller. "There's no hope for her. They found her this morning at the tennis grounds in Waldpark. She was hanging there, tied to ceiling beams, only flesh and blood left. The groundskeeper was making his rounds and discovered her in a toolshed that had been broken into. He thought she was dead, and despite her condition he had enough composure to call the police from the clubhouse. When he returned, he saw that her heart was beating."

She, Heller thought, she. Not Erwin, not Klaus. It was an unknown woman. He let out a breath. His heartbeat was calming.

"He could see . . . *it*? Her heart?"

The professor nodded. "Inconceivable, even for an experienced doctor like me. I've seen plenty of the most severe burns and skin abrasions, but that a person could still be alive after such torture—well, I would've thought it impossible until now. Her lungs were hanging exposed—just imagine that. But she's alive. However, I've decided against a blood transfusion as there's no doubt she'll succumb to her wounds within hours. It would be a waste."

"So why go to all this trouble?" Heller said.

The professor placed a hand on Heller's shoulder, sharing an unusual familiarity. "Why? Because she's a human being, isn't she? And because I cannot bear being responsible all on my own."

Heller stared at the professor, trying to comprehend what he'd just told him.

The professor nodded again. "From what I hear, you are trying to find a murderer. He's committed something like this at least once already and will likely do so again soon. You're dealing with a psychopath, which you're certainly well aware of. He's not doing this for fun. It's pathological. What I mean is, the killer feels something by doing this. Do you follow?"

Heller didn't respond. He only saw this half-dead woman before him. They now had to prolong her suffering in the vague hope that she might awaken to give them some kind of clue, if she even could. And what would he need to ask her? What crucial thing?

"We'd have to skip her next dose of morphine and wait until she reaches a level of consciousness where she's responsive. Though whether she's able to understand you, or could reply, or even nod . . . there's no way for me to predict that, Herr Heller . . . Herr Chief Inspector."

"Detective Inspector," Heller corrected.

"If this were a soldier at the front, I'd give him a final blow of mercy. A bullet to the head or heart."

Heller knew all about that. He'd experienced it intimately, one time after the heavy gas had seeped into the trenches and one of the new recruits inhaled it.

"Is there some other way to do that?" Heller asked, unable to take his eyes off the severely wounded woman. There would be too much to ask her. Did she know the man? How old was he? What did he look like, where did he come from, what did he promise her, how did he speak, where was he going? Would it even help him in this city now housing at least twice as many as normal, where chaos was routine? How would he even find such a person?

He glanced at the nurse and only now noticed that she'd been holding the victim's hand all this time. The nurse was young yet had already seen so much suffering, her face ashen. That's fright, thought Heller. Fright made faces ashen.

The professor had said something. Heller looked at him. "Pardon me, I didn't get that."

"We would turn off the resuscitator."

Heller stepped to the other side of the bed. Three fingers protruded from the bandages, slender, with fingernails trimmed short. Heller pulled himself together. It was crucial for him to keep a certain distance from the victims. He never let himself get too close to either the dead or living victims, otherwise they would not let go of him and would follow him home, crouching in dark corners of his bedroom and robbing him of sleep with their whispers.

"Then do so. And please see that she's taken to Dr. Schorrer afterward."

"Schorrer?" the professor asked. "Have you worked with him much? He seems the type who's likely lost any belief in final victory. This doesn't have the best effect on people's morale. The German Volk must be able to make it through the hard times as well. It separates the wheat from the chaff. Don't let yourself be influenced by him too much. Dr. Schorrer's transfer here seems more like a personal retreat. Still, scaremongering doesn't help. This war is far from lost. Nurse Ilka, you've heard what we need to do. And you also know everything you've heard does not leave this room." The professor turned, showing Heller an inquiring gaze.

"I need to take a look at her hair first," Heller lied.

The professor shrugged and left the room.

Heller carefully sat on the edge of the bed. "Nurse Ilka?"

The nurse looked at him with glossy eyes.

"What do you know about the Fright Man?"

The nurse lowered her head as if not wanting to look Heller in the face. "He creeps around the houses. He's not a human being. He's an animal. An ape from the zoo, some are saying. An orangutan."

Heller took the half-dead woman's three slender fingers, placed them in his hand, and gently pressed his other hand on top of them. "Would an ape carry a knife?" he asked Ilka.

"It means 'forest person,' I think—orangutan. How can I know what he can or can't do or what he's even thinking?"

"But why would he need to do it?"

"Maybe he's taking his revenge for being locked up all these years."

"You'd prefer that it was an ape, wouldn't you?"

The nurse nodded, and the two of them held the woman's hands now. "Because if it wasn't an ape, then it would have to be a demon. Herr Detective Inspector, my father was in the last war. And he said in the winter of '17 there were demons crawling out of the bomb craters during the night and taking those left lying wounded out on the battle-field. And they started screaming and pleading for the Lord to please show them mercy, screaming for their mothers they were, and—"

"Enough! Stop it!" Heller shouted.

Nurse Ilka stared in horror.

"Please, just stop," Heller repeated, softly this time. He didn't want to hear it, not here, not now. "Turn off that ghastly device, and we'll help her get to the other side. Would you like to pray?"

Nurse Ilka nodded. She leaned down to the device and turned it off. It fell silent with one last loud hiss. Then she folded her hands to pray in silence. Heller held the dying woman's hand and gently stroked her hair. If he never were to hear anything from his sons again, he would at least hope that they had just such a hand to accompany them out of this life.

January 1, 1945: Midday

"Karin, it's not the boys!"

Telling Karin the news had provided Heller with a nice diversion from the horror. But Karin only pursed her lips. He could tell from watching her that she didn't know whether to feel happy or disheartened.

"It's good news, believe me. They're smart boys and can take care of themselves."

Why was he always telling her things he couldn't quite believe himself? He still couldn't get that final hiss of the breathing device out of his head.

Karin was nodding now, shaking off her numbness. "Another murder?"

"Yes." She didn't need to know any more than that.

"So you're leaving again? You need sleep! And something to eat!"

Heller pulled her toward him. "I need to go to the crime scene."

Karin sighed. "I know, but at least let me make you a sandwich."

"There it is," the groundskeeper said, panting, pumping white puffs into the cold air. He pointed to a few sheds on the far end of the grounds. "I was only here as a precaution, what with so many strangers in the city. No one's played tennis here for years."

"Wait—you're Glöckner, aren't you? Caretaker at the nurses' quarters."

"Who else, Herr Detective Inspector?" Glöckner was trying to act natural.

"But what are you doing here?"

"I come by and have a look now and then. Honorary post, let's call it. Been doing so for years."

"How often do you come by?"

Glöckner puckered his lips. "Maybe once a week."

"Always at the same time?"

"No, only when it's on my way."

"Why are no cops here?" The fact that he had to ask Glöckner was bad enough.

"They ordered me to hold the fort."

From the clubhouse, they had to walk across the whole grounds, passing the covered and locked-up tennis courts. Glöckner walked by, flinging his right leg forward.

"Are you wearing a prosthetic?" Heller asked.

Glöckner knocked on the leg; it sounded like wood. "Accident at the switchyard. Used to be a railway man."

Soon they were standing at the door to the toolshed, which Glöckner kept pointing out as if Heller could somehow miss it. Beyond the shed was wire-mesh fence, forest beyond that. Heller glanced down at the fine reddish gravel. There had been lots of clues here, but they'd all been trampled on and covered up. No one had taken the trouble to secure the crime scene.

Heller carefully opened the shed door. Almost the whole floor was covered in blood. It was all frozen and covered with frost. The ambulance men had carelessly walked all over the place. They'd cut the rope used to tie up the woman, leaving the strands hanging.

Heller entered the shed and held one of the ropes, looking over the knot. It was a simple double knot, not a type of sailor's knot that could give him a solid lead. The rope seemed like the same used on Klara Bellmann.

The victim's clothing had been thrown in a corner. Heller bent down to pick it up. He carefully studied each piece. There were no clues about the victim's identity, not even a name sewn in. He took out his notebook and flipped back a few pages, which confirmed that these weren't Agnieszka Piotrovsky's clothes.

The underwear was missing. The previous victim's underwear was at the crime scene, same with Klara Bellmann's. Heller noted that too.

"Was the lock busted?"

"Broken off. This wasn't heavily secured. Just rakes and wheelbarrows, as you can see."

Heller had another look around and took his time, but he didn't spot a thing, not even a cigarette butt. "What's that out there?" he said, went back outside, and bent down. A glossy spot the size of a coin in the red cinder. He ran a finger across it. It was ice. He carefully clawed at it, loosening it from the ground, and saw little frozen bubbles in it. He crouched, searching for other spots. He didn't have to look long.

"Saliva," he said.

"The ambulance guys spat over there," Glöckner said. "I might have."

"Look here, though." Heller had no choice but to enlist Glöckner to test his theory. "This wasn't just someone spitting. This is a stream of saliva." He picked up another piece, let it melt in his hand a moment, smelled it, ground it down. "Saliva!" he confirmed.

"A dog, maybe, a big one?"

"Yours? Zeus?"

"No, he's never here with me."

"Ever?"

"Don't you see? There's no sign of dog paws. I can tell you one thing: I'm starting not to like this so much," the groundskeeper said, lowering his voice and peering around as if he were being watched.

Heller ignored him. He eyed a stretch of fence behind the toolshed. The bushes had been stomped on, the wire mesh buckled. He stepped closer and noticed a red wool thread hanging on an end of fence wire. He plucked it off, flipped open his notebook, and placed the thread inside.

Dr. Schorrer was obviously nearing physical collapse. His eyes had dark rings around them, and his cheeks were sunken. Yet he still held himself upright and showed no signs of weakening. He also looked resentful, as if repressing all his anger. His hospital building was just as full as Professor Ehlig's. The air was thick and sticky. No word was wasted among the passing staff, no second spent standing still. Heller had found the doctor outside his office and was expecting a stern lecture about wasting his valuable time, yet Schorrer said nothing and just waved Heller over.

"You see it?" Schorrer asked. He pointed around him. "You see it? This is our great German Volk now." He marched off and led Heller down to the cellar, where Klara Bellmann had been laid out to be examined. It was calmer down here, the nurses darting by, nodding at Schorrer. "This is what we've become. Constant state of emergency, unbearable conditions. Ripping up old sheets for bandages and cleaning rags, medications only for extreme emergencies, no penicillin. I'm telling you, Heller, this is only the beginning. The people see the signs yet they don't see a thing. They think they're suffering through adversity now, but they're about to get one nasty shock. This isn't hell yet, not like everyone thinks, not even limbo. It's only when the real end nears that the demons come crawling out of their holes and—"

"Don't you get started too," Heller said.

Dr. Schorrer froze. "Forgive me. I don't mean actual demons, despite everyone talking that way. People have gone completely insane. We're all so-called national comrades? Don't make me laugh. The German Volk? One giant gathering of mental deficients!"

"Dr. Schorrer!" warned Heller, his voice hushed.

Schorrer got ahold of himself, walked on, and pushed open double doors with both hands. He strode into the dissecting room with attitude. "Out, everyone out!" he commanded, and the two nurses cleaning tools at a sink rushed out of the room.

"What else can you expect?" Schorrer continued, his voice lowered. "Have you seen the latest posters? 'Hold On, Wonder Weapons Are Coming!' Don't make me laugh. I recently overheard two privates telling each other that Hitler has an underground city built where we'll all retreat to. Everyone's relying on Churchill and Stalin to start fighting one another. But I'm telling you, they've already divided up Europe, and our Reich is not in it, oh no, not anymore!"

"Dr. Schorrer, control yourself. Professor Ehlig has already been saying certain things about you."

"Ehlig! You know he was one of the first to join the Nazi Party? He knows Hitler personally. Nazi to the core. You can hardly expect the likes of him to make much sense."

Heller placed his hand on the doctor's forearm. "Listen. You've gone far enough. I don't want you risking my life too."

"All right, all right. Then come on."

Schorrer crossed the room, and pushed open a second door. The third victim lay on a dissecting table. They had mercifully spread a white sheet over her. Heller still only saw that blonde tuft of hair.

"The same scenario as with the previous victim. Those very sharp knives, large and small, which can be detected in various places. Possibly even the use of scissors. I'll spare you the sight; you can trust me on that one. Same with the eyes. The same killer, indisputably. But I did spot one thing, and I do admit I'm a little annoyed at myself for possibly not examining the previous victim thoroughly enough in this respect. I'll find you a spot where you can best see it." Schorrer moved over to the end of the table and yanked the sheet back far enough to expose the feet. Here the skin was still intact. The toes were black, frostbitten during the night.

"Here, look."

Heller moved closer and leaned down. "Bite marks?"

Schorrer nodded. "It's in other spots. I was reminded that you'd asked about any evidence of a cannibalistic act involving Frau Bellmann—and I'd rejected the notion quite harshly. I'm sorry about that."

Heller opened his overcoat and took out his notebook. He began drawing a sketch of the bite marks, as best he could. The odd formation of the upper incisors was quite noticeable: the incisor sat at a near right angle to the other teeth.

"But these are only bites," he said. "It doesn't exactly mean cannibalism."

"Well, I never said it did, did I?" The artery along Schorrer's neck had swollen. He still seemed upset, struggling to control himself.

Heller looked at his sketch again, adding one tiny change. "What about the other victim?"

"Cremated long ago."

"May I?" Heller asked, pointing at the head of the table. Schorrer gave him room. Heller pulled back the sheet and saw the young woman's face for the first time. Imprints still showed from the breathing mask and bandages that had covered the lidless eyes.

"People used to believe," Heller said, "that the last image the dead saw remained in their eyes, as if branded there. That's why murderers used to stab their victims' eyes out, because they feared they'd be recognized. But our murderer, he seems to want to be seen."

Klepp rubbed his face with both hands once Heller finished reporting everything to him. Klepp was sweating, and he smelled as if he hadn't changed his uniform in days. Heller had to wait a long time to see his superior, because Klepp was off doing "questioning," as his secretary, Frau Bohle, had informed Heller. Klepp had eventually entered the office with his knuckles red and sore; he dropped heavily into his chair while Heller recalled the blood he'd seen on that interrogation room wall.

All in all, Klepp was acting like he had far more pressing problems. "There are bites?" he said. "Possibly cannibalism? Do not let that be made public."

"It's between me and Schorrer. I found a wool thread that could be a clue."

Klepp thrust out his hand. "Give it here."

Heller flipped open his notebook, and Klepp plucked out the thread, took a good look at it, then placed it back.

"I also found traces of saliva. Right at the crime scene. Someone must have been expending a considerable amount of saliva. I couldn't detect any trace of an animal, but Glöckner, the groundskeeper, he owns a dog. I've instructed Oldenbusch to take any footprints he finds around the location. I can only hope it doesn't rain in the next few hours."

"You're using Oldenbusch? That's fine. Keep in mind, he's getting called up next week."

Heller thought he spied a perverse delight in Klepp's eyes. "Called up?"

"Our Volk now needs any and all hands who can use a weapon."

Heller was speechless. No Oldenbusch meant losing his last capable man.

"So, saliva traces?" Klepp continued. "From a human?"

Heller didn't bother responding. He'd gotten to know Klepp well enough to tell when he wasn't actually asking a question but simply repeating. It was his way of playing for time—before unleashing another one of his diatribes.

"Heller, this is the hour of the German Volk, the true German Volk. What you're now discovering is the offspring, what occurs when a pure Aryan race intermixes with inferior races. A race becomes infiltrated and weak. All these people coming into our city, who gave up their homelands to the Russians, who refuse to fight for the Fatherland, they all are the stuff of inferior human beings. Good enough to work in the fields, but not strong enough to be of service to our race. So here he comes, creeping through the night, snorting and drooling, hungry for that white flesh. A subhuman. A monkey. Thousands of the very same are now in town, just look. They're said to be Germans, but they're hardly any different from Slavs and Mongols, none of them able to prove their bloodline. This is our signal, Heller—we're the ones who must fight. The wops have only brought us bad luck, the Romanians cost us Stalingrad, and all these fringe and ethnic Germans only want to profit from our power. Now they come to us, wanting protection. This is our struggle, Heller, the final battle, and so let this be your very own battle, you against all these saliva-drooling and grunting subhumans."

Klepp eyed him eagerly. But Heller kept silent, staring back blank-faced. Klepp raised his eyebrows. "Well, what are we going to do about it?"

Heller had seen the question coming yet hadn't been able to come up with the answer.

"I'm providing you with even more men, retired old cops, thirty total. And Strampe," Klepp added, sticking to his guns.

That angered Heller. He didn't want the young SS sergeant. "Strampe? I thought he was indispensable."

"He still is, but in this case? He's my eyes and ears on the ground. You think I don't hear all the rumors? It only distracts people from the struggle ahead! So I want law and order in that goddamn neighborhood. The men will be armed, with carbines. Anyone without a pass and out on the streets during an air raid siren is suspect. Maintain calm, understand? No shenanigans. Results instead. Check open doors, search attics, cellars, abandoned buildings, any properties grown over. There must be a hideout somewhere." Klepp rose from his chair.

"One other thing, Heller. Several Jews got away from me after receiving their marching orders. Here in the area. An Aryan mother with two little Jew brats among them. They can't have gone far. Now get going, Heller!"

Heller stood.

"And Heller!" Klepp said, his tone threatening, his eyes revealing a certain shrewdness. "I hear you were interfering in an interrogation. Just what did you think you were going to do?"

"I—"

"I also know, on good authority, that you've mucked up the Gestapo's handiwork many times."

No one had ever dared speak to Heller like that. He kept his composure. Karin's words echoed in his head: just hold on, a little while longer.

"You are weak," Klepp droned on. "You're too lenient. Maybe once you were hard, say in 1915, but now you're old and weak. Because of people like you, the German Reich is now fighting for survival at its very borders. Because you are undermining all the Führer has created. Because you protect what needs to be eradicated, because false compassion determines your actions. I'm watching you. Now go find this madman, find that Jew-loving slut and her brats, and when you do find them, arrest anyone who helped them in any manner, even if it was looking the other way. The strong must eradicate the weak or our race will perish. Do you understand that?"

Heller nodded. "Eradicate. Understood!"

Klepp leaned over his desk, his face red and swollen. "You need to understand. Hard, merciless, fanatical to the death! Now get out of my sight."

January 6, 1945: Night

"Put out that fire," Heller said.

Bitter silence. Several dozen pairs of eyes stared at him. Wild-looking characters, haggard, destitute, stinking, their breath steaming, their hands and feet wrapped in rags. All their worldly goods tied onto carts, with more draft animals left. These people had filled the park at Walderseeplatz. Their desperate searches for firewood had stripped the trees of any branches at a reachable height.

Heller was standing close to the fire himself, feeling its warmth on his face and hoping to savor it as long as possible.

"That's an order!" he repeated. "Put that fire out. If you don't follow my instructions, I'll have to arrest you all."

Soon the people got moving. They feebly started stamping out the fire at its edges, yanking out larger branches. They kept silent, but Heller knew what they thought of him.

"Have you all reported in with the Strehlen Station collection point?"

"They sent us here," someone said in the darkness.

"You're going too slowly," Heller said. "Pour water on it."

"That's our drinking water," someone said.

"There's water at Fürstenplatz. Do it, I'm ordering you!"

Someone grabbed the pail and poured water over the fire with one full swing. A steam cloud full of ashes rose into the air, hissing, making Heller step back in a hurry. He got covered with bits of ash anyway and angrily patted down his overcoat. Karin had just washed it after happening to come across some soap—drying it had cost her several days of coal.

On top of that, there had nearly been a scene at the coal distribution point after Karin received more than a hundredweight with her coupon. Someone was complaining about her in a low voice. But the man distributing coal had said, "You have a nice day, Frau Detective Inspector," and after that no one dared scoff at her.

"Go to the collection point tomorrow," Heller said. "They're doing medicals there."

"Place ain't there no more," said a deep male voice in Silesian dialect.

Heller ignored him. He withdrew and left the people to their frigid night. He didn't feel good doing it, knowing how the people were suffering. He was freezing himself. Temperatures had risen above freezing days ago, but a bitter frost had returned to permeate all.

Today he'd read Hitler's New Year's speech in the newspaper and wondered how many still actually put faith in his babble. Yet he also knew that people were only too happy to believe in his words. People needed to believe in something. So why stop now, right when it was becoming most crucial to do so? Otherwise, they'd have to question their whole lives over these last few years. They'd have to question just what they were thinking when they voted for Hitler, when they kept receiving their allocated food ration cards, when they had to hand over all available metal that first time and buy government bonds, when they had to donate their furs and overcoats, when they were called upon to eat only potatoes with the skins on, when those first death notices arrived and the next ones and the next, until eventually so many were coming that it became all too clear that every one of them would be affected at some point.

Heller headed toward the river and crossed the paths of several of his men on patrol so he could get their updates. They were constantly having to force refugees to put out their fires and warn residents to black things out correctly. The only person not appearing was the Fright Man, not even when the air raid sirens were at full alarm. Had their patrols scared him off? Or was his next victim already in some attic or cellar and just hadn't been discovered yet?

Heller looked at his watch, having to hold it close to his eyes. The little moonlight they had was much too weak. It was nearly midnight.

Hungary had switched sides, declaring war on Germany. Fifty thousand soldiers were stuck in Budapest while the Russians blasted the city into rubble and ashes. He wondered if his Klaus was among all those soldiers.

Heller was now waiting on Holbeinstrasse. One of his men would be showing up in the next few minutes, at the stipulated time. He stepped in place for warmth, pivoting around because he wasn't sure what direction his man would be coming from. He wore as many layers as possible under his coat, yet the cold was finding its way in, creeping through the soles of his shoes, to his ankles, up his legs, and into his belly.

Then the shrill peep of a whistle sounded, and a shot rang out. Heller started and tried to make out which direction it came from. Another whistle sounded. It was coming from the north. He took off.

He reached Dürerstrasse, where he heard the brief rattle of a submachine gun firing. He knew that was Strampe and changed direction since the shots were clearly coming from farther behind him, possibly Zöllnerplatz. Someone was shouting, "Over here!" More whistling. A flashlight lit up, then was extinguished immediately. Heller rushed along Zöllnerstrasse toward the square, but the incident seemed to have moved on, suddenly behind him now. More shots, from pistols. "Don't move!" someone barked. Heller stopped and ran back the way he'd come. Suddenly someone was peeling out of a building entrance, running away from him.

"Halt!" Heller shouted, grabbing for his pistol. Right then a bright headlight flooded the street, a motorcycle approaching. He went to move out of the way, but the person fleeing did the same and right in his direction. Heller's men were now running up from both ends of Holbeinstrasse, cutting off the fugitive, who turned back, running right at Heller. The motorcycle braked, squealing tires no more than twenty yards behind him. The machine gun rattled fire. Plaster scattered from the building behind Heller, and a window pane broke. The man fell to the ground, silent. Yet a second, longer burst of fire followed. The bullets ricocheted off granite slabs, whizzing aimlessly, striking doorways and walls. Heller had thrown himself to the ground and tried to find cover behind a lamppost.

"Stop!" he shouted. "Cease fire!"

"That you, Heller?" shouted Strampe.

Heller pulled himself up, irate. He'd heard the lethal bullets whizzing right by his ear. "You nearly shot me, you moron!" he screamed. "Didn't you see me here, not to mention those two other men over there?"

Strampe, looking humbled, lowered his weapon. "All I saw was someone fleeing."

"That was me," Heller snapped, "running after him! Now turn off that headlight," he added, trying to regain his composure. The light went out.

Heller hauled his stiff legs over to the man lying on the ground and placed his fingers on his neck. The two reserve cops came over, along with Strampe.

Heller looked up at Strampe. "Dead." He asked the group, "What happened?"

"I was going down Fiedlerstrasse," the one named Fleischauer explained. "That's when I heard a bicycle clattering along. 'Halt,' I shouted, 'don't move.' He got spooked but pedaled faster. I ran after him. When I saw him turning into Lortzing, I whistled. I knew Ullrich had to be one street over on Holbeinstrasse. The fugitive tried turning right into Dürer but crashed, got up, and kept running. That's when I fired."

"He didn't say anything?"

"No, nothing. Then Peter showed up." He pointed at Strampe. "When the fugitive heard the motorcycle, he jumped over into someone's property so I shot again. Then he ran onto Zöllnerstrasse, so I made for Schumann, hoping to cut him off. Peter followed the fugitive onto Zöllner. That's all I know from there since I was just getting here up Holbein."

Heller stood before Strampe. "You see someone running away so you turn your light on, start pulling the trigger? A whole magazine? Can you explain why?"

Strampe lowered his head. But Heller wasn't fooling himself. He'd known it all along: it was fun for Strampe. No normal person emptied a whole magazine in the dark.

"I'm guessing you've killed plenty of people," Heller said.

Strampe raised his head and proudly jutted out his chin. So much for humility. "I was in Poland," he said, "under Obersturmbannführer Klepp."

Heller turned to the other men. "Have the dead man brought over to headquarters, right to my office. And where's that bicycle?"

"Must be where the man left it."

"I have it in my sidecar," Strampe said.

January 7, 1945: Early Morning

They had cleared off Heller's desk before spreading out a few blankets to soak up the blood. Then they'd laid the dead man there and covered his face with a thin cloth. Four of the twenty-three machine-gun rounds had struck him. One got him right in the heart, the other three in the chest and stomach.

Heller sat in his chair, a little farther away from his desk. He was exhausted and freezing despite the warmth of the office. Hopefully he wasn't catching that cold. Oldenbusch was with him. His marching orders had been delayed. He had a few more days left and could've easily just stayed home, yet here he sat in a chair on the opposite side of the desk.

Klepp was standing at the window, hands clasped behind his back, staring out at Pirnaischer Platz, at all the streetcars crossing the square and the always-busy traffic. Three swastika flags waved in front of the building.

"Look at it this way, Heller," Klepp began, and faced them. "It turned out to be a success in the end. All will be calm from now on. Excellent work. So it's a Frenchman. He who eats frogs also eats little girls . . . We would've had to hang the man anyway. Get this here finished up so you can finally devote yourself to more important work. And you, Oldenbusch, you'll go fight for our German Reich, our children, our future. This is an epic struggle between good and evil, and one day the world will be grateful that we sacrificed ourselves so dearly to put a stop to Bolshevism."

Klepp stepped toward the door, and Heller and Oldenbusch started to rise. "Don't get up!" he told them merrily and left the room.

Neither Heller nor Oldenbusch said anything for a long time.

"What next?" Heller finally said.

Oldenbusch stood, grabbed his chair, came around the desk, and sat next to Heller.

"Yesterday, in interrogation rooms 4 and 7, they beat two people to death," he whispered, so quietly that Heller could barely hear. "One was an older man, the other was said to be a woman."

Heller had known such things were happening. He'd known it for a long time. He'd been powerless to prevent it—there was no way to intervene without risking his life. He wasn't even sure he could trust Oldenbusch. He wanted to trust the forensics man, every part of his being wanted to, but reason forbade him. No one could trust anyone anymore, not friends, not neighbors, not colleagues. As Oldenbusch's direct superior, he should have explained why two people needed to be beaten to death during interrogation, that it benefited both the German people and the Reich, and that the strong had to eradicate the weak. The fact that he hadn't already could be considered treason. People ended up in concentration camps for such things.

Oldenbusch ignored Heller's uneasiness and kept whispering. "Klepp was at Gestapo headquarters twice yesterday, taking away detainees. One was choked to death on the way over. What a fucking pig, a real bastard. Be sure to watch out for him, Max. Once things really start getting tough, he'll string you up from the nearest tree."

"Goddamnit, Werner, be quiet. Why do I have to tell everyone to keep quiet?"

"What are they going to do? They're already sending me to the Eastern Front, and I won't end up in the rear. They need cannon fodder."

"Last night, Strampe fired a whole magazine at me."

Their eyes wandered to the desk, the shot-up body lying there.

"Strampe was shooting from the hip. I haven't been so close to dying since 1915."

Oldenbusch stared at Heller in shock. "Have to hand it to you, Max. You're staying quite levelheaded."

"I haven't been home yet. I'm scared Karin won't let me out of the house again if I tell her."

Oldenbusch made a face. "Word will get around. Better you tell her before she hears it on the street."

Heller couldn't take his eyes off the dead body. A gaunt man of twenty-eight, with relatively long hair and beard stubble trimmed with scissors. He was missing some teeth. His clothes, a brown coat and drab corduroy pants, were old and patched. His shoes were well-worn and splitting, bound with string to keep them together.

"A Frenchman, right? Prisoner of war?"

Heller shook his head. "Not a POW. Forced labor, in Germany since '42. Was building bunkers, first in Hamburg, then Wuppertal. Been in Dresden for over a year."

"Why is he here?"

"According to his papers, he was working in the hospital. He was repairing equipment, evidently, so maybe he's a mechanic or an engineer. He's had a permit to use public streets since '42 and was allowed to take the tram."

"So why run away?" Heller stood and went up to the table. Oldenbusch followed. Heller pushed the lapels of the dead man's slimy coat to the sides. He reached down into the shirt and pulled out a leather holder shoved behind his belt. He opened it and put it on his desk, at the man's feet. They saw two knives: a large one about twelve inches long and a relatively short one with a hand-carved grip and small blade. Heller lifted the smaller knife and held it up to the light. "So sharp, it could cut through paper." He lay the knife back on the leather flap. "You have those footprints from the tennis courts with you?"

Oldenbusch grabbed his leather case and pulled out some papers. They compared the prints with the dead man's shoes.

"No match," Oldenbusch said after a few minutes.

"You know something?" Heller said. "I can grasp that it was a good thing I did, letting that poor girl die. But now, sitting here, I wish I had at least tried talking to her."

Oldenbusch nodded at that. "So the shoes don't match—it doesn't necessarily mean anything. Everything got covered up at the tennis courts. The man fled, which did make him suspect, even with all his papers on him."

"Up until now, the killer had always found his victims during the air raid sirens. But there was no air raid siren last night." Heller watched Oldenbusch, eager for his take.

"The possibility of an air raid siren is more than fifty percent," Oldenbusch said. "He could have been gambling on it happening and was out on the prowl."

"On a bicycle?"

"Herr Detective Inspector, withhold your skepticism for a moment and consider possible alibis instead. Since he was working at the hospital, someone must have seen him in one of the cellar bunkers after an air raid siren. If no one saw him at the time of the crime, and he had no alibi, then follow up accordingly."

"I have to tell you, Werner: when I leaned over this man last night to feel for his pulse, I'm certain I had my other hand on his stomach. And those there"—Heller pointed at the knives—"I did not feel on him."

"Who brought the corpse here?"

"Someone called for a vehicle. I stayed until it came. They loaded him on and drove off. It was dark. I didn't get here for another hour."

They stared at the dead man.

Oldenbusch said, "You could be wrong, Max. You were worked up, because of Strampe. There's the bike too. What about that?"

"I'm having it checked out." Heller didn't add that the dead man's teeth didn't match the bite marks left on the third victim.

Oldenbusch pondered it all for a moment, then shook his head. This seemed to help him move on. He thrust out a hand to Heller.

"Max, it's always a pleasure!"

Heller reached for Oldenbusch's hand. He didn't shake it, but he didn't let go of it either. He was searching for the right words. He'd known Oldenbusch for ten years and had often been stern with him. But Oldenbusch's goodbye had moved him. What could he say that wasn't just hypocritical or didn't contain some false hope? Oldenbusch shouldn't be harboring any hope at all, not where he was now heading.

"It was a pleasure for me as well," Heller said. Oldenbusch tried to pull away, out of respect, but Heller kept holding his hand tight. Then he placed his other hand on top for emphasis. "Come back, Werner. I need good men like you around here."

The wind blew hard in Heller's face. He struggled to keep pedaling, and his hands were freezing despite his gloves. How absurd, to be riding a piece of evidence to go question a witness. But there was no way he was going to have Strampe drive him, so he had commandeered the bicycle instead. He hadn't told Klepp the details of last night's incident and hadn't filed an official complaint. Some might call it gutless, since a certain level of gutlessness was forcing him to take such a step. Something Oldenbusch said had confirmed it for him. He wouldn't put anything past types like Klepp and Strampe. They were murderers.

The only reason they couldn't be called out on it was because they were killing the enemy and traitors to the Volk.

Heller turned into Güntzstrasse to avoid the wind but got caught in a flow of bicycle riders, carriages, and people with pushcarts either coming from Albert Bridge or heading there. He was doing a poor job of avoiding all the obstacles, not having ridden a bicycle in years, so he turned off as soon as possible. He took a side street instead, and finally reached the spot where last night's incident happened.

Most people hurried past the bullet holes in the walls without noticing them. Many were carrying furniture from their homes, as the authorities had started urging people to vacate the inner city. A few boys were the only ones fascinated by the damage. They poked their fingers into the holes in the plaster, trying to pry out bullets.

Someone had rinsed the Frenchman's blood off the cobblestones, and the water between the stones had frozen into white ice. Heller halted and placed one foot on the ground, trying to re-create the scene in his mind. Where Strampe was standing, where the man came out of the building. It was a wonder Heller was still alive.

On a whim, he yelled out, "Hey, boys!"

The young boys turned his way.

"How come you're not in school?"

"Closed. Got no coal for heat," one replied.

"What happened here?"

"Killed someone last night. Right under my window," the boy said with pride. "Gunfire all over. Just like in the Old West!"

"My mom told me it was a spy!" boasted another.

"It was the bogeyman," announced the biggest one. He was ten at the most.

"No one can kill the bogeyman, you dummy!" countered another.

The biggest one shook his head. "Everyone can get killed," he said, then shoved his hands in his pockets and walked away.

Heller pushed off and continued pedaling. He still had one thing to do before he could finally ride home to Karin so he wouldn't have to make her worry any more than necessary.

Nurse Rita Stein wasn't in her ward yet, so Heller figured he'd find her at the nurses' quarters. It wasn't easy getting through the hospital grounds, as refugees occupied every available spot. Many had resorted to relieving themselves in the bushes despite signs warning against it. Heller soon had to dismount and push his bike forward. At the entrance, where a family with three small children was camped out, two nurses passed by laughing, arms linked as they continued on. Heller didn't know where to put the bike, fearing it would get stolen if he left it at the entrance. Unable to find any other solution, he picked up the bike and carried it up the steps to the front door. It was unusually quiet inside. He figured one shift was sleeping while the other worked. He sighed at the stairway awaiting him, then gave in to his fate.

Up on the fourth floor, still panting, he stowed the bike in the hallway and tried to recall where Rita Stein's room was, marveling at the brightly polished linoleum floor little more than thirty yards away from all those fugitives outside in their misery. He removed his cap, pivoted to get his bearings, then passed a big clock on the wall and yet another likeness of Hitler. It had to be down this way, he recalled, third door from the last. The door was cracked open. He approached, his steps halting.

"Frau Stein? Nurse Rita?" he asked in a low voice. No one replied; he heard nothing. He cautiously pulled the door open a bit more, taking a look through the crack. He instinctively reached into his overcoat pocket and pulled out his pistol.

Heller tiptoed into the room, his right foot brushing a pile of clothing on the floor. It was bloody, and so were the small towels next to it. One locker was open, and he spotted smeared red fingerprints on one door. He touched the prints with his index finger, then rubbed it on the tip of his thumb. The blood was fresh. He took one of the towels and stuck it in an overcoat pocket. He looked around the room, then got down on a knee and looked under both beds. Nothing. He crept over to the second locker, took a deep breath, and pulled on the door. It was locked. He left the room just as quietly and stood still in the hallway, listening, holding his breath. There was a faint sound, like someone gagging. He crept over to the washroom door on tiptoe and bent down to look through the keyhole, but he couldn't make out a thing.

Now he could hear it clearly. Someone was in agony. Or being tormented. He placed his free hand on the door handle, pushed it down, and opened the door as quietly as possible. The washroom was empty, but a thin stream of water was running from a faucet, and a bloody hand towel was lying on the floor.

A hoarse screech, coming from near the toilets, made Heller jump. He bounded over to the stalls. He spotted a wet hand towel lying there and could see bare feet under the stall door. He ripped the door open.

Rita Stein screamed with horror. She was kneeling at the toilet bowl. She jumped up and nearly tripped over the toilet. She grabbed onto the wall of the stall, struggling to keep upright.

Heller just stared, the door handle in one hand, his pistol in the other.

Rita was naked and wet, her hair down. She looked tired and worn out. A nasty sensation of embarrassment and guilt shot through Heller as he realized he was staring at her breasts and her pubic area. He bent down for the hand towel, handed it to Rita, and tried not to look at her.

Rita angrily yanked the towel from his hand, holding it before her body. She was furious and frightened but clearly too weak to voice her anger. As she tried to leave the stall she lost her balance, and Heller caught her from falling. He held her like that for a few endless seconds, his arms around her, her bare skin pressed against his coat before she elbowed her way free and stumbled out through the washroom and into the hallway. He then heard her door slam.

He stood there for quite a while, his eyes closed as the shame of it all burned away inside him, reddening his face and ears. He couldn't lose the image of her naked body. Only the unpleasantly sour smell brought him back to reality. He put his gun away, stepped into the stall, pulled on the chain to flush the toilet, and closed the door, only then noticing his cap lying on the red slate floor. He snapped it up and went out into the hallway.

It took all he had to knock on Nurse Rita's door. She opened it before he could say anything. There she stood before him, fully dressed.

"Please forgive me, I saw the bloody—"

"Doesn't bug me," Rita said. "Not the first time I've stood naked before the likes of you."

Her harshness stung. "Come again?"

"It doesn't matter. Now if you'll excuse me!"

Heller went to grab her by the shoulder but immediately let go. "Are you doing all right? You look exhausted. And you were throwing up."

"There are moments when my strength fails me, believe it or not. But don't go telling your friend Schorrer."

Her cynicism hurt his feelings. "Schorrer's not a bad person," he felt he had to say.

"Not true. You'd think he'd have me transferred to his ward for my skills, but evidently he's just wife hunting. That's been made clear enough."

"I'm sorry. I didn't know that was his intention. But a person can't exactly blame him, can they?"

Heller felt stupid for blabbering away like this. He only did it to hide his embarrassment. So he started over.

"I came here to question you about something. Then I saw those bloody things in your room. That's why I stormed in on you like that—I was afraid something had happened to you."

"We were doing an emergency amputation, and one of the younger nurses didn't clamp an artery well enough. So I had to wash and change. Then I felt like I was going to faint." Rita stared at Heller, her eyes sharp. "Is it true you shot that technician?"

"The technician?" It took him a moment to realize who she meant. "You mean Claude Bertrand? No, that was Strampe."

"Everyone called him 'Frenchie.' And who's this Strampe? Don't know any Strampe."

"Bertrand tried running from us last night. I didn't want him to die, but he shouldn't have fled."

"Yeah, I'm sure anyone trying to run is probably guilty. Look, I have to get going." Rita brushed Heller aside and headed down the hallway.

"Is that your bicycle?" Heller yelled after her. "It's a Diamant."

Rita slowed down and stood next to the bike. She flipped open the spring-loaded clamp on the rear rack and let it snap back down, then ran her finger along a paint scratch on the crossbar. "It is," she said.

"Bertrand was riding it. And he had a leather holder with two sharp knives on him."

"He did?" Rita stared at Heller, curious.

"Do you know if he talked with Klara Bellmann?"

Rita didn't answer.

"Come on, Nurse Rita."

"Yes. Just as friends . . . as happens in times like these."

She hadn't told him that back in December, when he'd asked her about Klara Bellmann's contacts. He took out his notebook and made a note.

"Where does everyone here go when the air raid siren sounds?" he asked. "Down to the cellar?"

"That, or the cellar of whatever building they're in. But that's hundreds of people. You'll never find out if he was in one of those cellars. There's an air raid siren every other day. No one would remember him."

"But he lived here."

"Not in the building. Lived over on Marschall, in some basement. I don't know the address. Some big white house. They'd assigned him a tiny room there."

"Did he and Klara Bellmann meet there?"

Rita shook her head. "Never. They only talked during work. I wouldn't know where else they might have met."

Her answer was elusive, but Heller didn't want to dig too deep. He was finally gaining a tiny shred of trust from her.

"Do you think someone around here could have been jealous of them?" he said.

"You have someone special in mind?"

"I need to hear it from you."

Rita shook her head again. "You don't really believe it was the Frenchman, do you?"

Heller sighed and picked up the bicycle. "Me? I never believe anything."

The Frenchman's small room was barely larger than one of the cells at police headquarters. It had a narrow bed, a little table, no chair. A bare bulb with a broad shade hung from the ceiling, and a narrow wardrobe stood in the corner. The shelf on the wall was just two thin iron brackets holding a single board, with a few books in French and a stack of letters.

Heller looked through them. His little French was enough to decipher that Bertrand was writing to his mother in France. Heller knew nothing about his hometown.

He put the letters back and turned his attention to the red woolen blanket on the bed. It was the first thing that had caught his eye when the caretaker had opened the door and led him in.

"Has he had this long?" Heller asked.

Herr Schubert, tall and thin, with a thick and curving Kaiser Wilhelm mustache, tilted his head. "I don't know."

"You don't know?"

"I was never in his room."

"Never once taken a quick look inside, say, walking past?"

"Sure, but a blanket?" Schubert shrugged.

"You must have noticed." Heller looked the man in the eye but decided not to press him. Better to change the subject. "So what was he like? Quiet? He have any visitors?" He plucked one of the stray threads from the thick blanket, flipped open his notebook, took out the wool thread from the tennis grounds, and compared them in the light.

"No. He was very quiet. Never requested anything, never acted suspicious or said anything derogatory."

"He have any female visitors?"

"That's forbidden."

At first glance, the threads seemed identical. Heller placed them in his notebook.

"Was he able to prepare meals in here?"

Schubert shook his head. "He got all that at the hospital. Sometimes he'd bring something back. Bread, a sandwich."

"You get any theft in this house? Anyone complain about knives missing?"

Schubert didn't know anything about that.

"Did he own a bicycle?"

"He was given one a while ago, yes."

"Given one?"

"Yes. That surprised us too. But he apparently required one for urgent errands, I believe, obtaining replacement parts for heating and the like."

"You don't know how long he'd owned the bicycle exactly?"

Schubert shrugged again.

"A week? A month? Longer?"

"Longer, I'd say."

"So do you know what it looked like? Was it a men's model? What color? Was it always the same bike or did he used to have a different one?"

"I'm not very good at recalling such things."

"So at night, whenever the air raid siren sounded, did he go down into the air raid shelter with everyone?"

"He often had the late shift. Was working on the heating and doing various repairs, which gave him special permits. But when here, yes, he was in the cellar during the air raid sirens."

"Not always, though?"

"Not always, no."

Heller felt around the shelf again, flipping through the pages of each book with the spines up. Then he lifted the blanket, together with the actual bedspread, and the mattress. He finally went over to the wardrobe and opened it. He found a few rolled-up stockings, underwear, long underwear, work pants, various sweaters, a cardigan. Cardboard boxes, more letters. Shaving kit, comb, tooth powder. A small round plastic case. He opened that to find an unused condom covered with silky white powder. Talcum. He touched it, rubbing it between fingertips. He tilted the case, then tapped on it like a salt shaker, watching the white powder float through the air like dust before coating the floor of the wardrobe in a fine film. Then he put the case back. He summarized: no whetstone, no receipt for any knife, no bicycle oil. No female hair, no blood. Though there was that white dusty powder. He pulled the wardrobe out a little and tipped it forward. Without prompting,

Schubert held it so Heller could glance under it. But there was nothing underneath it nor atop it, nor under the bed, nor attached to the underside of the table, and no hiding place in the frame of the small double windows either. The floor was cement. The walls weren't hollow. Heller even stood with one foot on the bed, propped himself against the wall, and checked around the lampshade.

He was sweating a little. He clapped dust off his hands. "Was anyone else here? Inside this room?"

"Not that I know of." This meant little since the room wasn't ever locked.

"What about the toilet?"

Schubert stepped out of the room and pointed at a small door to the right. It was a tiny chamber without any hiding spots. Heller climbed onto the toilet bowl, lifted up the lid of the toilet tank on the wall, rolled up his sleeves, and checked around inside. Nothing. He shook the water off his hands and stepped down.

"What are you looking for, if I might ask?"

"When I find it, I'll let you know." Heller was irritated. Because he'd found nothing. No withered tongue, no eyelids, no little bits of skin, no women's underwear.

He needed Oldenbusch to examine the Frenchman's corpse for red woolen threads. "Do you have a telephone?"

"Upstairs in the foyer."

Heller nearly ran the whole way, found the phone on the wall, and dialed Oldenbusch's number. No one picked up. Then he dialed the switchboard and had himself connected to Klepp's secretary, Frau Bohle, because he couldn't think of anyone else to call.

He told Frau Bohle what he needed, and listened to her response. He fell silent, his face hardening. He couldn't believe this: Klepp's secretary had just informed him that the corpse of Claude Bertrand had vanished.

"How is that even possible?" Heller demanded. She didn't know. "Put in an urgent call to the city undertakers." He ground his teeth. "Frau Bohle, I know how awfully much you have to do, but this is crucial. See to it that the body is returned. Thank you."

Heller hung up. He saw Schubert standing there. "Bertrand's superior—what's his name?"

"Ewald Glöckner, as far as I know."

Heller perked up. "Glöckner? Was he ever here?"

"Sure. We play cards together. Skat."

"So was it Glöckner who would send Bertrand out on his errands?"

"I assume so."

"Did Glöckner have good knowledge of all the affairs going on at the nurses' quarters, and did he talk about it?"

Schubert pursed his lips, which shifted his bushy mustache.

"I'm just doing my job," Heller said. He felt bad for always having to say that. Yet Schubert was also wearing a Nazi Party pin, while he was not.

"This or that detail did come up once in a while, yes."

"He ever mention the name Klara Bellmann?"

"With regard to Claude Bertrand?"

"Or at all?"

Schubert shook his head, but Heller wondered why Schubert had first answered with another question. He kept at it. "You know, the nurse from Berlin."

"Oh, right, her." Schubert acted as if this were just dawning on him. "He did, yes. Once he was quite angry because she'd blamed something on him. He didn't like having to take that from the likes of her."

"The likes of her?"

Schubert hesitated, looking unsure how to talk himself out of this. "Well, she was generally regarded as, as—"

"A floozy?" Heller said.

"You could put it like that, yes."

"What did she try blaming him for? What was the situation?"

"He didn't exactly tell me."

Heller didn't believe him. When people felt unjustly treated, they tended to report every detail. Maybe Glöckner had been rejected by her, a supposedly easy girl. Men turned down like that all too often got insulted, had their precious honor wounded.

Two hours later, Heller was sitting in his office, staring at the wall. His zeal had waned. No one had been able to locate Glöckner. Now he felt drained and extremely tired, his arms heavy.

Seeing the ever-growing masses of refugees had sapped him of his energy. The Russians were getting closer all the time, the flood of refugees never ceasing. What then? Would he and Karin have to flee too? And where would they go?

Yet that was so far off, so unreal, that he couldn't even picture it. What bothered him far more was the missing body. No one knew where the dead Frenchman was, and no one knew who'd arranged for him to be taken away.

If only Heller had some confirmation that the blanket hadn't suddenly appeared in Bertrand's room only hours before, then he could accept that the man was guilty. Otherwise, he still had his doubts. The teeth imprints didn't match, and Bertrand didn't appear to have exhibited any oddly profuse salivation. But Heller had no idea how to express his doubts without putting himself in another dangerous situation. He had the inescapable feeling that someone was manipulating the case—and he couldn't do a thing about it.

He jumped when his phone rang. He picked up. Klepp was expecting him, Frau Bohle told him.

"Finally got this off the table!" Klepp said, giving Heller a crooked grin. Outside, the air raid sirens had started. "Lonely guy, this dead Frenchman, couldn't tolerate the German girls not wanting to mess around with him. If only he could've suffered more. But now there's calm, Heller, I promise you! Or do you still have your doubts?" Klepp glared as if goading him.

"No more doubts," Heller said in a placating tone. It was clear that Klepp would not accept any more doubt.

"I have told both SS Gruppenführer von Dahlen and Mayor Nieland about your extraordinary work. Both were very pleased. They want to honor you with a very important post. You'll be taking over the management and oversight of our trenches being built along the eastern parts of Dresden. I'm giving you a full transfer to the regular police force for this. Frau Bohle will hand you all the plans and documents as you leave. You've been assured a personal car and driver. As I understand it, a company of army trucks and drivers has been assigned for the job along with a troop of State Labor Service workers, all of them at your disposal. Your superior will be"—Klepp pushed some papers back and forth—"ah, here: Sturmbannführer Seibelt. Know him?"

Heller nodded. It was pure mockery. Klepp was humiliating him, and Heller had to take it. He couldn't refuse.

"Full alarm siren!" Frau Bohle shouted from the outer office. "It's an air raid!"

"Well, let's get to it." Klepp took one last look at his documents, then one of the building's air raid wardens came running up.

"Herr Obersturmbannführer, you must get into the cellar!"

Klepp strapped on his pistol belt, which had been hanging over the back of his chair. "Come on, Heller!"

Heller looked at his watch: early afternoon. Not a typical time for the English; the Americans flew by day. He wasn't rattled, though; he was too depressed for that. He only hoped that Karin was down in the cellar at home, which gave him a sudden guilty conscience—he hadn't been home since his night shift.

Loud, rapid footsteps sounded along the hallway. Frau Bohle had been down in the cellar awhile now, and as Heller headed down the stairs with Klepp, he wondered whether the Americans knew where the police headquarters was located.

"They need to team up with us," Klepp said in a low voice, "if they're going to take on the Russians."

Heller sped up, as Klepp was a couple of steps ahead. "Come again?"

"You heard me. Bolshevism is the greatest evil on earth, and the Allied powers in the west will soon regret having teamed up with the Russians. They'll be begging us to keep fighting so we can finally get those subhumans under control."

What about the Jews? Heller really wanted to ask. Weren't the Jews the greatest evil? But he kept quiet. Hopefully he wouldn't have to sit next to Klepp the whole time. Maybe the all-clear siren would sound before they got down there.

It got more crowded as they entered the cellar. This allowed Heller to shift to a different part of the room than Klepp, and he found a spot at the end of a long bench.

"Herr Detective Inspector!" A man about his age said hello to him. Heller nodded, trying to recall who the man was.

"It's Durig. We were in vice together awhile under old man Rust, God rest his soul."

"Durig, right. How are you?" Heller only faintly remembered his face, since all their current troubles were dulling his memory. It must have been twenty years.

"I'm getting by. Heard about your case. Can you believe it? This war's letting plenty of evil stuff reach full boil. Although, wasn't there a situation like this before the war? In Berlin, but even so. They called him the Slasher. Went down around '39, if I remember correctly. Hey, I hear you're under Klepp now."

Heller nudged him and gestured at Strampe sitting about four yards away on a stool with his back to them. People in the cellar were talking loudly from all their nervousness, but young SS Sergeant Strampe definitely had good hearing.

"Strampe," Durig whispered.

"I know, I know," Heller whispered back.

"Klepp's 'iron fist,' they say. Got a real thirst for blood. Sic him on a scent, and he never lets go."

Heller wished he could slap a hand over Durig's mouth. Strampe was sitting rigid, hadn't moved a millimeter. Could he hear them?

"He has no parents, went right from the orphanage into the SS. Klepp took him under his wing in Poland."

"Hey, Durig, you're married, aren't you?" Heller asked, loud and clear.

"Long time now, got two kids. Sent them with my wife to the country, out to Dippoldiswalde. Oh, hear that? It's the all clear already. Who knows where they dropped their load this time."

Durig rose while Heller remained seated. He wanted to see what Strampe did, if he would look around. But the young SS sergeant just stood up, patted his pants, straightened his jacket, and left the cellar. Heller wasn't surprised that he didn't even deign to look at him.

January 16, 1945: Late Afternoon

Heller stood there half-frozen as he watched the men digging. Older men, with yellow stars on their chests. Young men, captured Red Army soldiers, emaciated, their mirth sometimes concealed, sometimes not. Many sang and joked as they wasted their labor down in the trenches that crisscrossed the city.

"Boss man, *makhorka* for me?" one shouted and laughed, although he knew Heller would never give up a cigarette.

Heller gave him a brief twitch of a smile and went back to losing himself in his thoughts.

His new posting was a pure waste of time. One of the supervisors could easily get it done. All he did was walk back and forth, never knowing if and how he was supposed to speak with the Jews. Regular cops stood watch everywhere as civilians rushed past, dumb and blind to it all. The only ones content with their fate seemed to be the Red Army prisoners; that, or they'd given in to it.

"No sad, boss man," the young Russian shouted. "When you my prisoner, I give *makhorka*!"

Heller looked up. "I'm not sad—I'm thinking."

"Ah, yes. I try that, thinking. But it never fill stomach!" The young Russian winked at Heller and got back to devoting himself to his work. Heller chuckled.

Then he heard someone all worked up in a high voice: "Hang you lowlife Jews is what they should do!" A boy was standing near the Jews, wearing a Hitler Youth uniform and the insignia of a flak-gun helper. Wouldn't be long before he was drafted.

"Keep moving, march!" Heller barked at him.

Lunch break was next, and Heller never felt good about getting his hot meal ration from the canteen while the Jews had to eat the cold potatoes they brought with them.

Suddenly the sirens sounded. "Air raid warning!" shouted one of the cops. "Head for the shelter!"

"Jews out!" someone shouted angrily as they filed down into the air raid bunkers near the Zeiss Ikon factory. "Go find your Jew shelter!"

Heller looked for a spot between all the strangers. He didn't look up, didn't want to talk. In his head, he was with Glöckner, with Bertrand, and with Rita Stein. Had she told him everything about Klara Bellmann? Glöckner's fingerprints would still need to be taken and compared with any from the crime scene. Medical vehicles drove from the hospital to refugee camps every day, so it wouldn't have been hard for Glöckner to ride along on one of those trips and lure a young Silesian with a chocolate bar. Forensics would need to recheck each crime scene for red fibers, and Glöckner's cellar dwelling as well. Heller stared at the floor. It occurred to him that he still had the small towel from Rita's room in his overcoat pocket. It was torn from a sheet, fraying at the edges and leaving behind millimeter-long white threads, just like those in the nose of the first victim.

"What's that?" he muttered, and listened intently.

"Airplanes!" replied a man from a far corner. It had grown so quiet that he'd heard Heller's faint question. A buzzing, like a massive swarm of bees, was nearing them. And then they heard a faraway rumbling, of bombs striking.

"Far from here," someone whispered.

"No flak guns," said someone else.

The buzzing grew louder, making the cellar vibrate. The bombing strikes weren't coming near, remaining far away. Hopefully far enough from Karin too. She'd wanted to go into the city today, Heller suddenly remembered.

The buzzing faded, but the sirens didn't sound the all clear. Instead, an announcement came over the radio that a second wave was coming. At least they had a radio here. Without one, they'd be cut off from the outside world. The mood grew gloomy, everyone sitting slumped, heads hanging. It was clear that the factories were the target, whether they were producing artillery shells, locomotives, sewing needles, or camera lenses. Heller now wondered if those Russian POWs were still laughing and singing. Here it came again, a faint roar like persistent storm winds. Louder this time? Why hadn't they heard any bombs hitting? And then they came. Heller counted along, but gave up after a dozen. Just what were they hitting? Then he realized: the train stations.

The all clear sounded eventually and only then did Heller look at his watch: more than an hour had passed.

"Heller?" someone shouted. "There a Max Heller here?"

"Here!" Heller shouted back.

A uniformed cop came up to him. "Orders from Local Group Leadership East. Your men are being withdrawn to clear debris and put out fires. Have them fall in. Trucks are coming."

"Just the Russians or the Jews too?"

The uniformed cop hesitated. "Just the Russians. The Jews are to report to the duty station."

"They hit anything? Anywhere?"

"Friedrichstadt," the cop replied, and pointed toward the western part of the city, where black clouds of smoke were rising into the sky.

Heller came home in the middle of the night. That was after a second air raid warning, which kept him in a cellar shelter near Postplatz until 11:00 p.m. No bombs fell that time, yet what Heller had already seen was enough for him. They had stopped trusting the Russian POWs for anything more than sweeping up shards, securing windows and doors with boards, and slogging water for firefighting even though every possible helping hand was needed for locating people trapped under rubble. The Russians weren't singing anymore, yet Heller thought he could still read something in their eyes. A certain pleasure, a schadenfreude.

When he opened the door to their apartment, Karin was there waiting.

"Is it true—a couple thousand dead?" she asked, hugging him.

"About a thousand, but it's not official."

Anything "not official," Karin knew, was only for her to know.

"They bombed Friedrichstadt train station and the main station."

She let go of him. "You want something to eat?"

"We have anything?"

"I can fry some potatoes. Lehmann had set aside a piece of bacon for me. And I even got a hunter's sausage today and nearly half a pound of butter."

Heller thought it over. "No, let's not smell up the building right now. We'll do it on Sunday, for lunch. I'm not really that hungry anyway. I'll go wash, and we'll get some sleep."

"Max, today's only Tuesday."

"All right, then, tomorrow evening, how's that?" Heller wondered why Karin was acting like this. Something was different. There was a slight hesitation, a glance for a little too long.

"Karin, what's going on?"

"Didn't you hear? Magdeburg got bombed today. It must be completely destroyed. Max, you do remember? Magdeburg, all those years ago . . ."

Heller nodded. Magdeburg was a lovely memory that kept evaporating. Like a dream. A trip in May, so carefree, the boys still so young then, amazed at the steam locomotive, all the people so friendly. Now it was so different. Now it was war. And today he heard someone scream, "Jews out!"—a small red-faced man with thin hair and crooked legs.

He felt Karin watching him from a corner of her eye, and he stroked her arm to calm her.

"There's still some warm water on the stove," she said, and Heller went to wash up. He used the soap sparingly.

A little earlier, a cart had passed him. Ten bodies were lying on it, maybe more. He had looked away. He'd seen enough dead in his life; he'd been carrying such images around with him for thirty years. And then there was the building wall that collapsed on Adlergasse, a crackling sound at first, like gift wrap. A horrific sound. Everyone ran, and the gray cloud consumed them like an ocean wave.

Bent forward at the washbowl, Heller paused. A thousand dead, he thought, and here he was worried about a single murderer.

Heller's eyes popped open. He lay on his back. He couldn't remember awakening yet was now fully alert. Silence filled his ears. His heart beat hard, up in his throat as if it wanted to leap out of him. It was dark, except for a narrow strip where the window was. The blackout shade was not completely closed—Karin always opened it a crack after she turned out the lights. Hearing Karin sleeping beside him, he remained as still as he could, breathing evenly. She lay in a deep sleep.

Why had he woken up? He hadn't been dreaming about bombs or that ditch he couldn't get out of his head ever since Klaus told him about it. He wasn't down in the trenches either, as so often happened in his dreams. That constant, drumming barrage, sometimes lasting for days, had stayed away too.

He still had not moved. He didn't want to wake Karin; he wanted to listen to the night, to hear if anything was different. And something was. It was right here. In the room.

Heller squinted so no one could see the whites of his eyes in the darkness. He'd learned that as a kid reading Karl May Westerns. Old Shatterhand did that when creeping up on someone. Strange that it occurred to him now. He shifted his eyes to the right, toward the door gradually showing contours—a brighter rectangle against the dark backdrop. It was open. But usually it was closed.

He tensed up under their heavy down blanket and frantically tried to recall where he'd put his overcoat with his pistol. Out in the hallway, in the wardrobe there. He'd never contemplated taking the gun to bed with him. Now he regretted it.

His next option was to get into the kitchen, where they had knives. Yet all was dark in the apartment, much too dark. Then came a sound, a soft click, like a grain of sand hitting the floor, or the moist blink of an eye, or a dry throat swallowing.

Heller's heart was beating so hard he thought it might burst, his skin taut like stretched cloth. For Karin, he thought—he would fight for her.

Another sound, this time different. A soft hiss, like an atomizer, like a breath that couldn't be held any longer.

Heller parted his eyes a little more and turned under the blanket as if doing so in his sleep. Then he saw, among the darkest shadows along the wall, a figure. Blurry, with soft edges, almost sheer. He froze. His chest ached. Was this his adversary? The Fright Man? Was he hiding in the shadows, crouching there on the floor?

No, he did not believe in ghosts. And certainly not in the Fright Man.

Heller needed to act while the intruder still believed he was sleeping. He'd count to ten, then attack.

Heller started to count in rhythm with his breath: one, two, three, four—

"He cannot be killed," whispered a little voice, nearly inaudible and yet close to his ear, a cool breath hitting his face. Startled, he opened his eyes wide. A grotesque face was staring at him through equally huge eyes.

Heller swung. And connected. A shriek rang out.

Karin shot up. "What? Max! What is it?"

Heller was already out of bed and throwing himself at the intruder. It fought, floundered, screamed. He screamed too and pressed down on his opponent with all his weight. Someone was tugging at him, hollering at him. "Max! Max, stop it!"

It was Karin. She pushed by him and turned on the light. He gaped at the figure lying under him, whimpering.

It was Frau Zinsendorfer. She'd thrown her hands up in front of her face and was bleeding profusely from her nose. Her nightshirt and dressing gown were all red. Heller looked at his hands, which were covered in blood. He slowly rose, and Karin knelt down next to Frau Zinsendorfer, who slapped wildly at her.

"You cannot kill the Fright Man! You cannot kill him! He's a demon, he's still creeping through the streets. Creeping around and whispering and cackling. And one day he'll come get us. All of us!"

"Quiet, goddamn you, silly woman!" Heller barked at her. He was irate that she'd dared creep into their apartment, into their most private of rooms and right into his fears. He was ready to slap her. He stood up instead.

"Black that out!" someone yelled from out on the street.

Karin leaped up and shut the shade.

Frau Zinsendorfer wiped at her face, smearing blood across her cheeks and into her hair. "I will not be quiet," she hissed, and blood sprayed onto the Hellers' white bedding. "He's there outside, a dark demon, a being from hell."

"I'll have you admitted if you don't shut your mouth. You're mentally ill is what you are!"

"You tell him, you tell him!" Frau Zinsendorfer screeched, pointing at Karin, who was staring from the window as if frozen. They shared a glance for a moment, and Heller saw how his wife struggled with it, trying not to give in. Frau Zinsendorfer wheezed and sobbed hysterically at his feet.

"What does she want you to tell me?" he asked Karin.

Karin opened her mouth, then shook her head.

"All of us heard him, we've all heard him!" babbled Frau Zinsendorfer.

"Heard who?"

"The demon!"

Heller bent down and grasped Frau Zinsendorfer, furious now. "Be quiet!" he threatened, and as he let go her head hit the floor.

"You two heard him?" he said. "Both of you?"

Karin looked at her feet, ashamed.

"Tell me. What did you two hear, for God's sake?"

"It was during the air raid siren," Karin said. "We were sitting in the cellar. Everyone was silent. Everyone was afraid that something bad was going to happen since they'd already come once during the day. And then we heard him, as if he were standing right in our building, as if he were climbing the stairs. Herr Leutholdt wanted to go out and take a look. But then his fear got to him too."

"Karin, what exactly did you hear?"

"All of it," she said, flinging her hand in a despairing gesture. "Everything the people are telling each other. He was laughing loudly, like a madman, with this crazy joy. Bellowing, howling like a wolf. Then he was crying."

"He was crying, that's right," whispered Frau Zinsendorfer.

"That's why I took her in, Max. Because she was just so terrified. I told her she could come to our place."

"You should have told me!"

It was all his fault. He hadn't bothered inquiring about how her day had gone. Karin hadn't been upset because of Magdeburg. It was because of the Fright Man.

"Very well," Heller added and straightened up, smoothed out his pajamas, and buttoned his undone buttons. Then he helped up Frau Zinsendorfer. "Go wash yourself. And Karin, please make her some tea?"

Karin glanced at him. "What are you going to do?" she asked, though she already knew the answer.

February 13, 1945: Night

The nerve-racking howl of air raid sirens shrilled in Heller's ears. Full alarm.

He ran across the cobblestones. He slipped and stubbornly fought his way onward, not wanting to squander his energy shouting. Air raid sirens had sounded many times in the last four freezing weeks, during which he'd been roving the streets, night after night, despite his wife's speechless glances pleading with him to stay home. Of course he should've stayed with her instead of hunting down a phantom through the pitch-black alleys of the Johannstadt neighborhood where the first murder had taken place.

Heller leaped onto the sidewalk, his freezing hands balled into fists.

The endless howling was piercing and all-pervading. It penetrated his bones and his brain, allowing no other thoughts. Demons singing. And it seemed it would never cease.

He'd lost sight of the man yet again. Where now? To the left. Heller's shoulder grazed the corner of an apartment building, and he lost his step yet continued on. Sweat ran down his face, chilling quickly, his teeth chattering, his nostrils frosting over. Biting frost covered everything. He rubbed at his face, a nagging pain hammering at the inside of his forehead, growing worse every time his heels struck the sidewalk.

He'd lost his cap long ago. His overcoat hung heavy off his shoulders, and the tails smacked at his legs. The man ahead of him was wearing only pants and a white shirt, his upper body radiating steam that trailed behind him. Heller ran through it before it could evaporate; he was that close to him. Could nearly grab him.

The sirens, howling from hell, filled him with such fear. You could scream just not to hear it.

Heller had already heard the man's odd cackling and yelping twice now, from a distance. He had been following the noises, kept on listening for more, but to no avail. Yet it had strengthened his will not to give up, not after all those long freezing nights where nothing happened apart from having to see so many mute and dispirited people outside.

This time he'd gotten so close. This time he'd nearly had him. He had heard him howling, right as the air raid warning had gone silent. "Come here," the Fright Man had whispered. "Come over here, come over here to me. I have something sweet for you," came the purr, "delicious goodies, sweet goodies. Just come here, be a darling child." Heller had crept up, finding him in the darkness, and felt for the fabric of his sleeve. He dug his fingers in. Yet the man had torn himself away and given Heller a harsh slap in the jaw with the back of his hand.

Heller staggered onward, still tasting the blood in his mouth, yet he kept chasing the man through the darkness of the blacked-out streets. Were they running in a circle? All the buildings looked the same with their high dark walls. No light, not a soul around, the people all squatting in their cellars, squeezed together, filled with that fear, resigned to their fate. It was as if the two of them were all alone in the world. Only he and the other. Hunter and hunted.

Heller just missed a streetlamp at the last second, painfully knocking his elbow against it and losing his balance, falling back a few yards.

His eyes burned. He wheezed and gasped for air. But the other man wasn't giving up. He was steaming, a moving bulk, clumsy. His head tottering, all wide in the neck, chin jutting forward. His breath came in spurts, staccato. He didn't look around, just kept running as if the Devil were behind him.

The ground started vibrating. There were maybe ten yards separating them. Yet Heller's right foot hurt so much that he'd started hobbling and had to grit his teeth so as not to moan with every other step. He wouldn't be able to endure it much longer. He reached into his overcoat pocket and grasped at his pistol but could hardly feel it with his frozen fingers. The pistol got caught on the lining.

He yanked the gun in anger, jerking it back and forth, and suddenly got it free. He grabbed the gun with both hands. "Stop where you are!" he shouted. "I'll shoot!"

The howl of sirens was ebbing. No all clear? What about that other sound, this vibration? Could it have been rumbling thunder?

The fleeing man dared a glance back but kept running. His arms were flailing frantically, his breath pumping out, wheezing.

Heller took aim at full speed. He shot, a quick, sharp crack. Sparks bounced off the sidewalk. The man stumbled, toppled over. Heller was on him at once, about to pounce. But a foot struck him in the stomach, knocking air from his lungs. And the man was up again and bolting onward, running for his life.

Heller gasped for air. Everything went black for a second, but his rage won out. Hunching now, his guts stinging, he ran onward. He would not let him get away. He wouldn't aim for the legs next time.

The sirens had ceased yet that droning vibration still filled his ears. Was it his blood rushing through him and making him shake? Or was it airplanes? And where was the man?

Something struck his legs. Heller went down hard, fully stretched out, scraping his hands but somehow still clutching his pistol tight. The man kicked at him now, striking his kidneys. Then he gave up and fled again. Heller aimed from the ground, and shot twice. Hit him.

The man let out a hoarse scream, and his white shirt darkened. Heller sprung up. This was his chance. The droning grew louder, rolling nearer like a hurricane, filling the whole sky, making the earth quake.

"Come on, come on!" yelled a man who had emerged from an apartment building and suddenly blocked his way.

Heller tried to push by, but the man grabbed him by the arm. "Come on, in here! You need to get out of here. This one's serious."

"No!" Heller tried to free himself from the man's grip. Flashes across the sky lit up the street. "I'm a cop!" he shouted, and in the eerie glare he could see the desperate man disappear around the corner. That was no demon, nor monster. It was just a person. Bleeding and full of fear.

"You not hearing me?" insisted the man—an air raid warden—and Heller gave up.

This was terribly serious.

The flak guns fired away, but sporadically, having almost no effect against the rolling cloud of steel and explosives since most of their guns were at the front. Tracers soared into the sky, and spotlight beams reached into the night, found their first targets, sunk in their teeth. Buildings blocked his full view, but he could still see an unnatural glow above the rooftops in the west. There was a delay before the bomb bursts reached his ears. Hurtling his way. Whistling and shrieking.

"Come on already!" the man yelled, grabbing Heller's arm again.

Heller followed now. They heard the thunder rolling over them before they could reach the cellar. A massive blast hurled the front door shut as they entered, shattering windowpanes.

"Lord in heaven!" bawled the air raid warden, shoving Heller, urging him down the stairs.

Heller missed the last step, stumbled, fell against a wall, and ended up crawling through the door on all fours. Five, ten, fifteen, twenty solid hits after another kept him from finding his feet. The shelter door slammed shut behind him and was locked. Heller looked up and, under the light of two naked bulbs, was left peering at a row of distorted faces, at panicked eyes, mouths hanging open. There, among all the people pressed up against the bare walls of this small room, sat a child wearing an American Indian costume. What an absurd sight. Carnival season, Heller suddenly realized. And the next series of bomb strikes was already nearing, the tenth exploding really close by. The light went out. Heller's mouth dropped open. Little pebbles trickled down on him. He tasted dust and blood, and what he first thought was his ears ringing was actually the women and children screaming. But the roar of more bombs was already drowning them out. This was the very moment when Heller, who'd already been in one war and stopped seeking any consolation in God long ago, figured his life was over. He thought of Karin. It hurt not to be with her now. He would have held her in his arms, consoling her, thanking her for all their years together. He'd always wanted to die with her.

Not even those thoughts could last. What followed now robbed him of all senses, of any sensation of time and space. Bombs exploded one second after another, deafening all, allowing no breaths, no time to think. Explosions shook the cellar, hurling people all over. A shrill blare filled Heller's ears.

The bursting and quaking would not cease. Another close strike made all noise around him fade. All he heard was a piercing whistle. Now, he thought, now. Death was finally coming, to claim what it could not in the trenches.

He wasn't sure how long it had lasted. Maybe he'd lost consciousness, maybe he'd lost his mind. Far in the distance he thought he could make out people, hear them coughing, sobbing, moaning. This could not be. It simply wasn't possible. No one could still be alive. Including him.

Yet then he was sensing things again, feeling concrete under his stomach, tasting metal and stone grit, coughing, spitting, trying to pull himself up. His head felt so extremely heavy that he was barely able to lift it off the ground. Something warm was running across his face from his ears. He felt the back of his head and found a warm and sticky spot—blood.

Eventually the beam of a flashlight punctured the darkness. Heller squinted, saw nothing but a white fog. It was dust that refused to settle, with blurry movements within, like people floating in soapy water. He had such a horrible thirst, and sand grated between his teeth. Someone grabbed him, turned him over onto his back. The light beam blinded him for a second before moving on. He struggled to turn onto his stomach again so he could prop himself up on all fours but hit his head hard on something. He felt around in the darkness and grasped at a large chunk of concrete. Finally he pulled himself up, took a step, struck something soft.

"Pardon me," he said, but he couldn't hear his own voice.

He detected things rustling and feeling around, vague hands moving in the faint afterglow of the flashlight. There was whirring, recombining into words. Someone shook him. The harsh movement made him topple backward against a wall.

"Help us! We have to get out!" he finally understood. He pushed himself off the wall and followed the crouching silhouette scurrying through the dusty air, hunching over too. They felt their way along the wall with their fingertips. "Over there!"

"It's stuck!" someone screamed.

Heller wanted to grab hold and help pull the door open, but he couldn't get a grip. The men were already giving up.

"Dig our way out," Heller understood, as the shrill ringing in his head continued.

It's impossible, he thought, digging out like this.

"Someone will be coming soon enough," someone said to calm everyone.

"Just who might that be, jackass?" cursed another. "Don't you hear?"

It was completely still for a moment. Out from under the shrill piercing in his ears came a big wave of something, a great rumble. Heller knew the sound. Fire. Only now did he feel the heat radiating from the door.

"We have anything to pry it open with? An iron bar?" he asked. He could barely hear himself yet his words seemed to reach the others. They fanned out.

"Here. Over here," one shouted. "Come on!"

Heller followed the shout and the flashlight beam shooting around the room but ended up getting tangled on the same concrete chunk he'd used to pull himself up. Next to it, half-underneath, lay the air raid warden. The light beam only paused on him a second before darting up high to the ceiling from which the big chunk had fallen. One of the men was already climbing up there, reaching into the gap with his bare hands, but he leaped clear as quickly as possible to save himself from the avalanche of rock, debris, and wood that came tumbling down.

More dust welled up, enveloping them completely. Heller pressed his overcoat collar over his mouth and nose yet still breathed in dust, feeling it clogging his hair, coating his skin, stuffing up his nose. His throat turned raw; clearing it and spitting did no good. His thirst suddenly became overpowering.

"We must get up above," someone ordered. "On the double!"

The coughing in the cellar was multiplying.

That was one way to die: suffocating on dust. Now came the women and children, stumbling, stunned, feeling their way along as if blinded. All wanted to get away from here fast. No one was screaming anymore. They pressed and pushed in a silent panic, all white faces, looking up to the gap in the ceiling, ashen figures with dust covering their hair and shoulders, among them the little Indian.

Heller tried not to think about water, cold water, clear water. He bent down, picked up the boy, and handed him to the man who'd climbed back up on the big chunk of concrete. The man took the boy and shoved him up through the gap.

"Next! Where's Egon?"

Heller helped to push up another child and then another much too heavy for him. His back stung. He couldn't lift the women. A second man came up, braced himself, and pushed the women up while holding them wherever he could, no shame left here. Once all were up, the man with the flashlight made another round.

Heller waited.

"Everyone's out," the man shouted. "Is Alfred up? Hannah?" he then shouted, and got an affirmative reply.

Now it was Heller's turn. It took all he had to climb up onto the concrete chunk. He had to kneel and got dizzy looking up. His neck hurt more than his back. A brick must've hit him.

"Get going!" the man beside him shouted. "You gotta help me once you're up!" Then he bent down, cupping his hands to boost Heller. Heller stepped onto his hands, felt himself being lifted, and spread out his arms to grab hold of something. He was pulled up by the collar. The heat hit him. They carelessly released him, off to the side, and he stumbled and fell into debris. The last man was now being hauled up through the hole.

"Köhler?" someone asked.

"He's dead," came the reply, and a woman started screaming.

"Where to now?"

"To the Elbe!" The people were already climbing over the rubble that had once been their building, now piled yards high all around them.

Heller observed them like the stranger he was. He didn't belong to them, and they didn't take him along. Before he realized that it would have been wiser to go with them, he was left all alone. Alone in a completely foreign world. This was no longer his city, no longer his part of town, no longer the street he'd just been running down. It didn't even seem to be his planet anymore.

It was a hell of heat and thunder, of glaring light and dark shadows where black devils squatted and devoured people. The roaring was a relentless thunderstorm, a howling and sucking, a storm tearing at his coat lapels, at his hair, a blazing hurricane that wanted to ignite his whole body. A massive wave of fire was charging through the city chasms, shooting into the sky with wild spirals. Heller tried to shield his face, could feel the blistering air parching his skin, singeing his hair, trying to devour his eyes. It was total madness. No way up or down. No across. No escape. This was hell.

It took him forever to stand up. He dusted off his clothes as best as he could, then felt for his pistol out of sheer habit, as if he had all the time in the world. It was there in his overcoat pocket. He was alive, but the world around him didn't exist anymore. He felt strangely vacant, as if paralyzed, his thoughts frozen. But he couldn't stay here alone, with only a dead air raid warden somewhere below him, so he began climbing the mountain of rubble. He had to climb three yards up before he could see beyond the ridge.

Fires blazed everywhere he looked. Stray figures rushed through the inferno, stumbling like startled animals, falling over, pulling themselves up again, crossing each other's paths, and joining together only to immediately split up again. The flames got one. The person writhed around, turned to the fire, and withered in it like a scarecrow. Others were knocked to the ground by the force of the firestorm and sucked up into a whirlwind of flames. Never-ending mountains of rubble towered all around, immersed in glaring, flickering orange. Isolated dull explosions erupted, like absurdly bursting soap bubbles. The bricks and stones and wood cracked and broke under his feet. Less than a hundred yards from him, a single building wall had survived the bombings but now collapsed without any apparent sound, and the clouds of dust were sucked up by the boiling hot air and mixed with the reddish-brown fire clouds filling the sky. No actual street was visible anywhere. Above him the engines roared on as if the Devil himself were humming a melody.

Heller tasted ash and blood. As soon as he opened his mouth, his tongue seemed to wither. He could see only through the slits between his fingers shielding his face. He yanked his overcoat up over his head and slogged onward. He climbed over the remains of a house, dragging himself upward, skidded down into the void beyond, and landed hard on his ribs.

He then changed direction, helped along by a toppled chimney offering a better foothold, better progress. Crawling along it, Heller managed to make it twenty yards before the mountain of rubble dropped off into a bomb crater. He pushed his legs over the edge, trying to grab hold with his toes, then felt something give way under his feet. The whole slope began sliding away. He let go but was pulled down with it. Glowing hot bits of rubble peppered his collar and sleeves. He screamed and then lay there, on his stomach, at the smoldering rim of the crater. Ripped-out pipes poked out of the ground, and he stubbornly grabbed at them, hauled himself up, and used them as steps so he could reach a street. As he moved on, he suddenly became tangled in burning curtains that had been ripped from the windows and were fluttering around like red-hot birds. Again he fell, flailing to free himself from the fabric, and he rolled onto his side, feeling at cobblestone, then jerking his hands away since the ground was unbearably hot and glittering from millions of glass splinters.

A woman scurried past, blindly stepping on his ankle. She caught herself from falling and rushed onward in a panic, dragging a little girl by the hand. Heller raised his hand. Yet she didn't notice. Only the little girl turned to him as they headed on. And for one moment, the girl and Heller looked into each other's eyes.

That brought Heller to again. He wondered where to go. Heading to the Elbe was a good idea; the broad meadows along the river might provide enough shelter. But where was the river?

Was the woman running that way with the little girl? There was no getting through here. The street ahead was blown open. Going around the crater might be possible, but there was fire all around. Heller could barely stand now. The hurricane was pulling at him, trying to tear his overcoat from his body, and only on his knees could he make any progress. But the cobblestones were so hot he had to protect his hands with his coat sleeves. Fires blazed from the few buildings still standing, fanned by the storm winds, the flames stretching far out into the street. He saw streetlamps that had turned soft as butter and toppled over. He'd completely lost his bearings. Was this Holbeinstrasse, or had they climbed out on the other side? Were those trees burning over there? And where was that exactly? He suddenly spotted a figure crawling out from a pile of rubble. After a few yards, the figure rose and staggered toward him with short, teetering steps.

Heller was about to ask where they were, but the firestorm winds ripped the words from his mouth. The woman wore a long winter overcoat with only a nightgown underneath, and she stared right through him, her hair all singed away, even her eyebrows gone. Her coat was smoking. She tried to get by him, her eyes wide and mouth hanging open. Where was she trying to go? Behind him was all fire and debris.

"No, wait!" Heller shouted and went to touch her shoulder. The woman squawked something in a hoarse voice, turned to him, stiffened, and fell backward. Heller knelt down to help her, but she was dead. He recognized her now. He'd just helped her escape the cellar.

Heller turned away. A wave of nausea and fear surged through him. He didn't want to die like this. He didn't want to die at all.

Then he saw a manhole cover. He thought maybe he could hide down there. He crawled over to it, pushed away a chunk of wall with his foot, and grasped at the holes with his fingers. Seething hot air hissed up from the sewer system and scalded his fingers. The pain was so bad it shocked him out of his daze. Now he could feel with every fiber of his being just what had happened, how it was wrenching at him, how the flames kept seeking out more and more fuel. How his hair was frying, how the hot air was trying to shrivel his lungs and desiccate his eyes, how his oxygen was dwindling. All around him more of the remaining walls were giving way, flooding the street with debris and glass, the mountains piling up, insurmountable. But where had that woman with the little girl gone? Following her seemed like his only chance. He was now crawling close to the ground with his overcoat over his head, yet the heat from the road was nearly unbearable. A sudden intuition made him search for his pistol inside his coat, to toss it away. It was so hot the skin of his hand blistered instantly. And when he dared to stick his head out from under his coat, his hair caught fire. He slapped at his head with both hands and yanked his coat back over him. The thought occurred to him that maybe he should've kept the gun. He could've used it to put an end to his misery if need be.

Then off to his right he saw a street-level cellar entrance. He pulled himself up, ran ducking toward the fire pumping out of the building's ground-floor windows, threw himself down the stairs, landed hard, and found himself before an open cellar door. He crawled inside, gasping for air, yet all he breathed in was hot gas. He heard a high whistling, shrill like a boiling teakettle, then felt a strong draft, and he didn't hesitate to grope his way along in the darkness. Crawling toward the whistling, he found a breach in the wall leading to the next building. He got up, stumbled blindly with his arms out in front of him, found another opening, and tumbled over something soft and lifeless.

"Hello? Hello?" Heller stood again, feeling around. After a dozen more openings, he spotted a shimmer of light ahead. He figured he'd gone several hundred yards, maybe a whole block. He reached an exit door, and was completely out of breath. Dark bundles lay all around. As he peered closer, he realized they were dead bodies. They looked as if they were sleeping, the skin of their faces like parchment. To get out, he'd have to climb over them all. But there was no other way, he needed to get back outside. He couldn't get enough oxygen no matter how much he breathed. Desperate now, he pushed himself onward and crawled over the dead.

Finally outside, Heller found himself at a large intersection. The fire wasn't drawing as much fuel here, yet a gust of wind still knocked him to the ground. He crawled to the shelter of an advertising column with its posters glowing and smoldering but not on fire. He had no idea where he was. Nothing around him looked familiar. The column crunched and crackled with heat as if about to burst any second. He crawled away from it. Where was he supposed to head now?

He had to find a better view of things to get some idea of where the Elbe might be. To his right was a collapsed building, the beams of its roofing truss standing every which way among the bricks and remains. Heller began climbing them, on all fours. The loose bricks and rubble kept falling away under him, tumbling down and yanking him back. He held tight to the remains of a wall, balanced along a beam for some yards, then went back on all fours. He slowly made his way like this, passing smashed furniture, shreds of drapery, a single ski. As he went to support himself on a seemingly secure floorboard, it dropped away under his weight. A piece of wall collapsed too, plummeting down through the void, taking everything in its path. Heller threw himself to the other side, searching for something to hold on to and found a busted water pipe poking high up into the air. Suddenly there was a new noise. Like someone yelling. Heller crept toward the gaping hole in the debris. He lowered his head, listening.

Someone was screaming down there.

"I . . ." He had to clear his throat. "Hold on!" he shouted as loud as he could, but only a croak came out.

"Help! We need help!" someone screamed.

Heller couldn't help them. The people down there were buried under several tons of debris ten yards deep, and it was impossible to do anything for them. He needed to help himself. He needed to get up higher onto the crest of this mountain of rubble so he could get his bearings.

"Hold on, help's coming soon!" he shouted again. Then he climbed onward, feeling his way along, trying beams and remains of walls. After what felt like an eternity, he reached the top and gazed all around. To his horror, he saw that the entire world was on fire.

He turned away from the sight and stared up into the bloodred sky for a few seconds before he dared look at his city again. He couldn't believe it. All of Dresden was burning, as far as the eye could see. All around him were only craters and mountains of debris, fires blazing away. Black clouds of smoke climbed up into the sky only to be slashed apart by the hot storming winds. And still the engines kept droning high above him, the flares zooming into the sky, and still the bombs kept bursting into glaring eruptions of light while the sound of their detonation was drowned out by the thundering all around. He shut his eyes, desperately trying to block out the boundless horror of it all. His chest burned hot, and a pitiful sob rose in his throat. He shoved up his coat sleeve and checked his watch through the tears in his eyes.

It had stopped dead. He laughed hysterically. How long had it taken to turn a cold and still wartime winter night into an inferno? He had just been chasing down a murderer through the streets, and now those streets didn't even exist. Nothing existed around him now. The world was a blazing heap of ruins.

Karin! Heller started. For God's sake, what was happening with Karin?

He looked around, as if electrified. In the distance, where a huge gust of wind was slashing away at the black smoke, he could make out a church steeple. That could be Trinity Church. So directly behind him must be . . . He whipped around so fast that he lost his grip. He toppled forward and landed hard, but he didn't care. Somewhere over there in that firestorm had to be Gruna, his neighborhood, his building, less than two miles away.

"Karin! Oh, God, Karin!"

Heller hurried back down the mountain of rubble, obsessed by the notion that Karin needed his help, and that, even worse, she surely thought he was dead. Down to his right he spotted a wide street, the pavement torn up, the cobblestones tossed all over the place, the few cars along the road glowing white. Trees were busted off like matches and lay across the street. He could see streetcar tracks, pulled up, bent like wire. He might be able to get his bearings using them. All he had to do was somehow make his way down to that street. He clambered first to the left, then to the right, found something that appeared to be a cable, and grabbed it. He yanked his hand away in shock—it was a stray power line. But then he reached for it again, since it was unlikely it still had power. He pulled on the line a couple of times, yet when he went to lower himself down, the surrounding rubble gave way, and he tumbled downward. He got hit by debris multiple times and was left lying below.

Soon rapid footsteps headed his way. Someone tugged at him. He struggled to open his eyes. Everything buzzed and ached inside.

"Stand up! Please!" A boy of about twelve wearing a loose army overcoat and a Hitler Youth uniform shook him, his face smeared with tears and soot, a far-too-large helmet hanging over his face. "It's my mom!" he screamed.

Heller stood and shook his head. "Come with me!" Heller said.

But the boy kept tugging at him. "No, I have to find my mom!"

"She'll be all right," Heller said, coming off like a pathetic liar. "I need—we need to get to the Elbe, we'll be safer on the meadows." He took the boy by the hand, and the boy clamped on tight, clawing at Heller's coat sleeve.

"Our building is gone and all of them are lying there not moving anymore!" he screamed.

"I know, my boy, but we must get going. Come on." And Heller dragged him along like the mother had done with the little girl before.

"Why would they do this to us?"

"This way!" Heller said, and pointed ahead to divert the boy's attention.

Yet the boy had already seen what he never should have. He started wailing and tried to take a long arc around the charred remains that used to be human beings. So many were lying here, and Heller didn't have time to avoid them all. He lunged over them taking long strides, holding the boy's hand tightly.

"Why are they doing this? Those pigs," the boy howled and gagged as if about to vomit. "What'd we ever do to them?"

Heller stopped and shook the boy until he finally turned his eyes away from the dead and looked Heller in the face. "Stay quiet, and keep walking," Heller barked. "You think a true German soldier starts blubbering like this when he's facing the enemy?"

It was idiotic reasoning, but at least it brought the boy back to his senses. He was sobbing hard, gasping for air, and trying to choke back his sobs. His whole body trembled. Heller knew all too well that German soldiers were lying there in the trenches bawling and shudder-ing with fright, and it disgusted him to be lying to the boy for a second time. Yet the boy had to go with him; Heller couldn't just leave him behind. They couldn't be sure more airplanes wouldn't be coming in the night, dumping their bombs wherever they spotted fires blazing. Heller ran onward without another word, and the boy followed.

Soon they reached another square. A delayed-action bomb exploded. Trees snapped in two, red-hot stones flew all around them, and shards of brick and roof tile rained on them. Heller found cover.

"You know where we are?"

"Fürstenstrasse." The boy gasped for more air, wheezing.

Fürstenstrasse? Impossible. All these ruins, these absurd remains of human dwellings. Grosser Garten park crossed his mind—all those poor animals in the zoo.

"Listen to me, please," the boy pleaded. "My mom is in the hospital. She's a nurse." He wanted to take off, but Heller held on to him.

"What's your name, boy?"

"Stölzel, Bernhard."

"Bernhard, we need to . . ." Heller fell silent. What else could he do? He needed to reach Karin, while the boy wanted to find his mother.

"Please! Please. Just let me go."

Heller let the boy loose, and he ran off, leaving Heller alone again. Hundreds of newspaper pages from a destroyed newsstand swirled in the air, then evaporated in the heat. Thin branches of trees sizzled as they burned out. A small group of people, appearing out of nowhere, silently walked past him. They had blankets over their heads. None of them noticed Heller, each alone in their misery. An old man dragged a handcart down the street. Only the brim of his hat was left on his head, and his whole back was bare, his clothes consumed by fire. If he'd been fully conscious, he'd have been screaming in pain. Grimly determined, he pulled and yanked whenever the little wheels got caught on debris. There was no point. Whatever he pulled along on his little cart, all curled up like an embryo, was gone beyond all hope. He would gain more ground on his own—his only chance of surviving was to leave the cart where it was.

Heller knew that he too could gain more ground all on his own. But he had made his decision. To find the streets of Gruna, he would head farther up the Elbe. When he looked that way, he saw only fire and destruction. Yet he had no choice. He started running now. He was still alive, and he needed to find Karin.

Heller trudged through Blasewitz, heading for the Striesen neighborhood, and had to make wide detours. What used to be a brief stroll took him more than an hour. Everywhere people were crawling out onto the street from cellars. Some just stood there, stunned, staring at the inferno. Others reacted reasonably by digging away at the destroyed homes in search of survivors. Some in uniform were giving out commands, and the first dead were carried onto the street, while other people attempted to save their belongings by hauling dressers, kitchenware, and clothing onto the street. Heller hurried on, speeding up as he got closer to Gruna. He forgot the pain in his ankle, ignored the burning in his throat. His chest kept tightening, his stomach hardening to stone. He tried not to think about what he'd seen. Tried not to imagine what could have happened to Karin. Yet in his thoughts he kept seeing her suffocating and burning to death and screaming his name over and over.

As he neared Schandauer Strasse from Bergmannstrasse, his pace slowed until eventually he halted. All he could get out was a rasping moan. What used to be his neighborhood had been razed to the ground. The outer walls of some buildings still stood, like backdrops for a stage play. The firestorm raged hundreds of yards high, the wood of the roof trusses glowing red, great bursts of sparks spewing out like volcanic eruptions. A streetcar stood at the intersection, nearly unscathed, but there was no longer a track to follow.

A few people hobbled his way. None were crying, none screaming. Apart from the dull thunder receding and the rumbling of fires, an eerie silence now reigned. The sirens had ceased too. Suddenly Heller lost all strength in his legs. He had to sit down. Two female Red Cross helpers rushed by. As he sat there, on a half-yard stretch of curbstone uprooted from the ground, everything dulled, every noise a long way away. His sight blurred as if his eyes were now trying to shield him, to protect him from so much misery and despair. He felt nothing anymore. He smelled only himself, the scorched leather of his shoes, the seared wool, his singed hair. Blood, flesh, dust, fear, death.

"Max?"

It sounded almost bashful. Unbelievable. Heller looked up. Karin stood before him. She was wearing her slippers, her long gray skirt, and a half-scorched cardigan. Her hair was gray with dust, her face black with soot, one eye swollen. He slowly rose.

"Max?" she asked again, as if she couldn't believe it. Heller just nodded, took her fingers, and caressed the back of her hand with his thumb. Then he touched her face, carefully stroked her hair. "Max, I had to . . . I can't even . . ." She fell silent. There were no words to describe what had happened.

Heller pulled her to him. Karin pressed her face into the crook of his neck.

And there they stood.

PART TWO

May 16, 1945: Early Morning

How strange people are, thought Heller. Every single one of them, including him. It didn't take long for it all to become so normal.

"What now? Keep it movin'!" someone shouted, squeezing by him. It was getting warm already this early in the morning, the sky free of clouds. Loschwitz Bridge was teeming with people. All of the other city-center bridges had been detonated just one day before the war ended, turning the bridge they called the Blue Wonder into a giant traffic hub. To cross the Elbe, people either had to take one of the ferries or travel this one single span.

Heller pressed on. He carried his backpack by hand, his empty metal mess kit inside. The Russians had been in the city for a week. A simple proclamation, posted at all public squares on May 10, had left him unemployed: the whole police force was disbanded.

His constant goal was to come up with food for himself and Karin—and for Frau Marquart, in whose apartment they'd been assigned lodging. They were now living in the Weisser Hirsch area across the river and up the hill, within earshot of a villa that had been requisitioned by Russian officers. Night after night, they heard the exuberant Russians singing and firing their guns into the dark sky.

They were getting used to that as well, along with the much longer walking distances, the constant searching for firewood to fuel their primitive steel cookers and always for food, and the soldiers of the Red Army everywhere, and the sight of their city completely destroyed.

Heller stopped and pressed his body to the railing to get out of the way, thinking they should all just be glad to still be alive. But were they? Were they happy? Shouldn't they be mourning the dead and the complete destruction of their baroque buildings, their art treasures and paintings? Was anyone mourning that? Anyone crying? For his neighbors and the people lying dead in the street? For his friends Hans and Armin and their wives? No, they didn't think about that. They didn't talk about it; no one did. Faced with so many corpses, they had had to burn massive pyres of the dead for days on end. What about those hanged from streetlamps? "I am a traitor to the Volk," read a sign hanging from the neck of one, "I colluded with Jews." Or that young soldier, executed for cowardice toward the enemy just hours before the surrender? No one talked about that.

Life had to go on, people said, and on and on. One must only look forward, letting past days, years, simply vanish from memory. There's no other way, people said, shrugging. The war was lost, but no one complained about that. Hitler was just a ghost now. It was unimaginable that someone like him had driven a whole nation into madness. No one talked about him now being dead. If anything, it was as if a heavy weight had been lifted, as if people had been relieved of some great burden. When the blackout rule got rescinded a few days ago and they'd seen their first windows lit at nighttime, Karin had cried with joy.

"*Davai, davai!*" someone shouted now, and laughter followed. Three Russians stood at the end of the bridge, sneering at Heller and waving him forward.

Heller pressed on. By now, the sight of the destroyed city was almost familiar to him. Karin had made them flee the city the night of the bombing raid. A medic from the Security and Assistance Service had first rinsed their eyes with boric acid lotion, and they'd received a little first aid from a National Socialist People's Welfare truck. They were planning to stay with a cousin outside the city, in Langebrück. On the way there, they could see the second bombing raid coming, and they witnessed it all, holding each other's hands, as well as the third raid from a safer distance the next day. Two days later, Heller had an emergency air raid truck take him back into Dresden, where he reported for duty. Even at that point, things were supposed to continue as usual. They sent him out onto the streets, where there was so much to do, and officials were called in from all of Saxony. Police headquarters had received multiple direct hits, and Obersturmbannführer Klepp, SS Sergeant Strampe, and Frau Bohle were reported killed along with many others. American planes had returned one more time in April, dropping their bombs on Reich Railway switchyards and repair facilities.

"*Stoi!*"

Heller's heart beat wildly. The Red Army soldiers were now blocking his way. They were barely older than twenty. One looked Mongolian, his cap riding on the back of his head as if stuck there.

"Paper!" demanded one. The other ripped Heller's backpack from his hand and pulled it open to look inside. He took out the empty mess kit, rummaged through the pack, and tossed the metal cookware back inside.

Heller raised his hands, trying not to worry despite all the people suddenly passing by him much faster. "No papers," he said. "Burned up. Fire." He gestured at the cityscape behind the Russians.

"Fascist!" said a second one, who chucked the backpack behind him, and the Asian one grinned.

"No, not fascist." Heller shook his head. He was acting like a hypocrite, since he'd been part of the regime for twelve long years, after all. At Karin's urging, he had burned his temporary police ID in the oven after the Soviet Red Army marched in.

The first Russian stepped closer. "Soldier! Fascist soldier! Ess-ess," he hissed and positioned himself behind Heller.

"No, not soldier. No SS. Leg kaput! Nineteen fifteen." Heller raised his right leg and pulled up his pants to let them see his scar.

"Not fascist, not soldier, not war, not Hitler!" The Russian mimicked him. Then he delivered a hard punch between Heller's shoulder blades, making him stumble back toward the two other Russians. They dodged, and Heller fell to his knees. He hastily grabbed his backpack. The soldiers laughed and cursed him in Russian. Heller knew he should be relieved to be let off easily, yet he still felt a need to set things straight. He had never been a Nazi, and he'd never wanted Hitler nor the war.

"Just keep going!" someone warned Heller, then helped him up and pulled him away. The man hauled Heller across Schillerplatz at a rapid pace, Heller letting himself be marched along without protest. They only halted once the Red Army soldiers couldn't see them.

"You got away, Maxi, you dimwit!" His counterpart gazed at him, his eyes smiling. Only now did Heller take a good look at his savior. But he couldn't place the face.

The man removed his cap. "It's me, Fritz. You don't remember? From your bowling days. Let it roll!" He eagerly shook Heller's hand.

"Fritz . . ." It seemed so long ago, like in another life.

"The old bowling alley's done for. We're now bowling over in Radebeul, every Sunday—come on by, but shhh! Meanwhile, don't let the Russians bag you." Fritz winked, gave Heller a slap on the shoulder, and headed off.

Bowling, Heller thought, rubbing his shoulders, shaking his head. What an absurd notion.

Today he had something completely different planned. He hadn't been able to sleep since he first started considering it. He wanted to return to the building he used to live in. He wanted to retrace the path he'd taken that very night. And he wanted to find that row of buildings whose residents had saved his life because they'd managed to break through cellar walls. He needed to do this. It might rid him of his nightmares.

Seeing ruins had lost its horror. They all looked alike, all reds and grays. It was astounding how little remained of a given building. A building that once had seven floors, home to twelve families or more, was now just a mound of rubble no higher than fifteen feet. They had all seemed like mountain ranges to him that awful night. The main streets were passable again. Some of the power lines had been repaired with stopgap fixes. The people and the authorities salvaged what they could, and the rest had to wait. Somewhere beyond one of the few habitable buildings, someone was beating dust from a carpet.

Crosses marked the cellars where people still lay buried. Both survivors and those seeking loved ones had taken to writing in chalk on buildings, since any notes pasted up came off after a few weeks of wind and rain. The hundreds of desperate messages on display never confirmed whether they'd found their loved ones or were falling prey to complete despair.

Lehmann family now living with the Schultes, Laubeg. Ufer Rd. . . . Stephan Müller is alive, Dornblüth. St. 12 . . . Hildegard Summschuh—where are you? —T. . . . Erna and children now in Dipps. Town . . . Inge, are you alive? —M.

Heller took a while, preparing himself for what he was about to see. All this time he'd avoided his neighborhood of Gruna, as well as Johannstadt. He had kept busy on the outskirts of the city, helping to mark up bombs that were duds, handing out food, taking missing-persons reports, organizing work crews, redirecting refugees. Most had come from Silesia. They only had bad things to say about the Russians. Many were supposed to be sent back to where they came from, so many thousands of sorry fates—tales of freezing, fear, and hunger. Such misery. Sometimes he just wanted to close his eyes and ears and never open them again.

And then there he stood, right where he and Karin had found each other. If she had taken a different route or if he had or if they had only missed each other by a minute, they probably wouldn't have seen each other again. He recognized the curbstone he'd sat on, in reality a chunk of building exterior. The wall behind it looked as if it could topple over at any moment. Every week, yet another building collapsed due to wind or rain. That night, he hadn't even noticed the streetlamps. They were all warped, bending far down to the street as if bowing in unison. The streetcar had been removed—he couldn't imagine how they'd managed that. He walked on and suddenly realized he was wearing the same singed shoes, the same overcoat, all charred, full of burn holes. A raggedy old man, ashen-faced, homely, emaciated. The wounds he'd barely noticed that night—his cuts and burns—were only now healing up.

His apartment building, like everything else, had come crashing down. The left-side wall still stood, though, rising high. Heller craned his head back and could see the wall of his living room, where their display cabinet had stood. One side of the cellar had been ripped open by a direct hit. He knelt down and took a look into the dark hole. Hard to believe that Karin had managed to climb out of there. None of the others had survived the explosion. What would've happened to him if he too had taken shelter in their cellar that night?

Heller forced himself not to see this as fate. They had gotten lucky, nothing more. He spotted something on the ground and stooped down. Melted glass. His overcoat had been full of it. His pants had been hanging off him in shreds. The metal of his belt clasp and the clips of his sock suspenders had seared into his flesh. He'd had to throw away his watch because the clockwork had melted and the glass had cracked.

He observed the mountain of rubble, now unsure. Did he dare climb around it? Karin didn't know he was here—he'd kept quiet on purpose. He wasn't really sure what he was hoping to find here. Maybe he would see someone familiar; maybe he would even find some object, a keepsake, pictures, tableware, some pieces of the dinnerware they'd inherited from Karin's mother. Something, anything he could use to provide her with some small pleasure, even just one of the nutcrackers they had kept in their display cabinet well after Christmas. He thought of his sons, of all their photos and letters now gone.

He tried to spot a way into the ruins of his building, yet kept hesitating. He eventually accepted that his plan was too dangerous. He couldn't go jeopardizing his life now—just for sentimentality.

Heller decided to take the most direct route to the city center. He reached Fürstenstrasse within a few minutes, and the Johannstadt neighborhood lay before him. He rubbed his sweat-soaked neck. The bombers had left a half-mile-wide swath of utter destruction. Whole streets had been wiped out, not a single building left standing. Only the spire of Trinity Church, which he had used to get his bearings, stood high above the expanse of ruins. The church nave was completely gutted from fire. It was tough to imagine anyone surviving this.

Suffocated. Burned to death. Ripped to shreds. Struck dead. Heat shock. German bureaucracy had managed to turn even these horrors into statistical categories. Even while the fires were still smoldering and many were still buried or trapped in their cellars, hoping for rescue, the administrative machine had already started counting, recording, measuring, classifying.

Heller regretted coming here. There was no point. He couldn't reconstruct that night of the bombings, couldn't re-create that route where he'd gone astray. He would've been better off filling his backpack with things to eat even if they were only dandelion leaves. The refugee camps were usually handing out food rations this time of day. Things got chaotic, and there was always a chance of scrounging something.

Closer to the Elbe River he could see the hospital grounds, and he recalled that the hospital had been hit but not destroyed. Maybe there was something to eat there.

A Russian army truck raced past him. Soldiers with rifles and submachine guns sat in its open bed. That was the police force now. And they were less timid. He'd heard about them shooting at people trying to steal food from a freight car at the train station.

All young German men were suspected of having been members of the armed forces. People were telling stories of arrests, of transports to Siberian POW camps, of SS men shot dead.

It was around noon when Heller reached the hospital, sweating from the sun beating down. The grounds were all hustle and bustle. Auxiliary train tracks were being laid for a connecting rail line as bored Russians supervised the work. A crane shovel was also piling up the ruins of a destroyed building. But those hospital buildings in better condition had been up and running for weeks now. And, somewhere, food was being cooked—the aroma made Heller's mouth water.

"Herr Detective Inspector!"

Heller whipped around. A young man on crutches moved toward him with cheerful enthusiasm. He was missing a leg. Despite the warmth, he wore a worn-out army overcoat with all insignia and buttons removed. "Herr Detective Inspector Heller, right?"

"It's just Herr Heller now."

"Seibling, Heinz. You remember? I'm a friend of Klaus's. From our sport club—SV Guts Muts!"

Heller now recognized him as one of his son's soccer buddies. His gaze wandered to the man's stump of a leg.

"Yeah, well, no more soccer for me," Seibling said. "Got this in France. Partisans. You heard from Klaus?"

Heller straightened. Did the young man know something? "What's wrong?"

"I just mean, do you know where he is? Is he still alive?"

Heller exhaled. The sudden thought of his sons had shot through him like a hot needle. He wished that he could believe they were still alive. But it had been far too long since he'd heard from them.

"Pardon me, I didn't mean to startle you, Herr Detective Inspector."

"Please. I'm not a cop anymore. There are no cops anymore."

Seibling nodded. "I thought you were here because of the woman."

"What woman?"

"Well, that nurse, just this morning. She'd only been here a few days. They found her dead in a cellar. Horribly mangled. But these Russians"—Seibling paused, since he'd let this escape his lips sounding too derisive, and looked around before continuing—"the Russians took away the man who killed her. They've surely hanged him." He then raised his voice. "If you happen to hear anything from Klaus, tell him hello for me. I'll probably get lodging in Albertstadt."

Heller nodded. He could only imagine what his sons must have thought when they heard about the bombings. They would have expected the worst.

"Wait," Heller said.

Seibling had already turned to go, so he pivoted back around on one leg.

"They arrested someone?"

"The man they arrested told them he'd only found her that way. He must be some kind of imbecile."

"Imbecile how?"

"Don't ask me. I just heard he chopped her up. You know how people talk."

"Which people?"

Seibling raised his crutch and drew a wide circle with it. "People around here."

"You said she was a nurse, right?"

Seibling nodded. "Silesian. Came from Breslau, had volunteered to be a nurse. I'd seen her around here a few times."

"The Fright Man," Heller muttered. But he had to be dead. How could he have escaped all those bombs raining down? Not to mention that Heller had shot the man.

"What's that?"

Heller looked up. "Nothing. What else are they saying about him?"

"He apparently had blood all over him. He'd surely lost his mind at the front. I know a few who've lost their minds." Seibling laughed as if it were all a big joke. "Hey, *tovarish*!" he shouted with a wave.

A group of Red Army soldiers had just been dropped off by a truck. One of them waved back, aiming his submachine gun. "Rat-a-tat-tat-tat," he said, imitating gunfire.

Seibling dropped his crutches and grabbed at his amputated leg, then he jumped forward on his good one and made the Russians laugh. His performance over, he picked up a crutch. Heller bent down for the other one.

"If you want to eat, you got to make friends, Herr Detective Inspector," Seibling whispered, winking at Heller. He hobbled off toward the Russians, taking long strides with his crutches.

Heller watched as the Russians let Seibling take two drags off a cigarette and slipped him something wrapped in paper.

Yet Heller's thoughts were elsewhere. He hadn't thought about the Fright Man since he tumbled down into that cellar that night. And now he of all people had supposedly survived? And the Russians arrested him? Just like that?

It's not my problem anymore, he told himself. A murderer had been arrested and would be punished. Heller's job now was to get some potatoes, wheatmeal, a little ground meat, or any sustenance at all into his mess kit through skill or begging.

Two buildings over, he spotted a small mobile field kitchen. A soldier crouched atop the two-wheeled trailer with a big ladle. More soldiers leaned against walls or stood off to the sides, policing the event by aiming machine guns with drum magazines. Hundreds of people were standing in line, silent, everyone hoping something would be left when their turn came. Each received a ladle of porridge without having to pay or show anything. Heller got in line. It moved forward in small steps, and the Russian was already having to reach deep into the large kettle even though there were about thirty people before Heller.

"They come at a new time every day," someone behind him grumbled.

"The clocks just run differently with them."

"Or not at all!" Restrained laughter broke out.

Heller turned around. "Did you hear about that murder?" he asked the old man behind him. Maybe he knew more. Rumors were practically the elixir of life in times like these.

The man gestured with his chin in the general direction of Johannstadt. "Supposedly she was found in the ruins, somewhere under there, in some cellar."

"Was it a nurse?"

The old man indicated a hospital building to their right, its busted windows patched up with wood and cardboard. "Go ask them if you're so interested. Now keep the line movin'!"

When Heller's turn came, the Russian gave him a dollop of porridge in his mess kit and accidentally spattered some on Heller's hand, then waved Heller on without caring. Heller stepped to the side, licked off his hand, and closed his mess kit. It would suffice as a meal for Karin and Frau Marquart.

Without thinking, he headed toward the hospital building.

A Russian soldier blocked Heller's way. "What do you want?"

"To speak to the head physician—a Professor Ehlig."

"*Nyet!* Go away!"

Heller didn't dare contradict the soldier. He stepped away, not knowing what to do.

"Are you sick or injured?" an older nurse asked. She'd just come out of the building and looked haggard, drained.

"I wanted to find out about the one who died—the woman from this morning."

"Poor Erika, my God. She'd come from Silesia and was staying at the main train station. It's not advisable for a woman to be out alone in the city."

"What about the man the Russians arrested?"

"He'd been our boiler man since mid-December. Wait, no, mid-January. A young man from the Eastern Ore Mountains, unfit for military service—stiff leg or something. He was always very quiet. He must've lured her into the ruins. Maybe he'd stolen some food and wanted her to . . . well, you know."

Heller knew. When a person was hungry, they would do anything for something to eat.

"Mid-January, you said? Do you know if he'd been in the city before that?"

"I don't. He'd been with us a couple weeks before I knew of him."

Heller nodded, suddenly not feeling well. Talking about last January brought back too many memories of his night patrols. "Do you know where it happened?"

The nurse crossed her arms. "Why are you so curious?"

Heller figured it was about time to make a little sacrifice. He reached into his overcoat and pulled out a cigarette from the tattered pack in his inside pocket. "I'm a . . . was a detective." He handed the cigarette to the nurse, who snatched it up and hid it inside her smock.

"With the police, huh? Don't let the Russians hear that."

Heller waved for her to continue.

"So they found her in a cellar at Dürerplatz, corner of Reissigerstrasse. He was calling for help."

"Who was?"

"Uhlmann. The boiler man."

"He was calling for help and the Russians arrested him?"

"That's Russian efficiency for you."

Heller knew this brand of efficiency all too well; it wasn't only Russian. "The dead woman—is she here? Erika, and what's her last name?"

"Erika Kaluza. Russians took her away."

"And the boiler man, Uhlmann—first name?"

"Erwin. But he's done for, believe me. They'll have made short work of him."

Out of habit, Heller patted at his pocket for his notebook and pencil, but he'd lost them the night of the air raid.

It didn't take Heller long to lose his way in the desert of stone debris. He found a road sign on the ground that told him he might be on Dürerstrasse, but the sign could just as well have flown through the air a good half mile. Once again, Trinity Church provided his only bearings. He reached a larger open area less covered by debris and guessed this was the square that used to be Dürerplatz. But he had no idea where Reissigerstrasse was. He saw two little boys plucking cigarette butts from the street. As he approached, they snatched up a few more butts and ran off. He found tracks in the dust—boots and the wheels of a truck—then he spotted the hole leading down into a cellar under a mountain of rubble. He bent down hoping to see something, but it was too dark. He'd have to climb down there. He hesitated for a long time. In his dreams, he was constantly running yet kept getting boxed in by fire and always ended up in one of these cellars, couldn't find a way out. He eventually mustered the courage, took a deep breath, rubbed at his stubbly chin, and, crouching, squeezed himself through the narrow breach in the wall.

This cellar hadn't saved anyone's life. Its walls were black with soot, and it stunk like boiled tar. The floor was sandy. Black chunks of rock and steel beams deformed by heat stood every which way, leaving no clear path through for a tall man like Heller. Yet it didn't take long to locate the spot where the woman had been found, hanging from the rafters. In that split second it all returned to him, that feeling of anxiety, that pressure bearing down on him, that urgent need to hit the streets, that knowledge of not having done enough. Blood had run onto the sandy soil and turned black. All other clues had been wiped away or tread over.

The killer had been caught, they said.

But could the Fright Man really have survived that night of bombing? Without any air raid shelter to protect him, and wounded by Heller's bullet? And why would he have called for help only to wait for the Russians to show up? Had they nabbed him by accident? Had he only been trying to talk his way out of it? Heller refused to accept it.

He crawled out of the cellar hole, his heart beating heavily, his stomach aching. He felt guilty again, because of his wife. He knew that he always carried through on his plans. And what he was planning now was sure to land him in hot water.

He needed to go see Erwin Uhlmann.

May 16, 1945: Afternoon

"Wait, Herr Seibling, wait!" shouted Heller for the third time as he followed the young man. Seibling had just exited the hospital and was heading toward the Elbe, swinging his crutches along. Heller was relieved to find him here among all the people working and hanging around. He didn't want the Russians taking notice of him again today.

"Herr Seibling! Heinz . . ."

The young man finally heard him and stopped, his open expression encouraging Heller, who could walk more slowly now, less conspicuously. He pulled a second cigarette from his smashed-up pack.

"Please do." He offered the cigarette to the young man. Seibling accepted it, fished a box of matches from his overcoat, and lit up. He took a deep drag, then raised his eyebrows in appreciation.

"Bulgaria Sport. Where did you rustle these up?"

Heller smiled. "The elderly lady we live with has no need for them now. Her husband fell in the fall of '44."

Seibling grinned. "Bulgaria Sport—you remember the line? 'Our Dear Adolf's oh-so-wonderful Wonder Weapon . . . just the thing for slaying the Soviet Satan!'" he said, laughing along and waving his cigarette like a composer.

Heller rubbed his neck, glancing around. He never did care much for slogans. But he couldn't blame the young man. Despite his happy way, Seibling seemed to be bearing more than enough worries under his long overcoat.

"Tell me something, Heinz. Where are the Russians detaining people? Could you find that out from your Russian friends?"

Seibling took another drag, nodded and laughed, then coughed. "I know where," he said. "Been there myself. Was trying to rip off an officer, which was not a good idea. You know the Heidehof? That hotel on Bautzner Strasse?"

Heller nodded. It was on the opposite side of the Elbe, a long way by foot if he hoped to get back home on time. A bicycle would be worth its weight in gold right now, yet the one he used to own lay buried somewhere underneath rubble, and using one without a permit was now a punishable offense.

Seibling rubbed his eyebrows. "You're not thinking of going there?"

Heller reached into his coat again, and gave Seibling another cigarette. "Here, for you. Thanks so much." He hoped Karin wouldn't find out about this. He could have gotten some food with those smokes. Information never filled anyone's stomach.

"You're welcome." Seibling rubbed his wrist, suddenly looking quite serious. "Herr Heller, you should let it go. I know you're a good man. I heard the Thomas Goldmann story. But the Russians don't know that. They're looking to do you in and wouldn't bat an eye."

Such warnings weren't new to Heller. Though it intrigued him as to what and how people knew about the Goldmann situation. Back in November of '44, he'd given Thomas Goldmann's mother a clear hint that the Gestapo was about to arrest her son. He'd done nothing more. It was only because he knew the Goldmanns—that, and he was sick of Gestapo shitheads. Yet considering all the mistrust that Klepp would soon harbor for him, it now seemed far more dangerous than he had supposed at the time. Sure, the Russians might have a reputation for brutality, but those creeps in the Gestapo had been working on a completely different level.

"The thing with Goldmann wasn't that big of a deal. And I only need to see this Uhlmann once, maybe talk to him if I can."

"Herr Heller, please. How are you going to make that happen? It's teeming with soldiers there. No one's going there by choice. No one ever returns."

Heller patted Seibling on his forearm. "You got out."

"Yeah, but only because I'm so foolish all the time. I'm a clown. They laugh at me and knock me down. I even lost my leg because I was fooling around. But you? You're no clown. And all because of some murderer? You don't know anything about this Uhlmann."

"What if he ends up not being the murderer?"

Seibling made a face. "So what? Herr Heller, so many haven't come back. And how many are now in Siberia? You shouldn't risk your life over this."

"You're right, my dear Heinz. Some of us are already bowling again, and others are beating out their carpets as if nothing ever happened. Too many others have gotten killed. But every person is different. You know what I mean? That's always been true. Because the so-called masses, they just happen to consist of all of us individuals—even if they did try to convince us otherwise for twelve long years. Tell me something, Heinz: Where are you living now? Just in case I want to see you again."

Seibling raised a crutch and pointed toward the vast fields of rubble. "In the rubble?"

"I have my hidey-holes," he said. "My treasures," he added in a whisper and grinned.

"Aren't you afraid of being robbed?"

"Not me. I have a guardian spirit."

"You can't really believe that."

"Oh, I do, my dear Herr Heller. People say it's all haunted here. Things reside in the ruins. I don't believe in the dear Lord anymore, but in a place where so many have died? Something will always linger on."

Seibling's words went through Heller's mind as he stood before the inn once known as Gasthaus Heidehof. It had taken him two hours to get out of the destroyed part of the city, across the Elbe, and up past the waterworks to Bautzner Strasse.

After crossing the river, he'd gotten the idea of first heading up to Weisser Hirsch to let Karin know what he planned to do. But he also knew she would never let him go, and for good reason.

He observed the chaos all around the large building, inside and outside the temporary wood-slat fence fortified with barbed wire, the jeeps and trucks coming and going, the couriers' clattering motorcycles, the dark clouds of exhaust. The noise was unbearable. It smelled of diesel, exhaust fumes, food, and cigarette smoke. At the barrier to the front gate, some sentries looked bored and others alert. Orders were shouted out, mixed with laughter. Young women prowled outside the fence, trying to catch the Red Army officers' attention while ignoring those advances from the common soldiers that always led to crude brawls.

Two trucks braked hard at the gate, and the sentries let the trucks onto the grounds after brief questioning. Heller craned his neck to see what was going on inside. Several Red Army soldiers leaped out from under the rear tarps and pulled down a half-dozen men with hands tied behind their backs as more soldiers came to grab them under the armpits and drag them into the building.

Heller looked at his new watch, which was given to him by Frau Marquart. It was already four in the afternoon. He hadn't eaten anything apart from a little heel of bread with a strip of old bacon that morning. His stomach growled, but if he wanted to be back home before darkness fell, he was going to have to act now.

Tomorrow would be too late. Tomorrow he'd have lost his courage. Tomorrow Uhlmann might already be dead, if he wasn't already. Heller took a few deep breaths. Then he got going.

At the front gate was a bored young Russian soldier. He wasn't carrying a rifle, though he did have a pistol stuffed into his belt. Heller cleared his throat.

"I would very much like to speak with the commandant," he said, his voice shaking.

The Russian only sneered.

Heller stood more upright and hoped his voice sounded firmer. "Pardon me, I'd very much like to speak with the commandant. Please, good sir."

The Russian tilted his head with curiosity. *"Gut sure?"* he recited. Then he shouted something to his comrade. During the conversation that followed, Heller kept looking from one soldier to the other, hoping to detect a lighter tone between the two. But it sounded serious. A third soldier in an officer's cap came over, his manner domineering and his hands clasped behind his back. He'd probably learned that by watching German officers, or maybe certain people just had that demeanor inside them.

"Problaim?" the officer asked.

"I'd like to speak to the commandant. I'm here regarding Erwin Uhlmann."

"Erween Oolmann? You be Erween Oolmann?"

"No. He's detained here. I'd like to speak to the commandant."

"What concern you Erween Oolmann?"

Heller took another deep breath. "I'm his father."

The officer shoved Heller in the chest. "Go!"

Heller lowered his head and avoided looking the officer in the eyes. "I would please like to speak to the commandant. It's very important."

The officer drew his pistol. "Turn around!" He pulled off Heller's backpack. "Paper!"

Heller spoke gently and hoped they didn't notice how frightened he was. "I don't have any papers. But I must speak to the commandant. It's urgent."

"Paper!" roared the domineering Russian.

Suddenly a window opened and a man shouted. The officer turned around, looked up, and replied to the man's question. Heller, who'd understood nothing, kept glancing at both soldiers. The young one winked at him.

The officer suddenly whipped around and grabbed Heller by the shoulders. He dragged him through the barricaded grounds and into the building entrance where the detainees had disappeared. Heller resisted as little as possible, even when roughly shoved up the stairs. The officer pounded on a door, cursing under his breath. When a voice sounded from inside, he flung open the door, reported in the military way, and shoved Heller into the room.

The room must once have been a large dining hall. Chandeliers hung from the ceiling, the walls were paneled chest-high, and Heller saw a mural above: hunting scenes, idyllic landscapes. A rope had been strung through the middle of the room with various blankets hanging off it, apparently serving as a room divider. In the front area was a single desk, where a young staff clerk sat pounding on a typewriter with clumsy fingers. His telephone wouldn't stop ringing, so the soldier picked up while typing with one finger, said something, hung up again. Right after that the door flung open with a bang and a young man entered, taking forceful strides. He wore brown uniform pants and a black leather jacket instead of the usual soldier's tunic. His black polished boots glistened. He was tall and slender, his straw-blond hair showed from under his peaked leather cap, and his bright gray eyes glared. He was clearly a political commissar, and Heller knew what they had done to captured commissars during the war. They'd shot them on the spot.

The man bristled at the sight of Heller. He barked a question at the staff clerk, which made another man appear from behind the curtain of blankets. Heller recognized him as the man in the window. He was a high-ranking officer—Heller figured he was the commandant. The two men conversed for a moment, then ordered Heller into the rear area. The Russians sat; Heller had to stand.

"Who are you? What do you want?" asked the young political commissar in remarkably good German.

"My name is Heller—"

The commandant cut him off. "You lie! You told the guard you're the father of someone named Uhlmann."

"I said that so I'd be allowed inside," Heller conceded. "I used to be a police detective—"

"Police?" the young commissar asked and stood. "Overcoat off!" he ordered.

The commandant showed no expression. Heller took off his overcoat.

"Shirt off!"

Heller took off his shirt. The young commissar started checking his arms. "What's this?" he demanded, pointing at Heller's old scars and freshly healed ones.

"The war, 1915. Grenade. And then the air raids. Here." Heller pointed out the window at the opposite side of the Elbe.

"SS," whispered the young commissar. The commandant growled.

"No. I was a detective. I was on the trail of a murderer."

The young commissar grimaced. "A murderer? You all are—"

"Zamolchi!" the commandant said, and the young commissar shut up.

"A man was arrested today," Heller said. "Erwin Uhlmann. He allegedly murdered a young woman. But I don't believe that."

The commandant said something in Russian.

"You don't believe that he's the murderer?" the young commissar said, then sat down again.

This shell game of theirs was ridiculous. It was obvious the commandant understood German and could speak it. Heller turned to face the commandant.

"Please, Herr General, I don't wish to be a burden. I simply don't want to see an innocent man punished without us knowing for certain—"

"We are certain!" growled the commandant. "He's to be executed, early tomorrow morning."

Heller knew they wouldn't budge. "May I put my clothes on?" he asked. He didn't want to appear servile, which wasn't easy in this situation.

The commandant nodded. The young commissar started urgently trying to talk him into something.

"Major General Medvedev would like to know why you believe he is the wrong man," the young commissar said.

"The circumstances don't fit."

"Were you in the Gestapo?"

"No. Never."

"Were you in your fascist Nazi Party? NSDAP? SS? SA?"

"No."

"Did you kill Jews? You know what a concentration camp is?"

"Yes, I know," Heller said, hesitating, his heart aching. "But I never murdered anyone."

The young commissar shook his head in disbelief. "You have no papers, you were police, you deny being in the SS and Nazi Party, yet you come here because of a strange man and all because you wish to save his life?"

Heller could only nod and bite his lip. A thought hit him hard: he hoped Karin would never hear of what he tried doing here.

The young political commissar appealed to Major General Medvedev again. The general didn't look very moved. The commissar sprung up.

"Come with me," he told Heller and gave him a reassuring look. "My name is Zaitsev, by the way, Alexei Zaitsev."

"Max Heller," Heller said, and followed the young man out of the room.

Zaitsev grabbed Heller roughly by the arm. "Well, come on, then."

He couldn't be much older than Klaus. Midtwenties.

"There." Zaitsev took Heller into a room, where five soldiers sat at typewriters and radio sets. They glanced up as Heller got shoved past them over to a window.

"Here, take a look."

Heller looked out at the hazy day. He saw the Elbe and the broad meadow on the opposite bank where they used to hold the Vogelwiese carnival, all brown and scorched, covered with bomb craters, shanties and tents, refugees' carts, and the bomb-gutted city for a backdrop.

"Well?" Zaitsev prodded Heller's shoulder blade.

Heller wasn't sure what the Russian wanted to hear, so he kept quiet. Zaitsev stepped next to him. "That there? It's Tula."

"I don't understand."

"I was born in Tula, same size as this city. Your city. Much industry. Tula was destroyed, looks just like this." Zaitsev side-eyed him. "Germans?" He shrugged and aimed a finger like a pistol. "Bang! All those there." He pointed at the Russian soldiers outside. "All of them out there killed Germans. Medvedev killed Germans. Germans mean nothing to me, you understand? Erwin Uhlmann means nothing to me, and the dead woman does not either."

Heller stared at him. He now understood but was trying not to show it.

Zaitsev stepped closer. Heller could smell cigarettes and leather. "I don't trust you," he said. "You have no papers, nothing. I will be watching you." Zaitsev then whipped around and glared at the soldiers. *"Rabotayte!"* he yelled, and they got back to work.

"Davai!" he ordered Heller.

The two of them descended the stairs. Constant hustle and bustle filled the hallways. Soldiers passed them, messengers ran their way, and plenty was carried around—typewriters, food, radios, water. Now and then they'd see men and women being led away in handcuffs. Heller heard screams coming from the basement.

That was exactly where Zaitsev was taking him. They walked down a lit basement corridor that stank horribly. Heller stole glances into the cells made of wood or metal bars. Dozens of prisoners were inside, sitting on straw.

"Traitor swine!" shouted an older man as he passed. Zaitsev didn't react, but Heller hesitated. "Beat you to death, you bastard . . ."

Zaitsev stopped at another cell. "Uhlmann?"

A young man started and pulled himself up using the wall. One leg was stiff.

"Don't give in, boy," someone whispered.

A guard unlocked the door, and the prisoner stepped out. He was a large young man, the type prone to gaining weight. A disgusting smell radiated from him, and he had blood on his hands and face. The victim's blood?

"Well?" Zaitsev glared at Heller to get on with it.

"Right here?" Heller asked, and Zaitsev's jaw tightened.

Heller said to the young man, "You are Erwin Uhlmann?"

"I didn't kill her—please tell them that!" The boy was frantically trying not to cry, and his despair and exhaustion were obvious.

Heller switched to his official tone for questioning. "You are the prime suspect. Answer the questions. Why were you found with the dead woman?"

"I was looking for wood in the rubble and anything I could use. Was bombed out, lost all I had. I was the boiler man at the hospital. The Russians were out patrolling all day, so I was going out at night."

"You're a plunderer."

"No, please, I only wanted to . . . I just needed something to barter. It was close to morning, it was getting light. I heard noises so I hid. But that thing, it was so . . . I don't know what it was. You have to believe me!"

"Tell me."

"It wasn't normal noises. Grunting and all these strange sounds, words like some different language."

"What language? French? Russian? Silesian? What?" Heller was growing impatient.

"No, not an actual language, completely different, more like cackling, someone's tongue clicking. I even tried getting closer. Then I made a noise, and that's when I saw something running away!"

"Something? So you saw it?"

"Only from a distance. It was leaping over debris and rocks. So I went over to where it must have been before . . . You must believe me . . . I got such a horrible shock, seeing this woman there with . . . with her . . . her . . . skin was peeled off, but she was still alive. Her throat was making this terrible gurgling sound. She was just staring at me. That's when I started yelling for help. And then soldiers came and arrested me."

"He had a knife," Zaitsev said as if that explained it.

Uhlmann stared, aghast. "Sure, but only a little one, just three inches."

Zaitsev stared back, unmoved. "And there was blood. Everywhere."

"But I was only trying to help her."

"Where were you on the thirteenth of February?" Heller asked.

"At the hospital, in the cellar, the women's clinic. Lots of people were there. And so many burned to death." Uhlmann shook his head and uttered a sudden laugh. Heller knew that well—people reacted like that when the horror was too great to comprehend.

"All done!" Zaitsev told them and shoved Uhlmann back into the cell. He turned to Heller. "The commandant will give you three days—before he's hanged," he said without caring if Uhlmann heard. "You be here early tomorrow morning, at seven. Come back upstairs. I'll give you a pass."

"What about the victim?" Heller asked. "The woman. Where is she?"

Zaitsev only shrugged.

Heller pulled out his metal mess kit and set it on the table. "That's all there is."

Karin opened it and shook out the contents into a little pot. "Have you eaten?" she asked, and Heller nodded. It was dark by now. "You're lying. I can tell. Frau Marquart was able to get some bread. I'll make you a couple of slices and cook off some old bacon."

Heller's stomach tightened. He was exhausted yet too shaken to be tired.

"You remember how it was during the war, Max? We thought we were suffering. And yet we still had quite a lot. Honey, potatoes, butter, marmalade. Now we're happy for a cube of sugar." Karin placed the pot on their wood-fired cooker and slowly stirred the contents.

Frau Marquart came into the room. "You made it back!" she said when she saw him, sounding relieved.

Karin turned and shot him a stern look. "Max, why were you at the commandant's?"

Heller didn't need to ask how she knew. Someone must have seen him, and news traveled like lightning. There was no way to fool Karin.

"There was another murder. They think they have the killer, but he's not the one."

Karin nodded.

"They actually want to help me solve the case, Karin. Just imagine!" He figured he should leave it at that.

"They had their way with the Walthers' daughter last night. Tried to kill herself after, the poor child," said Frau Marquart. She truly was a nice woman, and Heller liked her a lot, but she never knew when to shut her mouth and leave the room.

Karin took the pot off the stove and came over to the table. "Frau Marquart, we need some more candles. They'll be turning off the electricity soon."

It was just the right prompt—Frau Marquart left.

Karin gave Heller an accusing look. "I endured so much fear down in the air raid shelter. It wasn't for my sake, Max—it was for yours! I was so worried about you." She raised her head. "And now, after having endured all that, the war, the Nazis, here you go off to the Russians even though you know how they're treating everyone. Especially former officials, policemen like you. You're so goddamn pigheaded!" She folded her arms, glaring at him. They stared at each other for a long time.

"Maybe they could tell you something about our boys," she said.

Heller took her hand and caressed her cheek. Her hair was growing back, her skin looking less ashen. Despite all the misery around them, the end of the war had allowed her to blossom again. She had listened to the news of Hitler's death in complete silence, yet it seemed her spirit had been relieved of a great burden.

"I will try," he said.

May 17, 1945: Seven in the Morning

Zaitsev sat waiting for Heller in a flashy black DKW F7 convertible—the last thing Heller needed to be seen in. The young commissar rode on the passenger side and directed Heller to the back seat.

"Where to?" the Russian asked, almost cheerfully, full of energy.

"I'd like to go to the hospital, on the other side of the Elbe."

Zaitsev looked amused. "Last night, a young woman told me about this Fright Man."

Heller was amazed. Word got around so fast. "I didn't give him that name," he muttered.

They could only make slow progress. The driver kept honking frantically, driving like a beginner. People glared as the car passed, and all Heller could do was sit there frozen, looking straight ahead, feeling embarrassed. On the Loschwitz Bridge, they moved at a walking pace. The bridge had been hit repeatedly, and the roadway was only patched up for now.

Zaitsev turned around. "Have you ever wondered why this bridge still stands?"

Heller hadn't, and didn't guess now.

"You were supposed to detonate it, but that got sabotaged." Zaitsev laughed.

Heller wondered if he was drunk. The Russian officers in the villa above Frau Marquart's house had been drinking themselves unconscious every night.

At the hospital, the same bustle reigned as the day before even though it was still quite early. Seibling was nowhere to be seen. Zaitsev jumped out of the car. "Where to now?"

Heller nodded at a burned-out building that was obviously unoccupied. "Over there, I'm guessing. I'm looking for a man who was caretaker there: Ewald Glöckner. After that, I need to find out where the dead woman was living."

He looked around. A feeling told him he was being watched. But it was impossible to tell with so many people around.

He headed for the ruins of the nurses' quarters and waved down a nurse. "Excuse me, do you know Glöckner—the caretaker?"

"I haven't been here that long," she replied, trying to avoid Zaitsev. But the Russian grabbed her arm and pulled her to him.

"Where is the head physician?"

Heller placed a calming hand on Zaitsev's arm.

The nurse pointed behind her, her hand shaking. "In that building there, third floor."

Zaitsev let her go, and she hurried away.

The Russian's crude approach angered Heller. "You can't do it like that. And the head physician won't know who the caretaker is, let alone where he's living."

"Let alone . . . ?" Zaitsev apparently hadn't understood the phrase. "I don't think you have time to ask around like this. Who's she over there?" he abruptly asked. "The one against the blackened wall, to the left, next to the burned tree."

Heller turned around. He saw a young woman wearing a gray overcoat with black cuffs and a white knitted cap. When she saw she was being watched, she disappeared behind ruins.

"No idea." Heller pushed back his flat cap, wiped the sweat off his brow. It wasn't even 8:00 a.m. and it was already hot. Then he noticed Seibling. "Herr Seibling! Heinz!" he yelled. Seibling began to give Heller a friendly wave but then turned away once he saw Zaitsev and tried to rush off on his crutches.

Zaitsev snorted. "*Stoi!*" he hollered, and drew his pistol from his holster. All the people around froze. Seibling halted too. Then he slowly pivoted and, showing a tortured smile, waited for Heller and Zaitsev to reach him.

The Russian looked like he wanted to get rough. Heller stepped in front of him. "Leave him to me, please," he said.

"Heinz, pardon me," he told Seibling, who looked as filthy as he had the day before, his neck and face, his hands, and even his teeth black. "I just have one question. You know Glöckner, the caretaker? He was living at the nurses' quarters. Was he killed?"

Seibling started shaking his head, then his face suddenly brightened. "Wait, the caretakers have a workshop in building 19. It's nearly untouched. In the basement."

"Thanks a lot." Heller and Zaitsev started off, but Seibling held Heller back.

"Nice friend you got there," Seibling whispered. "He's one of the worst."

Heller freed himself with a smile and followed Zaitsev, who was already a good stretch ahead of him, his expression not revealing whether he'd heard Seibling.

It wasn't far to building 19, and the throngs of people parted in deference to Zaitsev. The workshop was easy to find. The men there started and sprang to their feet when the Russian pushed open the door, what with their military ways still so drilled into them.

"I'm looking for Glöckner!" Zaitsev roared.

No one replied.

Zaitsev placed a threatening hand on his holster. "Answer me!"

"He took off on the eighth," said the oldest man, who was at least seventy.

"He still have a place to live?" Heller asked.

"Nah, fire gutted it, whole nurses' building."

Zaitsev looked to Heller. *"Nu, i seychas?"*

Heller considered his next move. Glöckner was still alive but had disappeared. It would be impossible to find him, considering the general state of things, even if he were still in the city. That left the saliva evidence and those strange noises.

"We need to have a look at the last crime scene. And we need to find out where the last victim was living," he said in a resolute voice, hoping to hide his uncertainty from the Russian.

"Fine. The driver will take us. We go to the crime scene."

After briefing the driver, Zaitsev lit up a cigarette, and Heller tried to see what brand it was. Zaitsev misread Heller's expression and offered him one.

"Is it all right with you if I take one without smoking it?" Heller asked. Zaitsev gave a terse nod and shook a cigarette out of the pack. Heller took it and stowed it away.

"So you're serving a new master now?" Heller heard a woman say.

He hadn't dared to hope that he'd ever hear that voice again. He turned around.

"Nurse Rita!" he said, but Rita Stein's scrutinizing look spoiled his delight. "I'm still just doing my job."

Nurse Rita had become thinner, her face a little harder. He didn't want to imagine what suffering she'd been forced to see. "I hear it's another young nurse."

Heller nodded. "Erika Kaluza."

"Don't know her. It supposed to be the same killer? The Jew from Berlin?"

Heller didn't answer.

Rita softened her expression, as if realizing she might've gone too far. "It's completely crazy, isn't it? I've lost so many friends, so many lovely people, while others are spared. There's Nazis, the war profiteers, and that crazy Fright Man out there. Right when we all start forgetting about him, he returns. Suddenly everyone thinks they've seen him or heard him."

"He got away from me the night of the bombing," Heller said. "I almost had him. I even shot and wounded him."

"What Nazis?" asked Zaitsev. He offered Rita a cigarette, but she declined. "You know Nazis?"

"Everyone does, yet no one does!" Rita said. "And no one knows a thing. There's honor among thieves, as you know. And Professor Ehlig, that ardent Hitler worshipper, he's doing quite well by your people," she told Zaitsev. "He's dining with Colonel General Shishkov. Know the man?"

Heller watched her in awe. She showed absolutely no fear.

Zaitsev nodded and took a drag. "He is a hero."

"Today's heroes, tomorrow's criminals." Rita spat the words out, taking a big risk.

"What about Dr. Schorrer?" Heller said, trying to moderate.

But Zaitsev took Rita's lack of respect in stride. "History will decide that. Who is this Schorrer, Heller?"

"Dr. Schorrer was helping us with the autopsies. He'd been a front-line doctor in Poland, got himself transferred here. He'd spoken negatively of the National Socialists to me." Heller quickly added, "He and Professor Ehlig were not on good terms."

Rita gave a crooked smile. "Yeah, well. Many a man knows which train to hop on at just the right time. I need to go, duty calls."

As she moved to turn around, Heller surprised himself by taking her hand and squeezing it longer than necessary. "I'm glad you survived it all."

And then she surprised him, first by letting him hold her hand without resisting, then by blushing. "I'm glad to see you well too."

"Admit it: you don't know what to do next," Zaitsev said. It was true. Heller had insisted on seeing this soot-blackened cellar where the woman had been found, yet he hadn't been able to uncover any clues or leads that could help him. As for any saliva traces on the sandy floor, those had either been brushed away or dried up long ago. The crime scene only left him feeling more perplexed. Zaitsev stood inside the entrance to the cellar, smoking.

"Uhlmann said the victim was still breathing," Heller said.

"I have no idea. I first heard of this case because of you, Heller. We could ask my comrades who apprehended Uhlmann."

"I have to go back to the hospital and find out who knew Erika Kaluza. I need to question those people. I'm hoping your driver can help out."

Zaitsev flicked his cigarette butt toward the cellar entrance, looking annoyed. "Takes too long."

"That's how an investigation works. We don't have any new leads, which means we'll need to—"

Zaitsev held up a hand. He waved Heller over and whispered, "Here she is again." Then he stepped further back into the shadows and pointed outside. Heller recognized the young woman in her gray overcoat. She was hiding among the remains of brick walls and a ten-foot-tall interior wall that could topple any moment. She'd taken off her white cap.

Heller thought he might have seen that face somewhere before. But he didn't know where.

"I do not trust her," Zaitsev said, and drew his pistol. Heller knew what the Russian meant by that: Zaitsev didn't trust him.

"Let's find another exit. We'll creep up on her. There . . ." The Russian pointed behind them, into the darkness.

Heller shook his head. "I, I can't go in there."

"You have to."

"Please, you have to understand. I can't do it, I . . ." A massive ache filled Heller's chest.

Zaitsev extended his arm and pressed the muzzle of his gun right where Heller was aching. "Listen to me, *nemets*. I was buried alive in a foxhole for half a day, and I nearly went mad. But I'm still alive. My mother got ripped to shreds by a German shell, right before my eyes, and my sister was hanged by people like you—people just doing their job. Now follow me and help me catch this woman, otherwise I must conclude that you are conspiring together. Understand?" Zaitsev pushed hard, and Heller stumbled along.

"Now you listen to me," Heller muttered in anger, "I'm old enough to be your father."

"My father's dead too," Zaitsev hissed.

"After you," Heller said after a moment.

The Russian stepped back and grinned. "But of course."

It smelled of death and decomposition. They crawled through a narrow gap and blindly felt their way forward, shuffling. A vise had formed around Heller's chest and pressed on him until he couldn't seem to get any air. From somewhere far off, he heard explosions getting louder and the screams from another war. His boots were sinking into deep mud all over again, getting sucked down, and he couldn't move. He felt hands grabbing at him, grasping him tight, wanting him to remain here in this cellar, in this tomb stinking of soot, of burned flesh and hair. Heller grit his teeth and tried to remain calm, to keep breathing, even though the air was now filling with chlorine gas, acrid, poisonous. He clawed at his neck; the pounding artillery commenced. Mud was suddenly sloshing down on him. Someone grabbed at his neck, and he wheezed in horror.

But it was only Zaitsev's hand, shaking him.

"Come on, I found an exit." Zaitsev pulled Heller along behind him, Heller staggering as something crunched under his feet, cracking like a dry branch, and scattered into the air. Then he saw something. Light. He frantically gasped for the fresh air.

Zaitsev eyed him. "Go around that way, I go this way. Try and cut her off."

Heller crawled out of the hole. They had come out the other side of the destroyed row of buildings, and he breathed a deep sigh of relief. His panic had shaken him to his core. He unbuttoned his overcoat, took off his cap, and tried to hurry on, but rubble blocked his way. Just a narrow path passed through the mountains of debris, and every gust of wind could make a wall collapse. The pain in his ankle came roaring back as if reawakened by the bad memories, thirty years after the severe wound.

His route through seemed to last forever, and he couldn't imagine having to retrace his steps back through the connected cellars. He looked around. Suddenly he heard bricks knocking, breaking apart. He pivoted but missed the young woman by an arm's length. She'd evidently been hiding nearby, waiting for him to pass, and she was now running down what was left of the street. Zaitsev came over a mound of rubble, leaped, and slid down. The woman had already disappeared into a gap in the rubble. Zaitsev sprinted after her, but then he stopped. It wasn't wise to follow the woman alone down into a cellar, possibly into an ambush.

"Why did you let her get by?" the Russian barked in anger as he returned to Heller. "If it turns out you conspired with her, I will have you both shot! Now come with me, and tell me what you know about this Professor Ehlig. And what does the saying mean—'honor among thieves'?"

May 17, 1945: Shortly before Noon

"Back again already?" Nurse Rita asked Heller as he crossed the hospital grounds. She was holding a heel of bread. She looked Heller over, then broke off half and handed it to him. Heller wanted to decline, but she stubbornly held out the bread until he took it.

Heller, exhausted, sat down beside her on a low stretch of wall. The chunk of bread was small—he could eat it in two bites, but he only stuck a crumb in his mouth. Zaitsev had gone to speak to Professor Ehlig. It was becoming clear to Heller that the Russians were less concerned with solving a murder than with tracking down Nazis in hiding. And Zaitsev's driver supposedly hadn't been able to find out anything about Erika Kaluza either.

"Every day I'm hearing such horrible stories," Rita said. "Did you know about the concentration camps?"

Heller nodded. Many of the Jews who were sent to Theresienstadt, he knew, had allegedly died of typhoid fever or heart failure only a few weeks after arriving. Boys and the healthy even. It was obvious what was really happening there.

Rita looked him in the eye. "They were killing people, according to a system. Not hundreds. Thousands. I have patients here who are former concentration camp inmates. They're nothing more than skeletons.

They're going to die, and you can't do anything for them. Most of them have failing kidneys. And the things they talk about, such hunger and thirst and torture . . ." She lowered her head, gnawing at the piece of bread. "What about you? How's your case going? Making any progress?"

Heller sighed. "There are no clues, it's all destroyed. The Russian doesn't trust me. I'd really like to take another crack at the Bellmann case, go look up her relatives sometime. They must have survived; her neighborhood was pretty well spared. You know anything about Glöckner?"

Rita nodded. "He was helping out where he could after the air raids. Then he disappeared—the day before the Russians came."

"Wonder if he's still in the city."

"Why would he be?"

"His wife? His dog?"

"Both are dead." Rita stared at the ground.

Heller observed her carefully. Something had changed in the last four hours. "Did the Russians harm you? Are you not feeling well?"

Rita reached into the pocket of her smock and pulled out an envelope.

"I just got this. A soldier returning home was able to send it to me."

It was a yellow envelope. She handed it to Heller. The paper had taken a long journey. There was a photo inside, of a clearing marked off in the middle of desert sand, showing pristine white crosses. Army helmets rested on most. One cross read, in nice, neat letters, "Staff Sgt. Helge Stein, Aug. 25, 1908–Feb. 20, 1943."

Something made gentle contact with Heller's shoulder. It was Rita's forehead.

She had been fooling herself after all.

They sat there for a while. Heller didn't dare move. Then Rita sat upright and wiped at her face.

"Good thing he doesn't have to see all that's happening here," she said, taking the photo from Heller and stuffing it back into the envelope. "I was asking around for you earlier and found a nurse who was friends with the dead girl. She works in building 7, in the eye clinic. The building is half-destroyed; they made an emergency entrance on the side facing the river."

Rita handed Heller a piece of paper with a name: Irma Braune. "If you need me again, I'm now living in building 14 with most of the other nurses until our regular quarters are back in working order. Fourth floor, end of the hall to the right."

"I'm sorry, I can't find Nurse Irma," said the ward nurse, a stout woman of around fifty.

"She's supposed to be here."

"According to the schedule she is. And she was here earlier. This morning she came to tell me that the police wanted to question her about Erika. Maybe that's where she is now?"

Heller doubted that. "Where exactly is that?"

"At the police station."

"I am the police," Heller said. "When did you last see Irma Braune?"

"Two hours ago. But after that? Not that I can remember."

"Where does she live?"

"In Räcknitz, as far as I know. She was living there with Erika. I'd need to check . . ."

Heller stared at her to do so; she only stared back. He eventually won the staring contest, and she went off to the nurses' station.

"This street must've been Zeunerstrasse, there's a sign there." Heller pointed over Zaitsev's shoulder as the Russian gave the driver instructions. What used to be a short trip through town had turned into nearly forty-five minutes. They probably could've traveled faster on foot.

Here too was destruction wherever Heller looked. More than half of the buildings were fire-gutted; others had collapsed. Yet people had built makeshift lodgings, wooden sheds, shanties, tents. Others had set themselves up in bombed-out residences, covering the shattered windows with cardboard or boards. Laundry dried on lines as children played among the rubble. Looming on the building walls were those inescapable messages from survivors, written with chalk and white paint. The streets had been cleared just enough for vehicles to pass through.

"I'm looking for an address—number 8," Heller said to an older woman. She pointed at a building.

As the car halted, Zaitsev leaped out first but stayed in the background and let Heller do the questioning.

An old man was knocking bricks apart, stacking them neatly in front of the building. "Do an Irma and an Erika live here?" Heller asked him.

"They workin'," the old man said in a Saxon accent.

"Does Erika have relatives living here?"

"Nah, they come alone."

Heller wished he had a photo of Glöckner with him. "Have you seen any strangers around here in the last few days?"

"Strangers always comin' round. The authorities, they made bombed-out folks live here with us even though we bombed out ourselves."

"Did the two women have any male visitors? Maybe a man who has a pronounced limp, wearing a prosthesis?"

The old man shook his head. "Not seen a thing like that."

"Can I take a look at where they're living?"

"Sure, second floor on the right. Careful, though, stairs got a hole in it."

The women's lodgings consisted of two rooms. The doors were missing, the windows broken. Blankets and drapes kept it from being too drafty. The wallpaper had burned away. Two mattresses lay on the floor, and Heller found the nurses' few belongings in a trunk. A wash-bowl stood on a chair, a jug next to it still holding a little water. Heller found a few letters under the mattresses, then two hundred Reichsmarks under the trunk.

"It can't be coincidence that the Braune girl is gone as well," Heller told Zaitsev outside the building.

The Russian waved away the notion. "She got scared and took off. But she won't stay away forever. I will put sentries here and at the hospital."

They didn't have to wait long before a truck approached on patrol. Zaitsev signaled for the truck to halt, and two soldiers jumped out.

"Let's go, back to the hospital," he ordered Heller.

The trip back took even longer. Countless people and vehicles blocked the streets. Extensive repairs were being done to power lines. Red Army soldiers were out distributing food, large groups had formed at every soup kitchen, and just as many people waited around the freshwater tanks, holding their metal buckets and bowls. Off to the west, a large cloud of dust was rising. Yet another building wall had likely collapsed; that, or they were tearing another down. Nearly every week they were detonating another dud shell. More and more Russians were coming into the city, either to be stationed here or to be redirected to other cities. The columns of trucks, tanks, and ever-present horse-drawn carts blended in among the endless masses of refugees still trying to get to the west. And there was so much theft, plundering, rape, murder, again and again. Heller didn't want to think about all the madness. Instead, he couldn't stop thinking about that jug in the two nurses' room, how it still had water in it. Zaitsev had the car's top down, and the sun was beating down on them. Heller, who hadn't drunk a thing for hours, was incredibly thirsty but didn't want to admit it to Zaitsev.

They inched toward the hospital, which appeared in the distance like an oasis in a desert of rubble even though it was nearly destroyed itself. The streets were becoming more crowded, and they made even less progress. The Red Army soldiers had their hands full, directing traffic, redirecting trucks, waving through the cars carrying their officers.

As they crawled along, the driver steered into Fiedlerstrasse for the main entrance, slaloming around bomb craters, jolting them over potholes patched however possible, honking constantly, cursing and screaming. Zaitsev took it all with stoic indifference while Heller, who already had a headache, would've rather gotten out and walked the rest of the way.

The windshield suddenly burst, and the driver slumped over. The car hurtled out of control, crashed into a cart, and the engine died. Only now did Heller hear the shots.

"Get down!" Zaitsev shouted as he opened the passenger door and rolled out. More rounds struck the car, a tire burst, and another, and the engine hissed.

Heller got down low between the rows of seats but still felt exposed and defenseless. He too wanted out of the car yet didn't want to leave his cover. Another shot shredded the back of the driver's seat, and the driver, who Heller had thought was already dead, uttered a final moan and toppled to the side. More rounds pelted them. Zaitsev fired back as return fire from Russian rifles filled the air.

Finally Heller dared to raise his head. The people all around had thrown themselves to the ground or were crawling for cover while others ran off. He saw flashes coming from rubble in the distance. More rounds struck all around the car and into the wall behind them. Someone yelped from getting hit.

"Grenade!" Zaitsev shouted. Hand grenades exploded. Heller ducked down between the seats again, hands over his head for protection. Shrapnel clattered against the side of the car. A single shot rang out, another. Then it was suddenly quiet. Someone shouted in Russian.

Zaitsev pulled himself up, and Heller dared to leave his cover too.

He saw someone lying among the rubble. The attacker had tumbled out from the hiding spot where he'd been lying in wait. Yet no one ventured over. The shooter could have accomplices or might only be playing dead. Zaitsev shouted an order, gave his soldiers signals, and two, then three of them advanced while crouching and circled the man.

From the corner of his eye, Heller noticed someone exiting the shadows of a burned-out building and running up to the assassin. It was the young woman in the gray overcoat.

"*Stoi!*" barked Zaitsev, as he shot into the air. "Don't move. Do not get any closer!"

But the young woman had already reached the man on the ground and was tugging at his jacket. She looked up and, seeing the Red Army soldiers approaching, ran back inside the ruins.

Heller worked to climb his way free from the demolished car and bent over the dead driver, who was staring up into the blue sky. Heller then hurried over to the dead assassin.

Zaitsev had already ripped an MP 40 submachine gun out of the man's hands and seized two grenades. The man wore a nondescript gray suit and a flat cap that a head shot had left in shreds.

"Goddamnit, I wanted him alive!" growled Zaitsev.

Heller bent down, ignoring the blood and chunks of brain, and turned the dead man's head his way. "I know this man. It's Peter Strampe, assumed dead long ago."

"What?" Zaitsev held his shoulder. Blood trickled out between his fingers.

"Supposedly he and my superior were both killed in that first big air raid."

Zaitsev started bleeding heavier. He had to be in pain but wasn't showing it. "Well, someone had the story all wrong, at least as far as that man goes. Why did he attack us? Was it meant for you?"

Heller didn't have an answer. He bent down to the dead man again and sniffed the odor coming from his jacket. "You smell that?"

Zaitsev went down on a knee and had Heller hold part of the jacket up to his face.

"Strange, isn't it?" Heller said. "Smells like a mortuary."

"He could be wearing a dead man's clothes." Zaitsev shuddered and stood.

Heller stood as well. All he could think of was that night when Strampe emptied the whole magazine of his submachine gun, and of that bicycle going right into his sidecar. Had that bike even belonged to the Frenchman? It was odd how focused Klepp was on shelving the whole case so quickly. Heller was staring at the ground, lost in thought. He remembered Zaitsev and looked up.

"Come on, Zaitsev, we need to get you to a doctor. I'll tell you about Klepp on the way."

"Fine. Then take me to this Dr. Schorrer."

Dr. Schorrer didn't let on whether he was glad to see Heller still alive. He acted distant, and never bothered asking why they had sought out him of all people.

Zaitsev took off his shirt. His upper body was more wiry than muscular, with a large burn scar on his back. Schorrer pulled on rubber gloves and disinfected the bullet wound. The slug had struck his upper right collarbone and exited cleanly through shoulder muscle.

"You lucked out," Schorrer said.

The Russian kept silent, watching the doctor without emotion.

"It'll need stitches," Schorrer said.

"Go ahead."

Schorrer had the nurse hand him the right instruments and first sewed up the back wound. Zaitsev didn't even make a face. The doctor then sat facing him, to inspect the entry wound.

"Were you in the Nazi Party?" Zaitsev asked.

"I was not." Schorrer had to know what was at stake here. But he didn't let it show and kept doing his job.

"In the SS?"

"I was the head doctor in an army field hospital, in Poland. I was stuck in the rear," Schorrer said.

Zaitsev raised his head. "Did you ever take part in any Waffen-SS operations?"

"No. They had their own medical units."

"Was it hard for you to transfer back to Germany?"

"Well, for one, I'm not exactly young anymore. This isn't the only war where I served my country. And two, you didn't need to get shot just so you could interrogate me. I'm always happy to come down to headquarters or meet in my modest lodgings. So please let me finish my work now."

The Russian fished a cigarette out of his jacket, stuck it in his mouth, and gave Heller an urgent look. Heller looked to Schorrer, who nodded. Heller lit Zaitsev's cigarette with a match. Zaitsev took two long drags, made a face, and offered Schorrer a smoke. The doctor shook his head. "I don't smoke."

Zaitsev took another drag. "Do you know Obersturmbannführer Klepp?"

"Yes, I knew him. Heard he was killed."

"He might not have been."

Schorrer paused a second. "That so?"

"Strampe, his driver and bodyguard, was the one who shot at us today," Heller explained. "He was supposed to be dead already."

Schorrer had the nurse hand him gauze and bandages and started wrapping Zaitsev. "Thus all that shooting I heard. So, Klepp, huh? So the man left his post, turned deserter. And an Obersturmbannführer at that. The biggest blowhards are always the first to run."

"The last thing Klepp told me," Heller said, "was that we needed to team up with the Americans, to . . ." He fell silent. Zaitsev laughed and waved for them to continue—the discussion seemed to interest him.

Schorrer snorted. "Klepp saw how the winds were blowing—coming in hard from the east. He had plenty to answer for. Sounds like he made off at just the right time to save his skin and would have done so even if he were only half the weasel I took him for. A Jew recently told me that Klepp had been the most vicious of all the SS tracking them down in Dresden."

"So you think he got away?" Heller said. "Then why is Strampe still here? Why did he fire at me?"

Schorrer, now finished bandaging, held up his hands. "As I told you way back last winter, I'm a doctor, not a detective. Maybe Strampe still had a score to settle with you, or—"

"Or . . . ," Zaitsev interrupted. He was sitting up now, pulling his shirt back on. "Klepp is still here and has something to hide. Heller, you know where Klepp was living?"

"I think it was on Königsteinstrasse. But first we really need to find out whether this Irma Braune has been seen anywhere."

May 17, 1945: Evening

Nurse Irma Braune still hadn't shown up for work. And those bullets in Zaitsev's car left it unfit to drive. The commissar couldn't find a replacement right away, so they had to make their way on foot.

Heller's right ankle was becoming more painful, and he was all worn out. The soup and thick slice of white bread Zaitsev obtained for him didn't help much—he'd refrained from eating the bread so he could bring it home to Karin later in the evening.

The shortest-possible route was turning into a major challenge for Heller. Only narrow paths had been cleared between ruins, which meant the straightest line was often over the rubble. It was already pushing evening when they reached Königsteinstrasse, and Heller could only assume that he wouldn't be getting home tonight because of curfew.

He'd been going over the Strampe incident in his head the whole way over. He was fairly certain that the attack was meant for him, and that he was only alive because of that unlucky driver who got in the way of the bullets. Did Heller have to be wary of a sharpshooter at every turn, waiting to finish the job that Strampe had started? He snuck glances to all sides as they walked along.

"You are limping," said Zaitsev. He was smoking one cigarette after the other, which had made several children start following them. They wrestled over the half-smoked butts Zaitsev flicked away. "War wound?"

Heller nodded. "Nineteen fifteen, Belgium. I probably owe my life to it—for getting me home."

Zaitsev nodded again, and Heller was starting to think he did that whenever he didn't understand. A sliver of wood the size of a bread knife had gored his ankle back in 1915. For a while, it looked like they'd have to remove his foot—anything to get away from the trenches.

"Do you have children?"

"Two boys." Heller stopped. "It must be over there." He pointed at a large villa with a collapsed roof.

Zaitsev wasn't done. "Where are your sons?"

"Klaus was in Russia. Erwin was sent to the Ardennes in '44."

"Good," Zaitsev said. Then he whipped around and drew his pistol at the children. "Go away! Now!" he shouted. They turned and ran off.

Klepp's villa had four floors. A large overgrown yard surrounded the house, and there were two tall, fire-ravaged poplars. The fences were busted, all the windowpanes were shattered, and drapes still hung out the windows as if the air raids had happened yesterday. A part of the roof had fallen in, and a section of exterior wall along with it, as if a large and hungry beast had taken a bite out of it. A home like this had been well guarded, even during the final months of the war—any plunderers could assume a death sentence. Yet the same homes had been left unprotected after the Red Army started occupying the city.

Zaitsev stepped over a toppled wooden fence onto the property and began to circle the house. Heller followed at a distance. It worried him that they had no backup should someone be waiting for them inside the villa.

"I'm not sure what I hoped for," Zaitsev admitted once they were standing back outside the entrance. Apart from the destroyed section, the villa was more than habitable by present standards. Its proximity to the vast grounds of Grosser Garten park had protected it from the firestorm. "Why would Klepp go and hide out? Most members of the SS didn't do that."

Klepp had certainly not reacted like a typical SS man. Right after the air raids, Heller had seen the Nazi Party apparatus, the SS-controlled police, and the other agencies react by helping out, coordinating emergency efforts, and feeding people. Extra personnel had even been sent from Berlin to Dresden to help run things. That had all functioned well. At the same time, word was quickly spreading that leading party comrades and SS figures were often the first to flee from the advancing enemy. Yet none had probably absconded as early as Klepp, nearly three months before the war ended. Klepp must have either speculated that the end was coming much sooner, or he had been hiding something from his own people.

"Come on. We're going in." Zaitsev leaped up the first few steps.

"I'd feel better if I had a pistol," Heller said.

"So you can shoot me in the back?" said the Russian. He drew his gun, undid the safety, and crept into the foyer.

Klepp's home was a small palace. In the grand foyer, the floor was appointed with black granite tiles, and two curving stairways led up to the second-floor balustrade. Two huge sets of double doors opened to a salon on the left and a den on the right. Tracks in the dust hinted at stray animals and people, likely homeless and starving, in search of anything to eat. Nothing indicated that Klepp was still living here.

Zaitsev pressed himself to the wall, checked that the stairs leading up were all clear, and gave Heller a signal that he hadn't spotted anything suspicious. They started their tour of the ground floor. The study looked untouched—complete with swastika flag and Hitler bust still standing—but the kitchen and laundry room were completely destroyed, their ceilings fallen in. In the salon, the buffet cabinet doors had been flung open, the dishes and glasses either missing or shattered. The table had been smashed to bits by collapsed masonry.

They ended up back in the foyer. Zaitsev waved and pointed upstairs. Heller followed him, tiptoeing up the steps. Here were the Klepps' living areas—large, bright spaces, all cleared out or plundered, more footprints in the dust. Bedding and mattresses were missing from the bedrooms, the chandeliers had fallen from the ceiling, and papers lay scattered all over the floor. Heller bent down and saw tax assessments, insurance documents—nothing he could use.

Zaitsev seemed angered. "No one lives here. Doesn't look like Klepp was staying here. There's no point climbing all over. See that? Stairs to the next floor don't exactly look safe."

Heller didn't want to give up yet. He knelt in the dirt and looked under cabinets and beds. He then stood on a chair. "No one has taken shelter here. Which is strange. Every habitable location and building is being used, the spots under the bridges are overcrowded, and this place is just standing empty?"

"What did you expect to find here?" Zaitsev asked.

"I never expect anything. Otherwise, I only find what I want to find."

Zaitsev nodded, then shook his head. "My party, it finds what it wants to find . . ."

Heller had to keep himself from grinning. On top of one of the armoires, he'd just noticed a little wooden strongbox that he'd like to look in. But without Zaitsev. If he could only lose the Russian for a short time.

"Don't stop now," Heller said. "We're only here once, so let's use the light we have, give each room a thorough look."

"In that case, old man, I'm heading upstairs anyway. If you hear something, do not shout. Better to hide and wait." With that, the Russian was gone.

Zaitsev's arrogance was getting to Heller, but at least it left him privacy to remove the shallow little box from atop the armoire. It was not locked. There were photos and letters inside. Heller took out a few letters and read them, then leafed through the rest. They were love letters from Klepp to his wife, Magdalena. He missed her so much, he had written from Poland, her voice, her laughter. Mixed in were small poems, pompous stanzas full of roses, throbbing hearts, eternal love. Heller was amazed that this cynical member of the "master race" obviously had a far different side to him; he never would've thought the man capable. Heller held the photos up to the broken window's thinning daylight and recognized Klepp in uniform, in undershirt, with hunting rifle, with a dead deer, atop an armored car wearing goggles, shaking hands with a high-ranking officer, with a cow and six men in front of a country house, and Klepp in butcher's clothes and a long white apron, hoisting half a pig in each hand, posing like a weight lifter, feet planted far apart. There were also photos of him with a slim young girl: Klepp in uniform, his wife all in high-necked white, the collar up to her chin, a gentle face.

Heller heard something. He set the photos down and crept to the door. But it was only Zaitsev making noise up in the attic.

Heller leaned closer to the window and started with the last photos. He went through them one more time from the beginning. In the photos showing Klepp in wartime, he thought he could make out Strampe. Despite his size, he looked more like a little boy under his dark helmet, given his childlike features. Heller separated the photos he didn't find useful, which left him holding only a picture of Klepp with men from the butcher shop. Five of them were older, with massive walrus mustaches and flattops. A younger man was standing in the background, likely an apprentice. One of the older men looked like Klepp's father, and on the far left Heller saw the face of a boy of thirteen or fourteen, smiling awkwardly, as if unsure that he belonged there. The photo was slightly overexposed and already a little yellowed. Heller leaned into the light.

"Keep leaning out that window and someone will finally shoot you in the head."

Heller started and gave the Russian an angry glare.

"Just look at this," Zaitsev said. He stuffed both hands into his pockets, pulled them back out, and held them up to Heller. They were filled with rings, necklaces, and coins. "Hidden up in the attic, under the floorboards. There's plenty more. Seems the Obersturmbannführer made himself rich from the extermination of Jews. Must have been skimming from Hitler's war chest. Many wads of cash there, silver cutlery, candlesticks, watches, porcelain, everything a heart desires. Quite the treasure trove."

Zaitsev put the booty back in his pockets. "So this is why he went underground? Afraid someone might discover this after the air raids, and now he doesn't want to leave his treasure behind? Heller, you're not listening. What's with you?"

Heller, still looking at the photo, suddenly felt as if the walls were whispering to him, trying to tell him something. They would need to look in every possible corner. They would find something much bigger there in the shadows. This wasn't like Frau Zinsendorfer lurking around his bed in all her madness. This was truly menacing. He held the photo up to the Russian. "That one, far left. That's the one I was chasing, the one I shot."

"Are you sure? He's just a kid."

Heller nodded. He still had the feeling, like someone was eyeing him with a cold stare.

Zaitsev grabbed the photo, folded it, and put it away. "It's late. We need to figure out how to get home."

"Where do you live?" Heller asked.

"I live—" Zaitsev began but raised a hand in warning, placing a finger over his mouth. He reached for his gun, then moved over to the door and listened. He waved Heller over. "Hear that?"

Heller turned his head. All was still. The sun had disappeared behind the ruins a while ago, and it was curfew soon. Anyone with a place to live had gotten there by now or should at least have found shelter for the night.

Yet there was a noise.

"It's coming from downstairs."

Zaitsev tiptoed down the stairway. All was quiet on the ground floor.

"We never tried the cellar," Heller whispered.

"The outside door was under rubble," Zaitsev whispered back.

"There must be another way in, from inside the house." Heller led the Russian into the demolished kitchen and found a small wooden door painted white. It opened down to the cellar. He automatically reached for the light switch, but of course there was no power. A kerosene lamp stood on the highest step. Zaitsev quietly shook it, splashing the liquid around, and lit the wick.

They went down into the cellar. The walls were sandstone, the tiny windows plugged up with rags. Rugs lay around, blankets, pillows. Children's toys made of wood. Various bowls stood in the corners, with brownish water in them or worse. It reeked of ammonia. A leather ball, bones, pieces of clothing, everything a complete mess. Heller bent down and picked up something—women's underwear. Then he reached for the ball. He clearly made out bite marks in the leather. The wooden toys were chewed on too.

Zaitsev took the underwear from him. "You think this is from a victim?"

"Impossible to know," Heller said.

Zaitsev raised the lamp, took a few steps around. "No one's here."

They suddenly heard moaning, muffled but so near they both jumped to the side. It was coming from right below them. Zaitsev handed Heller the lamp and started clearing the layers of blankets and rugs from the floor. He eventually found another layer, of loose tar paper. He removed it to reveal a trap door, constructed of heavy wood, built into the floor. A large sliding bolt kept it locked. Zaitsev opened the bolt and lifted open the door. Below, they could see a dungeon of less than twenty square feet. A revolting smell rose up, and they held their hands over their noses and mouths. Zaitsev took the lamp and shone it down. On the damp ground, among shapeless rags, lay the young woman in the gray overcoat who'd escaped from them twice, her face familiar to Heller. Her hair was sticky with mud and blood, and she was gagged and blindfolded, her hands tied behind her back, legs bound.

"Don't be frightened!" Heller shouted. "We're here to help!" He knelt down and tried to reach for the woman. That wouldn't work. Like it or not, he would have to climb down into the stench. The muddy earth sucked at his shoes as he did. He grabbed the woman by the arms, yanked her up so Zaitsev could get hold of her, and together they hauled her up and out. Heller scrambled to get out of the hole, the thought of the door slamming shut with him trapped inside sending him into a mad panic. He desperately clawed his way out, helped Zaitsev remove the woman's restraints, and started on the blindfold and gag. She started screaming, gasping desperately for air, her eyes rolling around in a panic, her hands reaching for Heller's arms and neck as if seeking something, anything, to grasp onto, like someone drowning.

"Be calm, you're safe! What's your name? Who took you here?" Zaitsev pulled out his jackknife and cut the rope around her legs.

When she saw the knife, the woman started hitting Heller. She kicked frantically, trying to free herself from the Russian, who kept trying to get control of her legs.

"Calm yourself. I'm with the police!"

But the woman didn't stop. She kicked her feet loose and knocked the lamp into the pit, where it went out. In the ensuing darkness, Heller took a strong blow to the face. The woman ran away, just a silhouette at the cellar entrance revealing itself in the dark. Heller and Zaitsev found the stairs at the same time. Zaitsev pushed past Heller.

"*Stoi!*" he shouted. "*Stoi!*" Heller, keeping up with him, ran out onto the ground floor and made a hard left for the window to cut the woman off. But she was faster and already out into the street. The Russian aimed his gun.

"Don't shoot, for God's sake! Wait, Fräulein, wait!" Heller shouted after her. "Please, Fräulein, don't run away."

Zaitsev cursed. The woman had disappeared into the ruins.

"Don't move!" someone shouted in broken German—Red Army soldiers on patrol.

Zaitsev shouted back in Russian to call the patrol over. He gave Heller a serious look. "Let's take another look at that cellar. We've found your Fright Man, it appears. Or at least his lair."

The Red Army soldiers illuminated the hole with their flashlights. Zaitsev slid down into it, and his boots sank a couple of inches into the mud. Heller checked his own shoes and shook them.

"This is earth, just dug out, no cement." Zaitsev rubbed the walls. "And you see this here?" He pointed in disgust at a long bone. "There's more of them."

"Human bones?"

"I can't tell. He must have been holding his victims here."

"Then Klepp must have known." Why the bones, though? Heller wondered. Could there be more victims?

Zaitsev nodded and pulled himself out of the hole, using the edges to wipe mud off his boots. "You know anyone who can examine bones like this?" he asked.

"The only one I can think of is Schorrer."

"That's fine by me. I must take a closer look at that one anyway."

"Wait, did Professor Ehlig put you on Schorrer's trail?" Heller asked. "Ehlig was an ardent Hitler worshipper . . ." Heller shut up. This was one of those things he had sworn he would never do. If they questioned him as a witness, he would testify to the best of his knowledge and conscience. But anything else was just informing, and suspiciously like trying to gain advantage. And there had been more than enough informing to go around during the years of the Third Reich.

"You are naïve, Herr Heller, if you think your Dr. Schorrer is such a good man. That helps explain your behavior during the Third Reich. You are naïve."

Talk like this made Heller furious, especially coming from young Zaitsev, of all people, who seemed to believe whatever his party dictated. Yet he controlled himself and kept quiet.

Something hissed. Everyone glanced up the stairs, where a Red Army soldier stood whispering in Russian. Zaitsev waved Heller over, and they quietly went upstairs, followed the soldier in a crouch, and squatted near a window. Night had come, the stars twinkling, the passing clouds illuminated by moonlight.

Then they heard it. It sounded like an animal panting. Rocks and stones got knocked around. Someone was softly giggling, gurgling.

Heller cautiously raised his head above the window ledge. The nearest mountain of rubble was only a faint outline. Something rustled in the tall grass, the branches of bushes seemed to move, and then they heard a throat clearing, and again, louder. Then snorting.

"What is that?" Zaitsev whispered.

Heller listened to the darkness. Soon he thought he heard someone loudly sucking up their spit. Crying followed. It was weeping, nearly silent, like a child whimpering.

Zaitsev whispered a command to the soldier, who promptly left. Then Zaitsev moved in the other direction without telling Heller.

He was cautious yet still kicked a few stones loose. The noises outside silenced. Soon they heard hasty footsteps, twigs breaking, and the clunking of clay bricks. Heller crouched below the window in anger. Why did Zaitsev always have to be so impatient? If Heller had had his way, they'd have waited and watched in silence. Now they were squandering another chance.

He leaned his head against the wall, disappointed, and only now did he notice how hungry he was, and above all tired. Yet as soon as he closed his eyes, all the episodes from his day mixed into a tangle of car trips, shootings, screaming, and that nightmarish sensation of being buried alive. No wonder the young woman had been so panicked. Still, he wished she could've just kept calm.

Zaitsev returned and spoke to the same soldier. Heller rubbed the weariness from his face, thinking, That damn language of theirs—he'd have to learn to understand it somehow.

Zaitsev dropped down beside him, tapped a cigarette from his pack, and lit up. "He's gone."

"Did you see anything?"

"He was limping badly."

"Limping?" Heller thought of Glöckner the caretaker and his prosthesis.

"I've ordered the house guarded," Zaitsev said. "There's a billet near here—we will stay the night there."

"I was actually hoping to go home," Heller said.

"No, no home for you!"

In the darkness, Heller lost track of where they were. Everything was just as destroyed here, farther south in Dresden. He barely recognized any streets and could only guess where the main train station stood. Campfires burned on street corners. They were halted by soldiers several times before they finally reached a large building that had survived the air raids. It had five floors and might have belonged to the university. Armed guards stood outside, laughing, smoking, and drinking a lot. Zaitsev marched inside with impressive self-assurance. Heller followed at his heels, an uneasy feeling nagging at him. They climbed the stairs and entered a large hall. Thick clouds of smoke hung in the air. It stank like booze and unwashed men; the noise level was unbearable. Everyone carried a gun, and some men staggered around the room from boozing it up while others were already half-unconscious. Heller attracted angry and derisive stares, yet Zaitsev acted unconcerned and gave a rough shove to a man who didn't want to let them pass.

"Here, take a seat," he ordered, and sat Heller down at a table in a corner. Heller sat, trying to ignore all the stares. It took a brief eternity for Zaitsev to come back and set down a large bowl of soup. He pulled out two spoons from a jacket pocket and a piece of bread that he split in two, then he sat across from Heller and started eating.

"Well, what?" he asked, and pointed at the second spoon. Only now did Heller understand what he meant and began eating from the same bowl.

The soup had an amazing amount of meat, but it was so tough and unfamiliar that Heller couldn't get it down. He nearly gagged and had to keep pausing to chew it well enough. Zaitsev shouted something. A man came with a bottle that he handed to Heller. He took a big drink and nearly choked on it because he was expecting water, not vodka, and the soldiers standing around roared with laughter. Zaitsev smiled and drank down a quarter of the bottle.

It was getting late. Heller sat dazed in his chair, dead tired yet unable to fall asleep. Whenever he was just about to nod off, something clanked or someone shot into the air. Zaitsev slept bent forward over the table, his head on his arms. Seeing him like this, Heller was painfully reminded of his sons. Where and how were they sleeping right now?

Out on the street, the Russians got louder. Did these people never sleep?

The rest happened so fast. Two young women were shoved into the room. One of them already had a torn blouse and was making a futile attempt to cover her breasts. A couple of soldiers yanked down her skirt.

"Mama!" cried one of the women, and a bunch of men mimicked her voice. A soldier grabbed her and hauled her onto a table. Several soldiers pressed in close, and others left the room, yet the majority just stayed and watched.

"No, please, I'm pregnant, I have a child in me, please no!" screamed the young woman in pure terror. The other girl had already lost consciousness.

Heller jumped up without thinking about it. "Stop it," he shouted. "*Stoi!* Stop at once!"

An abrupt silence fell. The only sound was the woman sobbing.

"What you say?" snarled a soldier with his pants undone as he came over to Heller and brandished a submachine gun. "You dead, fascist!"

Heller stared back, his eyes fixed. He'd started this and was going to have to end it. "Stop it. You should be punished for this kind of behavior."

"I no understand, Hitler Youth! You make Russia kaput! My father kaput, my brother kaput. City kaput. Now I make Germany kaput, see? You kaput, woman kaput! With this!" He raised his weapon. He pointed at his genitals. "And with this. One word and you dead!"

"I can't allow it. Commissar Zaitsev! Alexei!" Heller looked to Zaitsev and noticed that he'd been awake the whole time, watching. Zaitsev rose sluggishly, and the soldier exposing himself backed away.

"You know, Heller, these men have seen it all. They were fighting this war for four years, without leave, without letters, without knowing if their parents were still alive. They've seen their wives and children dead, the old ones dead, cities burned down. These men have had such hunger, and thirst, and wounds, and everyone who becomes a friend has fallen, killed by a German bullet or a German shell. And so now they come here as the victors. They defeated the Devil, so they eat and drink and behave how they want. And you want to forbid it?"

Zaitsev had said it very quietly, watching Heller. But Heller didn't admit defeat.

"Zaitsev, you're an officer! You can't allow that." He pointed at the girls. "Those two there can't help it."

He had judged Zaitsev wrong. Zaitsev leaped at Heller, grabbed him by the collar, and hurled him against the wall.

"No one can help it!" Zaitsev roared, his spit spraying Heller's face. "A whole nation of people votes for Hitler. And suddenly no one knew anything, no one did anything, everyone just followed orders. You all say you're victims. Good old German order, that's all that matters." Still furious, he gave Heller another shove. Then he whipped around and barked at the soldiers. *"Zamolchi i odevaysya!"*

Grumbling sounded around the room. Zaitsev repeated the order just as harshly. Then he went to the women, heaved them up, and shoved them over to Heller.

"Here, you protect them," he said, then spat at their feet and stormed out.

The women pressed close to Heller. The naked one wrapped her arms around his neck, her body shaking with fear, while the other one looked listless and shocked.

"It's all right," Heller whispered, and went to pick up the naked one's clothes, yet the women clamped on to him and wouldn't let go.

"Here, take my overcoat." Heller pulled off his overcoat and draped it around the naked woman. Then he held each woman on either side of him and hauled them toward the door. A soldier stood tall before him, the barrel of his gun pointing to Heller's left wrist, which held the watch that Frau Marquart had given him.

Heller unfastened the watch and gave it to the Russian, who moved on.

"It's all right now," Heller said to the girls, though he had no idea how they were supposed to survive the night.

217

May 18, 1945: Morning

Dr. Schorrer waited until Zaitsev left his office. The Russian needed to use the toilet after forgoing his billet's overburdened facilities.

Schorrer stood, went over to the door, and shut it.

"You dragging this Russian around with you every day?" he snapped.

"I'm doing my work and have to rely on his help."

"You brought him here, and now he's set his sights on me."

"You hiding something?"

"That's not the issue. He wants his hands on a Nazi. He can't have Ehlig, not as long as he's on good terms with the Russian authorities. So he's latching onto me. You really aren't so naïve as to believe that any of this has to do with justice. You think that man's helping you with your investigation? Zaitsev wants to make a name for himself. He wants his medals. They're not a whit better than our party comrades were."

Heller was too tired to contradict the doctor, even though it annoyed him to be called naïve for the second time. He stepped to the table instead, laid out the large towel holding the bones they found in the hideout, and gave Schorrer an urgent look.

Schorrer pulled on his rubber gloves and sorted the bones. "This here, clearly an ulna. Here's part of a femur, broken off. This one could be from a pig or cow. And these here, now, these are human ribs." The doctor held the two broken bones up to his body. "See here." He pointed at scratch marks on the bones. "Knife marks. Someone scraping here. And this, right here, might be marks from human teeth." Schorrer made a disgusted grimace, though Heller doubted if anything shocked him anymore.

Heller took a closer look at the bite marks, hoping to tell how the incisors were positioned, but he knew it wasn't going to get him anywhere.

"Klepp had a cellar in his villa with a dungeon underneath. We found blood, feces, urine. We're assuming someone's been living in the cellar. I also found a photo . . . Zaitsev took it."

The two men stared at each other in silence.

"People . . . ," Schorrer began, sounding suddenly pensive. "They must think it can't get any worse. The war lost. Germany destroyed. Their Greatest Ever Führer of the Thousand-Year Reich dead. And yet despite all the hardship, they seem relieved."

Heller nodded.

"Pray to God," continued Schorrer, "that this impulse lasts awhile. We're in for more hard times. Next winter. My only hope is that it's not just turnips again."

Zaitsev burst into the room.

"I need that photo," Heller said.

Zaitsev pulled it out and gave it to him.

"Recognize anyone?" Heller asked, showing Schorrer the photo.

Schorrer eyed the picture, and the corners of his mouth turned down with contempt.

"Ludwig Klepp. Rudolf Klepp's son. Must be about twenty-one now." He pointed at the timid-looking boy at the left edge of the picture.

"How do you know that?"

"He was there in '41 for Operation Barbarossa, when we invaded the Soviet Union, but he was declared unfit for active service and sent home. Severely mentally ill. Not to mention a complete imbecile."

"Complete imbecile?"

Schorrer wiped the tabletop clean with a flat hand. "Klepp was always embarrassed by that. He really would've liked to kick him out. Considered him a weakling. Kept trying to get him to sign up for the Reich Labor Service. His wife surely put her foot down."

"How do you—"

"He came and asked for my help after I'd barely started my post here. Ludwig had severe diarrhea; Klepp thought it was dysentery. That's when I learned the story. Very distraught, the young man. Wouldn't let himself be touched at first. He kept twitching uncontrollably, and he would jump at every loud noise, laughing crazily in the process. Klepp was keeping him from public view by that point."

"And you're just telling me this now?"

"I had no idea you were gunning for Klepp."

"What did he look like? What sort of build did he have?"

"Built like his father—flabby, I'd call it. Ungainly, wide face. Dark hair, I believe."

"So, do you believe he's capable of committing murders like these? You met him, after all."

Schorrer didn't answer right away. He ran his fingers through his gray hair. "How does anyone really know what someone's capable of? It could very well be. His father was a butcher. He might have apprenticed with him, could've learned how to use knives that way. After the second murder, Klepp phoned me and asked how the investigation was progressing. He mostly asked about what you were finding out."

"Why didn't you tell me?" Heller asked, angry now. So Klepp was inquiring about him—maybe he'd been getting too close with his investigation. Did Strampe truly empty his whole magazine that freezing January night intending to hit an escaping Frenchman, or had he actually meant to kill Heller?

"You do know Professor Ehlig was campaigning against me behind my back. I was looking to keep my options open and was hoping Klepp might be inclined to back me if push came to shove. You can't trust anyone anymore, as you know. Every man for himself. And please, don't act so indignant. You yourself are the one setting the example."

"What does this mean—'gunning for'?" Zaitsev asked on the way to Klepp's villa.

Heller was having a tough time keeping up with him but didn't want to admit, not even to himself, that their long trips on foot were becoming more and more of a burden. His breakfast had been a lumpy milk soup, and a delayed nausea was spreading through him. On top of that, his guilty conscience was plaguing him—because of Karin.

"It's a figure of speech. Just means that you're watching someone."

Zaitsev side-eyed him doubtfully, eyebrows raised.

"That you're suspicious of someone," Heller clarified. "You really can't find us a working vehicle? And more people, if possible? Maybe even German speakers? And I'd really like to let my wife know where I am."

Zaitsev said nothing. He obviously had no intention of fulfilling Heller's requests.

Heller was unfazed. "If we're going to intercept Ludwig, those guards need to be withdrawn from around the villa." As they walked he detected movement from the corner of his eye, but among all the ruins it was hard to tell if someone was following them. Deep down, he was still reeling from Strampe's failed attack from the day before. "And don't let your men shoot him dead," he added.

Zaitsev pulled out a cigarette. "Believe me, I'm more interested in keeping the fellow alive than anyone."

Zaitsev was of course assuming that Rudolf Klepp was still alive, and he wanted to nab him. Whether Ludwig was the psychopath they sought was beside the point for Zaitsev. Heller couldn't hope for otherwise—he had to take what he could get. Meanwhile, Karin had probably been worrying to death about him and didn't have a thing to eat because he wasn't earning anything or bringing home marks. They should've moved to Langebrück, out in the country.

"Herr Heller, Herr Detective Inspector!" A woman came up alongside him. Heller winced. Why was she shouting his name so loudly? "Herr Heller?" She was probably fifty or older, had a cloth wrapped around her head, and wore a homemade dress of coarse fabric. "It's me, Hedwig, you know—Hedwig Borcher."

Heller, slowing, recognized his former neighbor from the building next door. "Frau Borcher?"

"My Otto was arrested. I don't know where they've taken him. He's been gone for two days. And he didn't even do anything!"

Her Otto, as Heller knew, had been the Nazi Party's local group leader.

"Herr Heller, you're such a good man. Tell them Otto's a good man too. He's helped so many, never did anything evil!" She tried to hang on to his arm. People were staring at them. Zaitsev pressed on, unmoved.

"He never hurt a single fly! I'm asking you, I'm pleading with you!"

Sure, good old Otto, the same one who immediately snatched up the apartment on the second floor just as soon as the Grünbaums were taken away. No one said a thing about it—otherwise some stranger would've gotten the apartment. Borcher, Leutholdt, none of them had done a thing.

"Frau Borcher, let go of me. I can't do anything for you." He could simply have lied, just so she'd leave him alone, could've just said, "All right, I'll see what I can do."

"Herr Heller, they're probably taking him to Siberia."

"Frau Borcher, we're on our way to important police business. Please leave me alone."

She finally let go, eyeing him with disappointment and anger. Heller hurried to catch up with Zaitsev.

At Klepp's villa, Zaitsev dismissed the guards. They hadn't noticed anything conspicuous during the night.

He and Heller agreed not to hide inside the villa. Heller found a spot in the ruins across from the villa, behind a stretch of brick wall, at about the height of the second floor. Zaitsev had climbed up into the closest house. They made sure that they had eye contact.

If Heller didn't pull himself together, his drowsiness would overpower him.

It was the middle of the morning. Farther down the street, someone had strung up a clothesline, and a woman sat next to it, watching over the wet laundry—a sheet, two pairs of underpants, stockings. On the other side of the street, someone was cooking outside using a primitive oven. Children were running around with tires, shooting each other with stick guns, playing hopscotch. Leaves rustled, and the fire-damaged stumps of trees were sprouting twigs and new greenery. Grass was growing in again. There was hammering and shoveling. A returning private with a gray backpack navigated his way down a narrow lane between collapsed buildings, taking careful steps. Heller watched him go. Then Zaitsev was waving forcefully at him, pointing at two trees near them. A large man in a white shirt and cardigan was standing between the trunks, as if about to relieve himself. Yet he just stood there, staring ahead. Then he continued on. Heller watched the man travel in a large arc, as if intending to take a back way into the property. He gave Zaitsev a signal, and then pulled back into the shadows. The villa was now blocking Heller's view. He climbed down the ruins and leisurely crossed the street so as not to attract suspicion. He crept around the villa's right side, keeping pressed to the wall. The man in the cardigan wasn't in sight. Heller had no other option but to keep going and really would've liked to know exactly where Zaitsev was. Then he heard a gentle rattle from inside the house. He couldn't make out what was going on. Was Zaitsev inside? Suddenly he heard a shot.

"Heller!" Zaitsev shouted.

A young man tumbled out the window, landing awkwardly on his feet and dropping his pistol. Heller now recognized him as Ludwig Klepp. As Ludwig bent down to retrieve his weapon, Heller charged. Ludwig spotted him and tried to sidestep, but Heller anticipated the move. They both toppled onto a mound of debris and shards, frantically wrestling for the gun until Heller was able to kick it away into tall grass.

Heller shouted for Zaitsev. "Alexei!"

Ludwig struck Heller's face with his forearm, then jumped up. But Heller had a tight hold on his leg. Ludwig quickly freed himself.

Gunshots rang out from the house. Heller, his view blurry, watched Ludwig run off, his arms whirling like a windmill. Heller pulled himself up and ran after the young man, intentionally putting himself in the line of fire.

Beyond the backyard was a mountain of rubble. Ludwig could scale that no problem. Yet no sooner had he scrambled up the hill on all fours than his jacket got caught and he tore at it, kicking loose rocks that tumbled down toward Heller.

Zaitsev sprinted up and passed Heller.

"Get down! Over there, cut him off!" ordered the Russian. Heller slid back down and ran along a cleared narrow path and soon had Ludwig in his view. Once Ludwig noticed him, he changed direction and headed off the path. Now Heller had to return to the ruins, which he'd really wanted to avoid.

"Zaitsev?" Heller shouted.

"Here!" he heard from the rubble.

Heller scaled yet another hill, balancing unsteadily on bricks and wood. In the distance, he could see Ludwig's white shirt slip between the remains of a wall. Zaitsev was about twenty yards behind Ludwig, stones scattering under his feet. He shouted something in Russian. Ludwig stumbled and disappeared, then Heller saw him climbing down into a cellar. Zaitsev ran right by the opening.

"No, Alexei, wait!" Heller shouted. The Russian stopped, looking around for Heller. Heller had already jumped down from the hill of rubble, cutting his hand on a sharp piece of wood. He now stood panting next to the Russian.

Heller pointed at the opening.

"Think it's a way through?" Zaitsev whispered.

Heller wasn't certain, but he guessed that the many single-family homes and villas around here were not connected underground. So he got an idea. He reached for a fist-size chunk of stone.

"Ludwig Klepp, come out with your hands up! I'm warning you. The Russian has a grenade!"

"Come out, or I'm throwing the grenade," Zaitsev shouted, playing along but not daring to stand in front of the opening. "I will count to three. *Raz, dva, tri!*"

Heller threw the stone into the gap.

Ludwig Klepp let out a roar, crawled frantically to the opening, and forced his way through. Zaitsev grabbed the young man and pulled him out. He threw himself onto Ludwig, frisked him for weapons, turned him onto his stomach, and wrenched his arms behind his back as Ludwig panted.

Heller bent down, ripped Ludwig's shirt out of his pants, and yanked down the waistband. Zaitsev gave him a questioning look, but Heller nodded with satisfaction: there was a clear scar over his kidneys. This was the man he'd shot the night of the air raid.

"Stand up!" Zaitsev ordered. He'd drawn his gun and aimed it at Ludwig Klepp. Ludwig stood up awkwardly, then thrust his trembling hands into the air.

"Don't shoot, please, please, please, don't shoot." The corners of his mouth quivered, and his eyelids fluttered as if he were anticipating a loud bang. "I didn't do anything, not ever, not to any Russian, not to anyone. I'm good for nothing. I just wanted a look."

Yet he swiftly whipped around and knocked Zaitsev's gun from his hand. Heller grabbed Ludwig by the wrist.

"Drop it!" shouted a hard female voice.

Heller turned around. A woman had stepped out of the shadows. She wore men's pants, an army tunic, and a green beret. She carried an MP 40. And from the way she was standing, she knew how to use a submachine gun.

Zaitsev had paused, crouched halfway down, about to raise his pistol. He stood slowly, not taking his eyes off the woman.

"Hands up, both of you. Ludwig, come here!"

Heller still held Ludwig's wrist. "Are you his mother? Magdalena Klepp?" She had seemed so gentle in her wedding photos, yet here she looked so tough and full of fight.

She ignored him. "Let him go!" she insisted. And Heller was now certain that this was Rudolf Klepp's wife.

"Do you have a gun?" Zaitsev whispered to Heller.

"It's back at the house," Heller whispered back. Zaitsev gave him an incredulous look.

"Quiet!" Magdalena Klepp barked at them. "You two get away from each other. You, Heller, stand by this wall."

Heller did as he was ordered.

"My family has suffered enough," she said. "Leave the boy in peace. He hasn't done anything wrong."

"That remains to be seen."

"You be quiet, Heller. People like you are worse than the enemy. You never did grasp the greater good! And now you're working for the enemy, for Bolshevism, just like Rudolf said. Ludwig, will you get yourself over here already?"

The young man nodded and went over to his mother.

"Your son is a murderer," Heller said.

"He's nothing of the sort. He's just scared. He's not meant for war. Come get in front of me, come on, both of you, this way. And Ludwig, grab that pistol there."

"Where are we going?" asked Heller.

"You really have no idea?"

Into their villa dungeon, Heller realized with wild shock. God, no, anything but that.

"Put your hands up, over your head. Anyone tries anything stupid, I'll shoot."

Zaitsev went first, hands over his head. Heller followed, with Magdalena and Ludwig behind them.

"Faster, go!" Magdalena ordered. Heller could see Zaitsev stealing looks around. Just then he lunged off to the side, threw himself into a deep crater, and was gone without a trace before the woman could react.

"See that, Heller? Such a true friend. Gone. Now I need to find something different for you. Go in there, to the left."

A large dark opening appeared in the busted-up cellar wall before him. Was she going to shoot him in there?

"In with you! Do it. Ludwig, you have to keep an eye out. I don't trust that Russian. Shoot to kill if you see him."

Heller was about to carefully grope his way into the hole when Zaitsev grabbed Magdalena from a dark recess. He hauled her to the ground, punched her twice. They wrestled for the gun.

"Do something!" she shouted at Ludwig.

The young man was clearly overwhelmed. He aimed the pistol clumsily at Zaitsev yet couldn't shoot without possibly striking his mother. Heller bent down for a board lying at his feet, whirled around, and struck Ludwig on the head.

Ludwig fell. Heller snatched Zaitsev's pistol and helped the Russian subdue the fuming woman, who resisted with astonishing strength. It took both men to wrestle the gun from her. In her rage she dragged her fingernails down Zaitsev's face, cutting him with two nasty scrapes. Zaitsev punched her in the face, and she sank to the ground, unconscious.

The Russian had lost his peaked cap in the fight, and he picked it up, then stood there cursing and spitting and shaking out his aching fist.

"The gun!" he said, thrusting out his hand, and Heller handed over the pistol. Zaitsev eyed him with mistrust. "You really have no other?"

"I already told you—it's at the house."

"You better not be lying," Zaitsev said.

Heller sighed and opened his overcoat, under which he wore his only shirt, now filthy and fully soaked with sweat. He turned out the pockets of his coat, and only then was Zaitsev satisfied. He then frisked the still-unconscious Magdalena Klepp for other weapons, finding a jackknife and a handful of ammo, which he stuffed into his pocket.

Ludwig was the first to come to. When he saw the Russian tugging at his mother, he let out a grunt and tried to crawl over and help her.

"Don't move!" Heller ordered. "Tell me, right now: What do you know about the dead women? Why the dungeon in your house? Was it you who locked her down there?"

"No. I didn't kill her. Those aren't women in there. No, none of it's true." Ludwig was twitching uncontrollably, his upper body quivering.

"There was a woman down there. You two locked her down there!"

"No, she was just . . . she'd been spying on us." Ludwig's eyelids fluttered—he wasn't telling the truth, and it was tough for him.

"You fled that night of the air raid. Why did you run away?"

"I was scared."

"But you do know who I am."

Ludwig nodded. "A policeman."

"And you knew that back in February during the air raid?"

Ludwig nodded again. He had a large lump on his head from getting hit with the board. It had split open and was starting to bleed. Ludwig grabbed at the damp spot, and his eyes widened with shock when he saw the blood.

"Why did you run off? Did you have a girl with you somewhere, a young woman?"

"Don't tell him anything!" Magdalena had come to. But Zaitsev hauled her up, wrenched one of her arms behind her back, and held her mouth shut with his other hand.

"He won't do anything to her, Ludwig," Heller said, and glared at the hard-nosed Russian. This was no time to be distracting the young Klepp. "So why did you run away?"

"Father couldn't know that I was outside."

"You'd rather get shot?"

Ludwig nodded. "Father was very angry at me, because I'm a disgrace. I wasn't supposed to leave the house."

"So why were you outside if your father forbade you?"

"Just because . . ."

Heller eyed the young man suspiciously. One of Ludwig's hands had started shaking uncontrollably.

"Where were you the last few nights?"

"Here in the rubble. I was looking for food and sleeping in a shack; that, or here at home."

"Where were you three nights ago? When another young girl was killed?"

"I was here."

"And you didn't lure Erika Kaluza from the hospital?"

Ludwig smiled at the ground, embarrassed. Then he shook his head. Magdalena Klepp was still trying to free herself from Zaitsev's strong grip.

"You didn't knock her down, drag her into a cellar, cut her open?"

"Cut her open?" Ludwig repeated, as if he'd never heard the words before.

"Peel her skin off?"

Ludwig tried fighting it, but his lips contorted into a wide smile.

Heller moved a step closer, keeping his eyes on Ludwig. "Did you cut off her eyelids so that she saw what you were doing to her? Did you let her bleed out like a pig?"

Ludwig grinned. "With pigs, you bash their skull in, hang them up by their legs," he explained, "and you stab them in the neck—in the carotid artery."

"Did you apprentice with your father?"

"With grandfather."

"And you learned how to use knives? A person has to learn it, right?"

"The knives must be sharp, always!"

"The women weren't hung up by their legs?" asked Heller.

Ludwig shook his head.

Heller leaned forward and whispered, "Are you the Fright Man? Go on, tell me. Say it. Don't be modest."

Ludwig giggled, and his eyes twitched. "I like it when people are frightened. Otherwise, I'm always the one who's frightened. Always. I was so horribly frightened of the Russians and the shooting. And I'm frightened of father."

"Ludwig, did you kill Klara Bellmann? The other woman?"

"Klara Bellmann? Yes!"

"And the other one?"

"Yes, the other one too."

"And what was her name?"

"I don't know."

"I found underpants in the cellar, from a woman. Are they from a dead woman?"

"I think so. Yes!"

"Ludwig, did your parents know about this?"

He shook his head. "No, no, they knew nothing at all!"

It was a lie, Heller knew. Ludwig wanted to protect his parents, at least his mother. "You're lying. They knew about it. They've known you're the murderer, and they wanted to protect you so you wouldn't get hanged."

"No, Herr Heller, I don't like getting hanged. Please. The others, they were always teasing me, 'cause I'm so chubby and 'cause I run so slow and 'cause I always put my hands over my ears when the Russians fire. And they were saying I'm a coward and not a good German soldier and a disgrace. And I never had friends. No one wanted to play with me. And my father, not even he wanted me anymore." Ludwig's eyes filled with tears.

"Show me your teeth!" Heller grabbed at Ludwig's chin, pulled down his jaw, and looked at his teeth. Both of his incisors were slanted. They would need to do an exact comparison, but they didn't have anything to match it to anymore.

"And that other nurse? Irma Braune is her name. She's been missing since yesterday. Was she in the dungeon too?"

"I don't know. I don't know her."

"Ludwig, listen. Those bones in the dungeon—who are they from?" Heller asked but got frustrated hearing Magdalena Klepp groaning. He turned and was appalled to see that Zaitsev had thrown the woman to the ground and jammed his knee into her while twisting her arm behind her back.

"What are you doing?" Heller shouted.

"I'm finding out where Klepp is!" Zaitsev got back to it, making Frau Klepp groan so loud her eyes rolled back.

"You're going to break her arm!" Heller protested as he held Ludwig back.

"I don't care. Go on, woman, talk!"

Ludwig's mother only moaned, and spit ran out the corners of her mouth. Zaitsev abruptly released her, letting her head drop into the dirt. Then he pressed his knee into her lower back, grabbed her hand, and broke her little finger.

She let out a piercing scream, which so alarmed her son that he tried crawling past Heller to get to her. Zaitsev drew his weapon. "Back! Heller, goddamnit, keep an eye on Ludwig."

"Alexei, stop it. That's torture."

"You don't know what torture is, stupid old man."

"What's that supposed to mean? I won't put up with it."

"Oh, yes, you will, and I will say whatever I want about torture, about the way the Germans did it, how they tortured partisans so they betrayed their comrades. I must know where her husband is, because I know he's in the city. He could be shooting at you again tomorrow, Heller, and then you will wish I broke every one of her fingers."

"But that makes you no better than all the rest. If you act the same as they do, what's the difference between you?"

"Revenge is the difference!"

"Zaitsev, think about it. Who are you getting revenge on? It's never on the ones committing the crimes, it's only on others."

"You all committed crimes."

"You know what I mean."

"All right, fine, you three wish to fucking preach to me about morality? You can all go straight to hell!" Zaitsev stood and drew his pistol. He fired into the air and shouted something in Russian.

"We're taking them both to headquarters, and you'll interrogate them according to your morally proper methods. You'll see. This woman will stay as silent as the grave, because she knows she has nothing to gain and everything to lose."

"We'll see." Maybe there was some way to appeal to reason.

"Please, please, don't lock me away," whispered Magdalena.

"Why shouldn't we?" asked Heller. "Tell me where your husband is, and maybe we can talk."

It was only now, with her hair showing from under her hat, that her features appeared gentler.

She lowered her head. "You don't understand. You can't understand. Don't harm him, please, don't harm him."

May 18, 1945: About Noon

Zaitsev smoked and glanced at Heller walking next to him. "What is wrong?"

"Why did she say that? 'Don't harm him.'"

They were on the way to the hospital. Zaitsev's wound had reopened while fighting with Magdalena Klepp, and he'd taken his jacket off. The bandage was soaked with blood, and he had to be in great pain, but he wasn't letting it show. Heller was amazed at how stoic Zaitsev was during the walk. They had started out a half hour ago, right after Magdalena and Ludwig Klepp were taken away.

"She was worried about her son," Zaitsev replied.

He saluted a Russian patrol surrounded by a cluster of children, the soldiers laughing and handing out chocolates as the children wrestled for the bounty.

Heller didn't respond. He kept pondering things until they reached the hospital.

They were immediately let through to Dr. Schorrer. "You again?" the doctor said, then saw the Russian's bloody shirt and sat down to work.

"Did you find Ludwig Klepp?" he asked Heller over his shoulder while removing Zaitsev's bandages.

"Yes, we have him. And his mother."

Schorrer paused. "Does this mean Rudolf Klepp is still alive? Here in the city?"

"You never wondered this before?" Zaitsev asked. He looked pale and exhausted sitting on the exam table, and Heller was practically relieved to see that the strain was finally getting to him. Zaitsev was only human too.

Schorrer snorted. "Sure, but why would he be so stupid? He could have at least made his way to the Americans. He would've had enough time."

Zaitsev's face had gone all white. Schorrer must have noticed, yet he kept focusing on his work.

"Maybe he's one of those unrepentant types," the Russian said. "Where were you exactly in Poland?"

"Near Warsaw. We had a large field hospital in a suburb." Schorrer sighed. "You need to start looking after yourself, my friend. This is no small wound. Then there's the heat and the way you're exerting yourself. You could die from infection."

"It will be fine," Zaitsev muttered, wiping sweat from his brow.

"Maybe you'd like to lie down for a few minutes? We have a quiet room here."

Zaitsev shook his head at first, but then he consented. "Very well. Heller, go find yourself something to eat. That pass of yours will get you something."

Outside, the heat immediately sapped Heller's energy. An excavator was operating nonstop, and diesel exhaust from the emergency power generators mixed with the swirling dust. The sweat stuck to his forehead. He looked around for Seibling, hoping to send him to Karin so she'd finally know he was all right. He looked around for Rita too, but he didn't spot either of them.

At the public soup kitchen just outside the hospital grounds, he received a slice of bread, soup, and a cup of tea for the usual amount of occupation marks and one Reichsmark fifty. He ate and drank standing, sweating inside his overcoat—he wouldn't set it down for fear it would be stolen. People pressed into him as they passed, one man complaining of getting too little for his marks. Someone stood close behind Heller.

"Beg your pardon," Heller said. Yet the man with a full thick beard wouldn't budge. Heller grew alarmed. Could the man have a knife on him? Was he one of Klepp's crew? He could slit Heller's throat no problem before disappearing into the crowd. Heller, starting to panic, grasped the spoon in his hand like a weapon, which only made him look ridiculous.

"Max, don't you recognize me?" the man whispered.

"What . . . who are you?"

"It's me, Werner!"

"Oldenbusch?" Only now did Heller recognize his former colleague. He laughed with relief and hugged him, completely out of character.

Oldenbusch whispered, "Are you in some kind of trouble, Max? Do the Russians have it in for you?"

"No, Werner, don't worry. You remember the Fright Man? I'm still trying to find him. And to make any progress, I have to work with the Russians."

"The Fright Man? He's still running around here? Figured he'd be long dead by now."

"That's what I thought too. But now we have a good lead. We're right on his heels." Heller couldn't tell him much more than that. "So tell me, Werner, how are you? How did you manage to get out of the army unscathed?"

"Please, Max, not so loud." Oldenbusch took a careful look around. "I'm lying low until things quiet down. I was in Luga. When I got on the train to the front, I got sick with a bad case of the runs. I was completely dehydrated. They thought it was dysentery and sent me to a field hospital. We kept getting moved around. When it turned into complete pandemonium, I took off and stayed in hiding with people

I knew. I've been back since Friday, looking for relatives and friends. I also asked around about you. Someone told me you'd been out and about with the Russians. You need any help?"

Heller shook his head, smiling. "No, Werner, keep a low profile for a while longer. I'm happy to see you alive and well. Right now, I have to make sure I hurry back to my Russian." He shook Oldenbusch's hand.

"Where can I find you, if I might ask?" Oldenbusch said.

"Weisser Hirsch area, on Rissweg, lady named Marquart."

Oldenbusch laughed. "Weisser Hirsch, where all those Red Army generals live? Always in the lion's den—it's just the way I remember you, Max."

When Heller returned to Schorrer's hospital building, chaos had taken over. Several Red Army trucks were parked at the entrance, and soldiers were leading the nurses to the trucks, where their fellow nurses already sat crying or staring ahead, ashen with fear.

"They're going to take us all away, send us to Siberia!" one said as Heller pushed through the crowd.

"What's going on?" he asked one of the Red Army soldiers, making sure to hold up his pass from Major General Medvedev. The Russian shrugged and pointed at a woman wearing a white nurse's smock over her Red Army uniform.

"What's going on?" Heller shouted to her.

She answered gruffly in Russian and shoved him aside. The first truck started up and drove off. But more soldiers were coming out of the building and leading away staff.

"What's going on here?" Heller asked a nurse holding her head high as a soldier shoved her past. The soldier pushed Heller away from her.

"They think we're killing patients," she shouted over her shoulder. "We're supposed to be interrogated."

"Patients?"

"Yes, from the concentration—" A violent blow silenced the nurse. They heaved her onto the truck and shut the gate, then the truck drove off with the others.

Heller stormed into the building, heading for Schorrer's floor. All he saw were highly agitated staff running around and no sign of Rita Stein or Dr. Schorrer. He stopped a nurse. "Where's Dr. Schorrer?"

"Russians took him."

"What about the political commissar, the injured one? Where's he? He needed to use Schorrer's quiet room."

The nurse pointed at a door. Heller stormed inside.

Zaitsev was sleeping, and not even Heller's violent shaking woke him. "Zaitsev, wake up." Heller resorted to slapping his face and raising his eyelids, but his pupils showed no reaction. The Russian couldn't be aroused—his breathing was flat, and Heller could barely feel a pulse. He rushed out to get a cup of water from a container in the hallway and splashed it in Zaitsev's face, then rubbed it on his neck and wrists. After what felt like an eternity, Zaitsev's eyelids started fluttering. He groaned and feebly raised a hand.

"Voda," he rasped. Heller grabbed more water and helped Zaitsev sit up to drink. Zaitsev had barely emptied the cup before he threw up on the floor. Heller held on to him so he didn't topple off the cot.

"Voda!"

Heller went to get water yet again. This time Zaitsev kept it down. "I'm doing better now. Sleeping is not good," Zaitsev groaned. "Do you know what 'Zaitsev' means?"

Heller shook his head.

"Rabbit. And a rabbit must always bounce."

"Hop. Our rabbits hop."

"Hop. Yet another funny word you have. Help me up."

Heller supported the Russian and helped him to his feet.

"They've arrested the nurses," Heller said. "They say they were killing former concentration camp inmates. Schorrer is gone too. Nurse

Rita probably. Just yesterday she was telling me that few of the former inmates could be saved. They were all dying of failing kidneys."

Zaitsev just stared. He didn't seem to understand a word. He was having trouble supporting himself on the edge of the cot. "Well, we must go to headquarters anyway."

"You're not walking," Heller insisted. "I'll go see if someone can drive us."

Soviet headquarters was completely overcrowded, yet Heller's initial impression of disarray turned out to be false. Everyone seemed to know what needed to be done and was working away. Zaitsev had pulled his uniform jacket back on despite the dry heat of early afternoon. He was either just keeping it together for his comrades or had recovered from his dizzy spell surprisingly fast.

He proceeded to storm into Medvedev's office without knocking and engaged in a sharp exchange of words with an officer Heller didn't know, all right above the head of Medvedev's staff clerk. The two men didn't like each other, that much was clear. The staff clerk soon rose and withdrew to the window.

"Ask about the nurses," Heller said.

Zaitsev glared at him. "I already did. Professor Ehlig has complained to Colonel General Shishkov about the treatment of his staff. His staff will now be released after questioning. So you need not worry about your fellow German comrades."

The officer interjected, his tone aggressive. He pointed at Heller and Zaitsev, clearly trying to maintain his authority over the fuming Zaitsev. Heller thought he heard the names Medvedev and Klepp a few times. The officer parried Zaitsev's continued verbal assault by shaking his head. Things suddenly got loud behind Heller, as armed guards stormed into the room, but they quickly lowered their weapons when they realized the disturbance was only two of their superiors having a heated dispute. Heller retreated to the window anyway.

Medvedev's staff clerk was holding a bundle of papers pressed to his chest like a shield. "What are they saying?" Heller whispered to him.

"Ovtcharov not let Zaitsev see woman," the clerk whispered back.

"The Klepp woman?"

The clerk shrugged. "Ovtcharov is NKVD. He say Zaitsev responsible for politics, not purging Nazis."

The Russians were saying much more than that. Their tempers grew increasingly aggressive until Zaitsev even drew his pistol. Everyone in the room pulled back. The officer drew his weapon. Zaitsev spoke in a menacingly quiet tone.

"He threaten to report Ovtcharov," the staff clerk interpreted for Heller. "Because Ovtcharov know where SS man is, will not tell Zaitsev."

Zaitsev didn't look like he was going to back down. Only Major General Medvedev would be able to get control of this situation.

"Where is the major general?" whispered Heller.

"Eat. Officers' mess."

Heller looked out the window. He spotted something outside. "Zaitsev," he shouted.

"You keep out of this, Heller," Zaitsev hissed back.

"Alexei, let it go," Heller said to calm the Russian.

"He knows where Rudolf Klepp is," Zaitsev said, "and he will not tell me!"

"It doesn't matter. Listen to me, Alexei. One SS man is not worth shooting over." Heller then winked at Zaitsev, which finally made Zaitsev lower his gun and mutter something to Ovtcharov. Ovtcharov only smirked.

"Come, *nemets*, we're going," Zaitsev ordered, and he and Heller left the room.

They were barely out the door before Heller pulled Zaitsev to the nearest window. "Look! Over there."

In front of the gate to the grounds stood the young woman they'd saved from the dungeon. She was speaking to a Red Army soldier. She had a white bandage around her head, she was laughing and joking, and she allowed the soldier to touch her on the behind. She placed a hand on his chest, apparently speaking fluent Russian, and they whispered to one another. The soldier nodded, glanced around, and kept whispering.

"She's sounding him out. Whether he knows anything about Klepp. Now she's leaving."

Zaitsev nodded. "Let's go."

They ran off down the stairs, Zaitsev taking three steps at a time. Outside he whistled at a jeep, a repainted German army VW. Heller kept an eye on the woman until her white bandaged head disappeared among the hustle and bustle along Bautzner Strasse. Zaitsev waved Heller over, and he had no choice but to leap into the jeep as it slowly passed. They drove through the gate, turned to the left, and followed the young woman as she hurried down the street.

Zaitsev warned the driver to drive slower. At Waldschlösschenstrasse, the woman turned right. The driver followed at a distance. The woman suddenly vanished. Zaitsev stood on his seat and looked around.

"*Suka!* She spotted us."

"She couldn't have seen us," Heller said.

Suddenly the young woman exited the driveway of a building riding a bicycle, crossed the street ten yards ahead of them, and turned back into Bautzner Strasse, heading straight for the city center, pedaling furiously. She picked up speed on the downward-sloping street, and soon she was gone again, around the corner of the next building.

"*Davai, davai, davai,*" Zaitsev said, and the driver yanked at the wheel, made an awkward turn, and sped after her so fast that Zaitsev was nearly tossed from the jeep.

"Just keep going," Heller insisted as he searched for the woman's white head bandage. But it wasn't easy for the driver. The street was clogged with people and cars, and the jeep had to either swerve around spots a bicycle could snake through or wait for traffic to open up.

"There!" shouted Heller. He'd spotted her, the trails of her overcoat flapping in the draft as she pedaled onward. She kept getting farther away, her head just one white dot among many.

Heller tapped Zaitsev on the shoulder. "She rides into the ruins, we won't be able to follow."

As soon as she reached the Neustadt area, she turned into the rubble fields along Tieckstrasse, deftly dodging rocks and people, and disappeared. The driver followed as far as he could before the route became too narrow and the roadway too damaged.

"She must be heading for the Elbe," Heller said.

"No, think about it. She's taking the shortest route—where does this end up if we keep going this way?"

"The river? Königsufer. Kaiser Wilhelm Square!" Heller shouted. "Have the driver take us down along the river."

"But everything's destroyed around here."

"Then cut back to the Rose Garden, over by Löwenstrasse. I'll tell you the way."

Zaitsev agreed, the driver backed up and turned around, and they drove upriver along the Elbe. The traffic wasn't much better. Bombed-out locals and refugees were camped out in the Rose Garden and on the river meadows. Only the driver's constant honking made people disperse.

They headed back the right way but had to give up near the fire-gutted ministry buildings around Carolaplatz. Zaitsev punched the dashboard, and the driver winced.

Heller looked around. He could see the destroyed city skyline, the steamers half-sunk in the river, the now-vanished Belvedere Palace, what remained of the Frauenkirche, and the spire of Trinity Church standing all alone. He couldn't stand to look for long, and turned away before his emotions overwhelmed him.

Suddenly he realized where the woman was heading.

"Alexei, that smell, remember?"

"Smell?"

"Remember that strange smell coming from Strampe's jacket, when he was lying there dead? It's the slaughterhouses. That's where she's heading."

Zaitsev whipped around. "Where are they?"

"Farther down along the bank. She'll need to cross the river."

The driver had understood, and sped off.

They spotted the woman right before the Marienbrücke, the bridge completely destroyed. She had stopped along the bank, and was looking around. Their jeep halted at a distance, and Zaitsev and Heller stepped out. Zaitsev gave rapid instructions to the driver, who drove away.

They used the cover of a pier to inch their way closer.

"Klepp's hiding in a slaughterhouse?" the Russian said, sounding skeptical.

"It's not as dumb as you think. Large premises, all bombed, cellars throughout, with ways to escape on all sides. There! She has a boat."

The young woman was awkwardly hauling her bike into a rowboat. A man sat in the boat, holding the oars.

Zaitsev and Heller ran farther along the bank until they reached the harbor where smaller boats moored, their owners somehow still making a living with them. The woman's boat had already traveled nearly a hundred feet, out into the middle of the river.

Zaitsev bounded onto the first good boat. "Out!" he barked at the people just getting on, loaded down with suitcases and packs. "We need to get across! Hurry!"

The boat owner didn't bother trying to negotiate a price. It seemed to take forever for them to reach the opposite bank, and they nearly got carried past the slaughterhouses on the other side.

Zaitsev jumped out of the boat. "Let's go, *nemets*!"

They ran up to Pieschener Allee, the avenue parallel to the slaughterhouse yards. They crossed the traffic circle and were soon standing in the middle of the decimated grounds.

It was vast and bewildering. The young woman was nowhere to be seen. She could be anywhere. Or maybe she had a different plan after all? Would Klepp really have dared to remain so close to the city, right within reach of Soviet headquarters?

They climbed over debris and waded through murky puddles. Some buildings were partly standing, offering countless hiding places. Here too were people trying to find refuge, erecting little hearths for cooking, building campfires, and constructing shelters from boards. Elsewhere on the slaughterhouse grounds, some work was starting up again even though there was hardly a thing to slaughter. In civilian clothes, Klepp would have been able to mix in with people here and likely wouldn't be recognized.

"Should we split up? Or wait for reinforcements?" Heller asked, stealing side glances at Zaitsev. He didn't like how quiet the Russian had become. Even loud and irate was better.

The Russian suddenly raised his head, startled. "Did you hear that?" he asked and gave Heller a signal not to move. He pointed westward. Heller shook his head.

"A gunshot—I'm certain," Zaitsev whispered, and started running in that direction.

Heller could barely follow the Russian swiftly scrambling through the rubble. Soon Zaitsev crouched down and waved Heller over.

"There's an opening to a cellar," he whispered, pointing around the corner.

"You want to go down there? That's crazy. It's all a maze."

"I want that Nazi pig. All mine! Understand me?"

"It's stupid," Heller said.

"You know what is stupid? Unquestioning obedience to your Führer, right to the death." Zaitsev had likely meant this sarcastically, but Heller wasn't in the mood.

"What about you?" he snapped. "Isn't Stalin just your own brand of Führer?"

Zaitsev turned to face him, and they glared at one another. Heller stood firm until Zaitsev relented.

"All right, fine," he said, "take this." He pulled a second pistol out of his jacket and pressed it into Heller's hand. "A Tokarev, built in Tula, eight rounds." Without another word, he climbed down through the blown-open cellar ceiling and into the cold darkness that gave off a musty smell of stagnant water and decomposition.

Heller, amazed by Zaitsev's show of trust, stuffed the gun into his pocket, sighed, and climbed down after Zaitsev. They descended a mountain of rubble to reach rock bottom, much deeper down than Heller had guessed.

Little stones scattered and rolled down as they climbed off.

Their shoes sank into mud and sludge as soon as they stepped onto the cellar floor. All was cool and dripping and pattering, like inside a cave, with moss already growing on the rubble. Darkness loomed, surrounding the narrow shafts of light shining down.

"This way," said Zaitsev. Every footstep made a disconcerting sucking sound in the mud. The light soon dimmed, and Heller peered around for each new point of light ahead as the holes in the ceiling grew farther and farther apart.

"You smell that?" Zaitsev whispered.

Heller smelled an extinguished fire, steam mixed with ash.

They heard a whistle, then found cover and remained there a long while.

"Not meant for us," Zaitsev eventually said, then kept going, aiming his pistol. Heller used his left hand to feel along the slippery cellar wall, holding his gun out with his right.

"We have to watch out," he warned the Russian in a whisper. "This could be an ambush."

Zaitsev ignored him. Then they heard a scream. A woman in pain. Zaitsev crouched next to Heller.

"That's the ambush," Zaitsev whispered. Another scream. "They know we're here. They want to lure us in."

"I told you we should've called for reinforcements."

"Well, we're here now."

Heller shook his head in anger yet had no choice but to keep following the Russian, peering into the darkness all around them, trying to find any point of reference to fix his eyes on. He lost contact with the wall. Then the whistle sounded again.

"Take cover!" Zaitsev hissed, and Heller threw himself into the mud. A volley of gunfire shredded the darkness. Water sprayed, and mortar and stones trickled down on them.

The echoes faded. Quiet and blackness returned. Heller couldn't see or hear Zaitsev.

"Alexei?" Heller whispered. Shots rang out again. The shooter had to be to their right, judging from the muzzle flashes that had lit up the room—just enough for him to make out that they weren't in a corridor anymore but had entered a large underground hall supported by heavy columns resembling logs. But he didn't spot Zaitsev.

It turned silent again. Heller raised his weapon, then reconsidered, since he couldn't know where the shooter was now. It was too dangerous firing into the darkness on a hunch, and it might give away his position.

"There you are, Heller." It was Rudolf Klepp's voice.

Heller started, but he didn't reply.

"We lost the war because of people like you. Traitors to the Volk. People like you doomed us to destruction. Now you're cavorting with the Ivans. I should've done you in when I had the chance. Should've hanged you from the first good tree."

Heller lay motionless in the mud. It was his only option.

"You think we don't know everything about you? We know where you live, where your wife is right now. We'll get her and do to her what we always do with traitors."

Heller broke out in a sweat. He needed to maintain his calm, couldn't let himself be provoked. Where was Zaitsev? Why wasn't he saying anything? Had he been hit?

"This here is my very own Reich, Heller. So you keep on hiding—go ahead and shit yourself just like back in the trenches. You should've croaked there like that. That was your destiny. What a coward! Got out of the whole thing with one little wound."

Heller gritted his teeth.

"We're going to create a new world, Heller. Neither of your boys will have died in vain! I'm not giving up. That's why I'm here. We'll start underground. But we'll be back out in the light soon enough. That's when we rise up, against the Bolsheviks, and a tribunal will make people like you—" Several shots rang out. Klepp went silent.

A machine gun rattled away, and erratic fire spread across the cellar floor. Whole stones burst from the columns. Heller pressed himself to the floor. Then it was calm again, and the ringing in Heller's ears stopped. A hasty clattering sound revealed that the inexperienced shooter was trying to insert a new cartridge. The next second, a hand grenade exploded where Heller judged the machine gun was. Someone started screaming. Shots were fired sporadically, and Heller crawled along until he felt a column. He went into a crouch, listening. The wounded person was still screaming, and Heller couldn't get Klepp's words out of his head; did he really know something about his sons?

"You're not getting out of here alive, Heller, if it's the last thing I do," Klepp yelled. Yet he also sounded exhausted, panting heavily between words.

"Klepp!" someone shouted. It was Zaitsev, from a completely different direction than Heller had guessed. He was alive. "We have your wife! She betrayed you. She told us you're here. Give it up! She doesn't want anything more to do with you."

Klepp said nothing. There was only the wounded person screaming, though the voice was waning. It gurgled and rattled.

"Is that true, Heller? Heller? Is that true?" Klepp sounded frantic. "I have that Jew bitch right here. I'll cut off her ears, her fingers, every last one. Heller, listen to me. Heller?"

The person started screaming again, a woman. Heller sprang up, started running while crouching—and slammed into the next column. More shots came, and he threw himself down. The shots zipped across the room.

"Hold your fire!" Klepp yelled, his voice alarmingly close. "Hear me out, Heller. We do a deal. The girl for my wife."

Heller couldn't reply without giving away his position. And the Russians would never allow an exchange like that—Klepp had to know as much. Yet Heller didn't want to have this young girl's death on his conscience as well. He thought he could hear her moaning. And Klepp kept silent, waiting it out. Heller was trapped in absolute darkness, between two columns, with armed foes all around him.

"Obersturmbannführer?" someone whispered, and Heller could hear others speaking softly. And then it all happened so fast.

A glaring light flashed on, shots rang out. Russians shouting. Heller pressed himself to the floor and tossed his pistol away.

"Hands up! Drop your weapons!"

A whole unit of Red Army soldiers had infiltrated the cellar. They ran, ducking among the spotlight's beam, releasing brief bursts of fire. When they spotted Heller, one stomped on his back, and he felt the hot barrel of a gun on the back of his neck.

May 18, 1945: Early Afternoon

The sun beat down on Heller's neck. He sat on a block of stone next to the cellar opening that the Red Army soldiers had infiltrated. He had taken off his wet overcoat. Zaitsev stood off to the side, smoking and observing the scene with a dispassionate expression. The Red Army men were carrying out one dead body after another, six men, all in civilian clothes. The Russians had discovered their hideout in the catacombs, together with crates of food, guns, and bazookas.

One of the dead was Klepp. He had a beard, had let his curly hair grow longer, and had become skinny. Heller probably wouldn't have recognized him on the street. Klepp's throat was cut. Zaitsev's doing, quite obviously. He'd been cleaning his knife with a cloth, out in the sunlight near the cellar opening.

A military truck neared, braked hard, and threw up a whirlwind of dust that settled on everyone standing around. Ovtcharov, the NKVD officer, climbed out of the cab and walked over to Zaitsev with his legs still a little stiff. Zaitsev pushed his peaked cap to the back of his head and awaited his comrade with hands on hips. Ovtcharov was snorting fury. He asked Zaitsev something. Zaitsev held up his index finger, clearly enjoying his success.

"Let me go!" said the young woman. Two soldiers were leading her out of the cellar. She was holding her right arm. Blood ran down her face from the bandage around her head. Zaitsev blocked their path, said something, and the soldiers let the woman go.

"Who are you?" Zaitsev said.

She ignored him and instead went over to Heller, who had stood up. "Why did you have to interfere like that?" she said. "That was my business and mine alone!"

"We were looking for Klepp, just like you," he said.

"Just like me? That's a laugh. Who do you think you are? Why haven't you been arrested? You're a filthy pig just like Klepp!" She screamed at the Red Army men now. "Go on, arrest this man. He's just as much a murderer!"

Heller held out his hands to calm her. "That's not true. Please." If only he could figure out why she seemed so familiar.

Ovtcharov had drawn his pistol. He grabbed Heller's arm. "SS?" he asked. "You SS?"

"No. Zaitsev, tell him it's not true. You heard what Klepp said."

Zaitsev turned away. "I have no idea what is true. You know this man Heller?" he asked the woman.

She went up to Heller and held her fist to his face, overcome with rage. "Yeah, I do, he's a pig just like all the rest. And that one over there, that beast, he killed my parents." She pointed at Klepp's corpse. "But you took even that from me—even my revenge!" She was swaying now.

Heller was ready to catch her if she fainted. "But he was going to finish you off," he said.

She only screamed at him. "You be quiet, you Nazi pig!" She started sobbing, then she sank to her knees. Ovtcharov gave an order, and the soldiers trained their guns on Heller.

"Listen to me. I've never been a Nazi," Heller said. "I know you. Help me remember: Where have I seen you?"

The woman looked up, and the blood ran down her nose and dripped from her chin.

It suddenly occurred to him. "You were in the interrogation room. With the Gestapo man. I was the one who knocked on the door."

"Yeah, and what did you do about it? Did you help me?" the woman asked. "No! You simply left."

Heller fell silent, staring at the ground. She was right.

Ovtcharov and Zaitsev started deliberating again, this time in a more peaceful tone. Zaitsev was looking worn down and barely objected anymore. Heller could guess what that meant: he had fulfilled a need for the political commissar and now wasn't worth it to him.

"*On ne fashist,*" the young woman muttered.

She looked up and reached out for something to hold. "*On ne fashist,*" she repeated.

Zaitsev and Ovtcharov nodded at each other, yet neither offered her a hand. So Heller bent down and took her hand.

Ovtcharov was letting Heller go. He turned away and started ordering his men around.

Zaitsev came back over to Heller. "I will release that Uhlmann fellow if it makes you feel better."

Heller gave him a half-hearted nod.

"This does not make you happy?" asked the Russian.

"I can't get Magdalena Klepp out of my head. That one thing she said."

Zaitsev made a face. "Come on, Heller. It's all fine now. Can't you ever be happy?"

He didn't wait for Heller's answer. He ordered his men back in the truck, climbed up, tapped his cap with two fingers, and Heller and the woman were left all alone.

"You have to help me; my arm is broken," she said. "I didn't even get a shot off at him. They'd already found me out. One of them held my arm on a rock and then stepped on it." She looked at him. "What's your name, anyway? And who are you?"

"Max Heller. Former detective inspector."

"My name's Constanze Weisshaupt. You'll have to excuse me for back there. I got really angry."

"It's all right. Do you know a doctor?"

Constanze shook her head. "I found a room with a woman in Radebeul. She's been putting me up the last three months. I'm sure she can help."

"I know a doctor, but we'd have to walk through half the city."

"I'll make it."

They started on their way.

"You're a Jew?" Heller asked after a while.

"Half. My father was Aryan. He refused to leave my mother. So we had to live in a Jewish building in Tiergartenstrasse. He was a doctor, only allowed to practice on Jews at that point. Klepp had it out for him; my father had a fortune. They took my mother away last December. She died of tuberculosis two months later, even though she'd been in perfect health before that. Father got ordered to the Gestapo last January. He never came back."

"So they thought you knew where his fortune was?"

"After you interrupted the interrogation, they let me go. I did get another summons soon after, but then the air raid came. I tore off my yellow star and fled."

"And from then on, you intended to take your revenge on Klepp . . ." It sounded like a statement of fact, but the truth was, he needed her to confirm that this had all been worth risking his life for.

Constanze Weisshaupt had understood. She looked him in the eyes.

"A man like that shouldn't be allowed to get away with it. I wanted to make him suffer. When I happened to see you with that Russian, I thought you were helping them hunt down fellow Nazis. I was hoping you would lead me to Klepp. That's why I followed you."

"Are you the one who gave Klepp that scratch on his face?"

"No, not me, I never would've survived that. When you're getting beaten, you simply have to keep still until they tire out."

"Who attacked you and locked you in that hole?"

"Klepp's wife and some young man. He said they needed to kill me."

"Why didn't you want to talk to me?"

"I was scared," Constanze said. "Can you imagine? Being all confined down there, getting buried alive? Having to breathe like that, think like that, until the very end, without being able to move? And how could I know what side you were really on? It was just a few days ago that the Russians' new best friends still had their swastika armbands on."

"You speak Russian?"

"I was born in Görlitz. My father practiced medicine there until '34 and always said it never hurt to know Russian. I know: Maybe we should go find my bicycle, and you can ride? I can ride on the handlebars."

"With a broken arm?"

"It's better than walking."

"So, Görlitz, you say?" Dr. Schorrer was examining Constanze Weisshaupt's arm. He had received her and Heller without saying much. "A Dr. Armin Weisshaupt? Never crossed paths, though he must've been around my age. It's a clean break. A nurse can splint it; you won't need me for that." The doctor gently set down her arm and waved a nurse over. Both women left.

"Did you get rid of your Russian yet?" Schorrer asked Heller.

"He's happy now. Klepp is confirmed dead."

"There you go."

"No, what I meant was, Klepp was just killed a little while ago. He was hiding out in the slaughterhouses with some men. I still don't understand why he didn't flee well before the Soviet Army took Dresden."

Schorrer gave it some thought. "Taking off wouldn't have been easy for him. He was quite well-known. They would've accused him of desertion, then tried and shot him on the spot. Maybe he only had a moment to decide and got it wrong. It's actually not a bad idea, faking one's death, since at the time it was certain the Russians would be advancing on Dresden within a few days. No one could've predicted that the Russians would get bogged down in Breslau first and then set their sights on Berlin. How was he supposed to resurface after? And what would've happened to his wife and son? It all seems plausible to me."

Heller reached for the water jug and poured himself some. He felt sapped, unbelievably tired, and his stomach ached from hunger.

"But would the whole family have known about the murders?" Heller asked. "Would Magdalena Klepp have allowed her son or her husband to murder like that?"

"Well, some women can show even less mercy than men," Schorrer said.

"And where is Irma Braune? Shouldn't we have found her in Klepp's house?"

"Irma Braune? Who's that?"

Heller shook his head. He had no energy to explain.

"So I hear the Russians hauled you away today too?" he asked instead.

"They did. And everyone thinks it's your fault."

Schorrer tapped at his desk pad.

Which explains all the reserved behavior, Heller thought.

"It wasn't me. I had nothing to do with it. I was surprised myself. Was Rita Stein there too?" Schorrer straightened.

"No, she wasn't."

"Really?"

"Why? Are you interested in her?"

Heller recalled Rita Stein telling him about Schorrer's advances on her. Maybe he hadn't given up hope.

"No, I barely know her. I'm also married, by the way, been so for twenty-five years."

"I don't like that doctor," Constanze whispered.

Heller was escorting her outside. He had decided to take her home with him. For one thing, it was impossible to get back to Radebeul. For another, he was hoping to use her bicycle.

"He seems like one of them to me," she added.

"Like a Nazi?"

"That starched behavior, so affected. His detachment. I'll bet he profited from the war like the rest of them, bet he doesn't suffer from hunger, probably has plenty stored up somewhere. And he can sell medication and bandages. The other thing is, I'm surprised he didn't know my father. Görlitz is not that big of a town, and Father met with the other doctors almost every week. They came to our house, and I always used to sit and listen in. There definitely was no Schorrer among them."

"What am I supposed to do?" Heller asked.

Constanze thought about that for a while. "Probably nothing you can do. People like him, they always survive and find a way to get ahead. It's inevitable."

May 18, 1945: Late Afternoon

Karin was furious, but she tried to hide it. She eyed Heller's filthy overcoat without comment. Then she politely greeted Constanze and didn't say anything about how they now had to provide for yet another person. She set a bowl of potatoes on the table, small and cooked with the skins on.

"Did you have to?" she asked Heller later, once they were alone.

Heller took a deep breath and avoided looking at her. So Karin grabbed his chin, turned his face to hers, and made him look at her, carefully reading his eyes. "You still aren't finished with this," she said, and let go.

"No, I'm not."

"You could've been killed."

"I know."

"Where's your watch?"

"Some Russian took it."

"Nice if you could've gotten marks for it," Karin said. "For all the work you've done."

She was the only person who could criticize him for such a thing, considering all that she did for them. And Karin was still staring at him. She placed her hand on his forearm. "This going to last into the night?"

Heller took her hand. "I don't know yet. I can't stop thinking that solving the case has something to do with Klara Bellmann. I need to go back and see her relatives again."

"That night of the air raid, when I came crawling out of that cellar and you weren't there, I thought about just throwing myself into the fire."

Heller looked at his wife, held her face, and kissed her on the mouth. He stroked her hair. "But you didn't, did you?"

The wind cooled Heller's face as he rode Constanze's bicycle. She'd said he could borrow it if he needed to. Heller was wearing a light jacket from the deceased Herr Marquart's surplus of clothes. He was able to get through the various military barriers easily because of his pass—without it, a man like him wouldn't have been allowed to ride a bicycle. It was a lovely and mild evening, yet he felt uneasy. Every man standing idly on a corner could be an assassin. Every concealed hand could be carrying a weapon. Every civilian could be a lone member of Klepp's gang. Rumors about the shootout had been spreading, and he was hearing the craziest stories at the checkpoints. A whole German regiment had supposedly engaged the Russians in battle.

On his way to see the Schurigs, he took a detour around Soviet headquarters, as he didn't want to run into Zaitsev. He took Wilhelminenstrasse and Charlotten and rode Radeberger to Jägerstrasse. The buildings were mostly undamaged here, yet they lacked electricity and water, and people were filling up at public water pumps. An old man was chopping a table into firewood. Otherwise, it was only women around, wearing head scarves and dresses made from coarse fabric.

He encountered Frau Schurig in the stairway of her building, a smile flashing across her face when she saw him.

"Herr Detective Inspector, I'm so happy you made it. I'm happy about everyone who's made it! I can't help you right now, unfortunately. My husband is inside, and he's got such a bad case of fluid in his legs."

"I'd just like to take a look around Klara's room one more time," Heller said. He drew two cigarettes from his jacket.

Frau Schurig took them and slid them inside her smock. "As you like, but people are living there now. They were sent here. Very taciturn. From Breslau."

"What about the furniture?"

"All like it was. But I can't imagine what you're looking for. Oh, there was a young woman here a little while ago. She was looking for something too."

Heller leaned forward. "A young woman?"

"That's right. Today around noon. She said Klara had wanted to keep it safe for her."

"Did she find it?"

Frau Schurig nodded and waved Heller into the apartment. She led him into Klara's room, where two scared children stared with wide eyes.

"Here." Frau Schurig knelt before the wardrobe, and pulled out the larger lower drawer. "It was tacked under here, with those little kind of staples."

"What was?"

"It was cardboard, real flat."

"A folder? Hanging file folder?"

"Could have been."

"This woman, did she introduce herself?"

"It was a nurse. I think I'd seen her and Klara together once."

Nurse Rita. Rita Stein had been here? What was Klara keeping that Rita needed to have?

"Did Klara ever tell you anything, ever talk about her work?"

"Not much. She resented us for asking about her divorce papers. But you do realize we had to, didn't we? It would've been dangerous to take her in otherwise. Forbidden, wasn't it? We'd have been risking our lives."

"She didn't say anything? Nothing at all? Think about it, please."

"No, she didn't. I'm sorry."

The ferryman demanded three cigarettes from each passenger and two extra for a bicycle.

"How ya think I'm payin' for all this diesel?" he told them when they complained.

But Heller paid no attention to all the bickering on the overcrowded ferry. He was too busy putting himself in Klepp's shoes even though it wasn't getting him far. Something had to have kept the Klepps tied to the city. There had to be something else, something more than that plunder in his attic, something that had crept up to the house at night.

Heller had to push the bike across the Vogelwiese riverbank meadow and was only able to climb back on near the hospital. Was it even Rita who'd visited the Schurigs? She hadn't been at the hospital, yet hadn't been taken away by the Russians either. Did Rita have some secret that Klara knew? Could the murders of Klara and the other women be separate cases after all? Or was there more to it somehow?

Zaitsev had believed there was a clear adversary, someone who'd known about everything from the beginning. That had to have been Klepp. Either him, or his wife, or his son, or all of them together? And yet something didn't fit. It didn't fit those noises that he himself had heard. Ludwig Klepp was traumatized, fearful, submissive, and definitely a little insane. Still, he hardly seemed capable of acting without clear instructions. His spirit, his will, had been broken, whether by his father or the SS. Had Ludwig just been trying to prove himself to his father? Or was there something else that Heller had overlooked, all because the man in him had taken a liking to a certain nurse?

He climbed off the bicycle and pushed it the last hundred yards to Klepp's villa. He saw no sentries. If it were up to him, he would've had the building guarded day and night.

He waited awhile, observing the house from a distance, and only dared approach the property once the sun was slowly sinking behind Grosser Garten park. He carried the bike into the house and hauled it up the stairs. Then he began his tour.

The cellar door was still open, but there was no sense in searching the dark basement as he didn't have so much as a match on him. So he devoted himself to the ground floor. Russian soldiers had trashed Klepp's den. The Nazi flag was shredded, Hitler's bust lay shattered on the floor, and the desk had been broken open, its contents gone.

Heller clambered around the bombed rooms as well, yanking smashed furniture from the debris without knowing what he was looking for. An interior wall suddenly collapsed with a loud crash, so he let that be and went upstairs. He carefully went through each room, but there weren't any other hiding places he could see. He continued upstairs before trying the attic. The upper rooms had been cleared out, their doors left open. Rainwater had soaked into the walls and floor, wallpaper hung down, mold was growing in corners, and the floorboards had warped.

The way up to the attic was dicey, as it involved climbing over a stretch of busted wooden stairs kept in place by a single suspect piece of wood. He only made himself do it because he knew that Zaitsev had made it up to the top.

Heller first had to place his right foot on the railing so he could stretch far enough to reach the ledge above him. He pulled himself up that way and found another toehold on the protruding beam in front of him. He swung his body, and hauled himself up. He now sat up in the attic, trying, for the moment at least, not to think about how he was going to get back down. He continued on, holding on to roof beams he ducked under to reach the part of the attic where the roof was damaged and the floorboards ripped up. Here in the floor, Klepp had been storing long metal crates of weapons. Zaitsev had had to tear out a whole floorboard to open one of the crates.

Heller stood transfixed, because only now did he understand what Klepp had been up to. The crate was full of jewelry: necklaces, rings, brooches, cuff links. It wasn't just a modest cache of stolen goods; this was an actual treasure trove. Heller bent down and pulled something out that he wasn't able to recognize at first. He let it drop, disgusted. It was gold teeth. Klepp had not only been a thief—he was a killer, committing robbery homicide. Some of Constanze's parents' things might even be here among all these goods. And this was only one of at least six crates. The Klepps hadn't even bothered hiding the porcelain and silver candlesticks. They were lying in an open wooden crate, just like all the everyday, superfluous household stuff that people stowed away in the attic. If it had come out that Klepp was withholding all this from the German Reich, he would've been put on trial. So was this why he had taken off right after the air raid—because he was afraid his treasure would be discovered?

And yet this still didn't have anything to do with those women being murdered. Heller gingerly returned to the stairs, where he was now forced to realize that the way he'd come up was not the way he would have to get back down. He lowered himself over the ledge until he was hanging by his outstretched arms, then he swung back and forth until he found enough momentum to bridge the distance between the stable stretches of stairs. He let go, landed on both feet, and grabbed onto what remained of the railing, which—luckily—supported him. A sharp pain shot through his knee.

He limped back into Klepp's bedroom and went through the letters scattered on the floor, then sat down in a corner and began to read. Yet after a while he grew tired and, having learned nothing new, had to put them aside. It was too odd reading such heartfelt declarations of love from a man who was a murderer and had just died that day, all to a woman who was now sitting in jail facing a nasty future. Heller knew what the Russians did to SS men and could only imagine how they treated their women. He could assume that Magdalena Klepp was facing prison with hard labor.

The light was dimming inside. Swallows were circling the house, releasing their shrill cries. Somewhere in the distance, he could hear the hollers of drunken Russians as they happily fired their weapons into the air. Little fires flickered among the ruins. Heller felt strangely weak, alone, and depressed. That dark dungeon far below him seemed like a bad dream, waiting to drag him down.

Heller woke with a start, his legs still asleep. It was now dark outside. He heard the wind rustling leaves in the trees and whistling through exposed attic beams. He pulled himself up, massaged his numb legs, and waited for the tingling to lessen. He felt something moist on his right hand. He rubbed his palm, sniffed it, and pulled back in disgust. Then he leaned forward and ran his hand along the floor. He discovered more moist spots, from a slimy substance. He comprehended at once and froze in horror. He promptly pressed his back up against the wall, not moving for the longest time, listening. But nothing stirred. He was alone. Or so he thought.

It had been so close to him. It had watched him sleeping. Had it touched him? Smelled him? Heller tried to breathe calmly, to slow his pulse. Sweat covered his forehead, but he didn't dare wipe it away. He didn't dare do a thing.

And yet? It hadn't done anything to him. Although it had been so close. If only he had a pistol. He couldn't just remain here like this the whole night, paralyzed, hoping something would happen, that nothing would happen. His ankle was hurting already. So he started moving, slowly, silently, away from the doorway, inch by inch, to the wall with a window, across from the door. There was something on the stairway. He thought he could see a face, eyes staring at him through the bars of the railing.

"Who's there?" Heller asked.

"Ha-ah," it groaned.

"Who are you? Glöckner, is that you?"

The shadow moved, and something struck the wood of the railing. Bam, bam, bam. It was its head.

"Stop that!" Heller stayed against the wall. It gave him support, kept his back safe.

The creature began panting and crawling on all fours, away from Heller's line of sight. Then he heard it approaching again, coming around the railing. He peered around frantically for a way out, a weapon. Then it was standing in the doorway.

"Ooh! Oh-oh! Ah!" The voice rumbled and gurgled and sounded full of phlegm and snot. Saliva spattered on the floor. It kept panting.

"Go away!" Heller blurted. The bad dream was here, and he saw no chance of driving it away.

"Ooh." The figure came toward him, head lowered, its hair and beard wild and tangled, hands contorted at the joints, fingers clawing spastically, its back all crooked.

"Go away!" Heller said, and gasped.

It kept panting, laughing and crying at the same time. From the corner of his eye, Heller noticed a beam of light on the street and heard tires crunching.

"Hey, *nemets*! Max?" It was Zaitsev.

"Ah, oh!" the creature roared and swung hard, hitting Heller with a stinging blow that left him half-stunned. Then it pounded frantically on the wardrobe, pushed it over, and rushed out.

"It's coming down, Alexei, watch out!" Heller said, holding his chin. He got to his feet and staggered toward the door. Yet there it was again. It grabbed him by the jacket, lifted him up, and tried to bite his face. Its teeth were black, the stench from its throat revolting. Heller pressed his forearms to the creature's face, and it bit him on the knuckles. Then it let go of him and stormed into the next room.

Zaitsev came running up the stairs. Heller was holding his bloody hand. "The window!" he shouted at Zaitsev. A dull thud confirmed his hunch. Zaitsev stormed back down the stairs and took off in pursuit.

Heller dragged himself out to Zaitsev's jeep, which was still chugging idly, and sat in the passenger seat. Zaitsev soon came back, jumped into the vehicle, threw it into gear, and wheeled them around, the tires grazing rubble.

Heller asked, "How did you know I—"

"It occurred to me that you didn't have your watch anymore," Zaitsev explained, surprisingly calm. "But my comrade returned it to me after I asked nicely. I was going to bring it to you."

"Did you go see Karin? Did she tell you where I was?"

"You weren't there. That told me enough."

"Where are we heading?" Heller asked.

"To see Magdalena Klepp. So she can tell us about this beast."

May 18, 1945: Just before Midnight

They had no problem getting access to Magdalena Klepp. Glaring light bulbs lit up the basement corridor, and the guard opened the door to her cell. Magdalena was lying on a cot.

"My God," Heller groaned when he saw her. Her face was battered, both eyes swollen shut, blood running from her ears. Her right hand was bloated and blue. She lay doubled up under a thin blanket, her other hand pressed to her crotch.

"She, she needs to see a doctor," Heller said.

Zaitsev stood at the cot and touched her shoulder. "Frau Klepp."

She screamed in shock, pulled back, and pushed herself up against the wall in panic. Heller shoved Zaitsev aside and sat on the edge of the cot.

"Magdalena, it's me. Heller. I want to help you. But you have to tell me who this creature is. I'm not supposed to hurt him, is that right? Is that what you want?"

"Please don't hurt him," she whimpered. "He doesn't know any better."

"Who is he? Tell me!"

"My little Harry. My Harald."

"Your son?"

Magdalena felt for Heller's hand. Warm blood stuck to her fingers. "He's Hilde's son. My sister. He was such a tiny baby, and he saw the world with these unbelievably huge eyes. He's never understood a thing. Even today he doesn't understand. And yet he laughed and he cried and he was still a human being. She gave him to me so I could protect him. She trusted me with him, with her little darling. Oh, you should have seen him."

"Is he insane? Mentally retarded?"

"They would've killed him, because in their eyes he was inferior! That institution near here, up at Sonnenstein Castle in Pirna. They would've killed him. I made Rudi swear that he'd protect him. My Rudi didn't mind. He's a good man. He really would do anything for me."

Heller changed the subject. "Tell me about the dungeon in your cellar."

Magdalena moaned. Her mental agony seemed worse than her physical pain.

"We needed to lock him down there. We could barely control him anymore. You couldn't explain anything to him. He always felt such fear, he hit and he bit. He missed his mother."

"So where is your sister?"

"She's dead," wailed Frau Klepp. "She died in an air raid, in Freital. How was I supposed to explain it to him? He cried and felt such despair and was always wanting to go look for her. We had to lock him in at night. He wasn't always this angry, you have to believe me. He's only recently become this angry. Don't hurt him, please, don't hang him! He didn't really mean to kill them. He doesn't understand what he's doing. Don't kill him, please. Please give him a kiss from me. Oh, dear Lord, what have we done?"

Magdalena Klepp was beyond distraught, her face in her hands, sobbing and trembling, smearing blood all over herself.

Heller saw Zaitsev about to intervene, but he held up a hand. Then he gently pulled Magdalena's hands from her face. "But if he was locked up," he said, "how did he get—"

"I let him out whenever the air raid siren sounded. I never slid the bolt when Rudi was gone. If the bombs happened to hit us, I simply could not allow him to die in that hole. And sometimes he'd run off. We couldn't stop him. We had to go out there and search for him before Rudolf came home. Ludwig usually found him. Ludwig knew how to lure him back with chocolate. But my Harry went missing after that big nighttime raid. At first we thought he was dead. Then he came to visit at night sometimes. He brought food with him and . . . sometimes he brought home . . . arms or a leg. He'd found them in the rubble."

Heller looked to Zaitsev, who subtly shook his head. He didn't want to believe it.

Magdalena tried to sit up. "What about Rudi? Have you found him? Don't kill him!"

"He's dead," Heller said.

A terrible, nearly animal scream rose from her throat, as if her soul was trying to force its way out. "Oh God, my dear Lord. It's my fault. I made him stay here, until Harry was back for good."

"Did Rudolf know that Harry sometimes used to take off?"

Magdalena sighed. "There were two or three times, yes, when we couldn't find Harry in time before Rudi came home. So he went out and helped us catch him. It's tough to subdue him when he's afraid or angry."

Heller was now able to piece everything together into a logical picture. This was why Ludwig had run from him during the air raid that night. It was why Klepp had been so exhausted and had that scratch on his face. It was why he didn't leave the city, for the sake of his wife. It was why he had manipulated the investigation, because he'd wanted to protect Harry.

"And the young woman, Constanze Weisshaupt?"

"She was following us, obsessed. She wanted to wreck everything. We lured her into the house and knocked her down." She grabbed Heller's hand again. "They didn't torture Rudi, did they?"

Heller threw a quick glance at Zaitsev, then he shook his head.

"We will take you with us, you and Ludwig," Zaitsev said in a low voice. "We must find this Harald."

"I can't," Magdalena whispered. "I'll die."

She pushed back the blanket, and Heller saw that her lap was soaked with blood. The straw mattress was sopping from it.

Heller shot up. "She needs a doctor, now. This makes you no better than the Nazis," he fumed before Zaitsev could even shake his head. "I understand your need for revenge, Alexei, I do. That's part of being the victor, you have the power. But this is about being humane."

Only now did Heller notice that he'd grabbed Zaitsev by his jacket and was shaking him. The guard at the cell had unshouldered his rifle and stood ready to fire. Heller let go of Zaitsev's jacket, and Zaitsev yanked it down taut.

"Do you know where Auschwitz is?" Zaitsev asked Heller.

Heller was irritated the Russian had remained so calm. "In Poland," he finally said.

"I was there, in the concentration camp . . ." Zaitsev fell silent for a moment. Then he continued. "One cannot describe what happened there. If you saw it, Heller, you would never wish to be a German anymore. They killed people there. With purpose, according to a system. Their goal was to kill as many human beings as possible with the least effort and expense. And they did this right up to the day before we arrived. They did not know what to do with all the dead after a while. There were mountains of them! Mountains of dead, Heller! They were doing research on the prisoners. Performed experiments on them, tortured them. Tested how much a human being could endure. They cut off their legs and infected their wounds. There are no words for what I saw there. Because that did not belong to this world. I do not believe in

God, Heller, not as a good Communist. But I do believe in the Devil, in human form. And he wears a German uniform. There are many, many such devils. So do not tell me what is humane."

Zaitsev took a deep breath. He was having trouble acting clear-headed again. "We must catch this maniac," he said. "I will take Ludwig Klepp with me. You go with her to the doctor—I will get you a driver. Heller, you are taking full responsibility for her."

"Don't hurt him, please, don't kill him!" Frau Klepp pleaded again.

"I must have the whole region combed through. But you, Heller, must do me a favor after: Dr. Schorrer. He is mine."

"Schorrer? What does he have to do with this?"

"I have my reasons, Heller."

"Then just have him taken away."

"I do that, and Ovtcharov from the NKVD gets him. But he belongs to me! And you're on good terms with Schorrer."

"So I'm supposed to sound him out? Spy on him? Why?"

Zaitsev was already in the doorway. He came back over. "There was no large field hospital near any suburb of Warsaw. But at Auschwitz-Birkenau, there was a Berlin doctor with the name Schorrer. He applied for a transfer out at the beginning of '44, and it was granted that June. Yet there are no documents placing him in Auschwitz, no photos, just one mention in a personnel file. There will be no more honor among thieves—to borrow your own words, Herr Detective Inspector."

Droves of insects hovered around a spotlight on the hospital grounds. The diesel generators chugged away. Heller had handed the severely bat-tered Magdalena Klepp to the sentry in charge with an accompanying letter signed by Zaitsev. The man then made a call, which produced two extremely sleep-deprived nurses and a female Russian doctor who took Frau Klepp with them.

Another guard stopped Heller at the next building, but one glance at the paper he showed was enough for him to pass. Heller went up the stairs to the second floor. A night nurse approached him in the hallway.

"Can I help you?"

"Detective Inspector Heller. I need to see Dr. Schorrer."

"He's not on duty."

"Then open up his office for me."

"Well, I'm not sure if—"

"Do what I say!" Heller demanded. He needed to get Zaitsev answers. The fact that the Russian had loaned him another pistol showed just how vital the matter was to him.

The nurse obeyed, opened up the office, and went swiftly on her way.

Heller switched on the light and began searching Schorrer's desk and cabinets. He found numerous documents about medical matters as well as instructions and guidelines from the Red Army that had been translated into German. Next to nothing personal. Under a stack of forms, he spotted a few faded photographs from the First World War. He could barely recognize Schorrer in them, assuming it was the doctor he was seeing.

He recalled his first conversation with Schorrer. The doctor's Fifth Guard Grenadiers regiment belonged to the Fourth Division, which was stationed in Berlin. Schorrer came from Görlitz, as he had told Heller. It wasn't necessarily unusual for someone from Görlitz to serve in a Berlin regiment. There were more than Dresden men in his own 101st Grenadiers.

A noise made Heller spin around. His hand automatically slid into his jacket pocket, where he had the pistol.

It was the night nurse. "Do you need help with anything? Did Dr. Schorrer forget something?" she asked.

"Forget?"

"For his trip to Berlin. For his training."

"For training? He's traveling to Berlin?"

"That's what he said when he left. Apparently the Soviets instructed him to, on short notice. Probably for political indoctrination. He had a suitcase with him."

Heller leaped up.

"Where are his quarters? Building 14, right?" he shouted, already bounding out the door.

Things were quiet around building 14. There were no guards, and the front entrance was open as it didn't have a proper door anymore. Heller entered the dim, stuffy hallway. He started. There was something on the floor. At closer inspection, he realized people were camped out, sleeping—probably those who either had no other shelter or were sick and waiting for treatment. Someone coughed, and a head raised up. Heller felt his way along to the stairway and went up to the third floor. He counted the doors there, recalling that Schorrer's room was the fourth on the left from the toilets. Here too people lay all along the hallway. He stepped over someone sleeping and knocked on the door. As a precaution, he'd drawn his pistol and kept it pressed to his pants seam.

"Quiet," someone hissed.

The door wasn't locked. "Dr. Schorrer?" Heller whispered as he entered the room. A faint ray of light came in through a crack in the window covering. He tore away the cardboard used to replace the shattered panes, and light from the spotlights beamed onto the ceiling.

The spartan room had a simple table next to a long, low wooden box covered with a mat that served as both bed and seating. The open wardrobe had been moved from the wall and emptied. When Heller peeked behind it, he discovered a false rear panel, flung open. Whatever was stored back there, Schorrer had taken it with him and made a break for it. Zaitsev would not like that.

Heller sat down. His only hope was that the Russian would react rationally and not accuse him of helping Schorrer flee. Sighing, he stood back up and knocked a heel against the bed box. It sounded hollow. He pushed back the mattress, felt for the lid, and lifted it up.

He couldn't see much, but he did make out a bundle of leather. He kept the lid open with one hand, bent over the box, and pulled out the stiff material. His heart skipped a beat. He was staring into a grotesque face, pale, its mouth wide open. He recoiled in horror, the realization hitting him like scalding water: what he'd thought was leather was the withered skin of a human. He let go of the lid and jumped back in disgust, despite all his years and training in dealing with ghastly things, and then toppled halfway over the table, which scraped across the floor.

"Quiet, damn you," someone yelled from the hallway.

"Police!" Heller shouted. "Someone get some light in here, now!"

It didn't take long for a man to appear with a candle and a nurse with a kerosene lamp. The curious were now pushing their way into the room.

"Stinks in here," said one.

Heller stood facing them. "Out, all of you—only these two with lights stay. Out!"

"What is it? Something happen to the doctor?"

"Shine a light, please, but don't be frightened," Heller told the man and nurse once the others had left the room. He lifted the lid. He hesitated a second, then grabbed hold of the dried-up skin and dragged it aside. A body lay beneath it.

The nurse let out a gasp. "That's Irma," she whispered. "Irma Braune."

"Is she dead?" the man asked.

The nurse nodded but bent down anyway and felt for a pulse. She pulled back her hand. "She's cold."

"What's that?" Heller asked, pointing at a bright bundle of fabric in the box next to the dead girl. The nurse hesitated, then pulled it up and out. It was a small pile of cloths from torn-up sheets, each four inches square. They were just like the ones Heller had found in Rita Stein's room.

Heller lifted out the pile of cloths and smelled them. The faint residue of a distinctive odor lingered. "What's this smell like?" he asked, holding it up to the nurse.

"Chloroform."

Heller nodded. "Right. Someone call in the soldiers. No one comes in here. Take care of it, please."

"Will do," the nurse said.

"Where are you going?" asked the man, clearly not wanting to stay behind.

"I need to go see Rita Stein."

"She's not here," said the nurse, already halfway out the door. "She never came up after her last shift."

"She did too—she was here," interrupted a woman from the hallway. An agitated, whispering crowd of people had remained around the door.

"Never did trust that one," said someone else.

"So she was here?" Heller asked.

"Yes, I ran into her today, right here on this floor. Even though she lives one floor up," the other woman added. "I'm telling you, she was right there in Schorrer's room and making some racket too."

"They had something going on!"

"No, she'd mucked things up. The patients from the concentration camp, they croaked because of her. She was trying to pin the blame on Schorrer."

"They had something going on—I seen her come out of there before."

"True, I did see them sitting together before."

"I heard she made someone go away who tried to nab a head nurse job from her."

The people were growing more and more agitated. Everyone thought they knew the true story. Heller couldn't take it anymore. "Be quiet!" he thundered. Silence reigned in the hallway.

"You, with the lamp, come with me."

Rita's room wasn't locked either. The room was clean, with two books on the table, a jug, a cup. Heller opened her locker but found only a few items of clothing, a blanket, a piece of hard bread and equally hard cheese. In the lower compartment was a piece of soap. Heller gently ran his fingertips along the slightly dusty board.

"She took off," someone whispered. Assorted onlookers had gathered at the door again, pushing and shoving.

In a side compartment at the back of the locker, Heller discovered a little cardboard box. He carefully shook it. Something light was inside, rattling against the cardboard. He lifted the lid, and stared with interest at the long, narrow brown object, held it between his thumb and forefinger, pressed it, and smelled it.

"Dried meat," someone whispered.

Heller sucked in air. Klara Bellmann's tongue? He put it back and closed the lid.

"All right, who here last saw Rita Stein?"

A woman pushed through the group. "She was sitting on that low wall outside where the Russians always smoke. Schorrer and her were sitting together. He was holding her. I said good evening, and he nodded. They took off, I'm telling you. She even had a handcart with her."

"When was this?"

"Hardly an hour ago."

May 19, 1945: After Midnight

"Come, come. *Davai, davai!*" Heller impatiently waved the Red Army soldiers along. They spread out among the rubble, climbing over hills of debris and shining lights into cellar vaults and craters.

"Zhey can be anyplace," said a visibly bored female Russian army doctor.

"True, but they can't be far from the hospital. They have a handcart with them, plus the curfew is on. They're sure to be hiding out somewhere. You don't have any more people than this?" Heller was growing anxious and concerned. And he was angry at himself—for letting himself be so fooled.

"Zhey not leave city. All guards veell know."

"What about Zaitsev? Have you called for him?"

The doctor clearly didn't like Heller's tone. "I haff! So now, you let us do vork!"

Suddenly headlights were on them. A truck raced up and braked hard. Zaitsev jumped out and ordered everyone off the truck. Soldiers jumped down and lined up, and Zaitsev had them spread out. He then exchanged a few words with the female doctor.

"I never trusted that Rita Stein from the start," he whispered to Heller. "But you? You were in love."

"Don't go talking nonsense."

The Russian nodded. "You still are. Show it to me!" He thrust out a hand, and Heller gave him the box with Klara Bellmann's tongue. Zaitsev looked inside and snorted before handing back the box. "And yet you are still in love with her."

"I don't know what you mean," Heller said, lost in thought, his finger feeling at the rough cardboard.

"What do you think? Yesterday afternoon, when Schorrer bandaged my wound and I felt so bad after, was he trying to kill me? Maybe he put something in my water?"

"From the questions you were asking, he could've suspected you were on his trail."

"And he killed those liberated concentration camp inmates because he was afraid one of them might recognize him. Does that make sense?"

Heller nodded, thinking it over. He still wasn't sure what all this had to do with Rita Stein. What had she been up to with the doctor? What about the blood on her clothes that time Heller surprised her naked in the washroom? Had it been fresh blood? Was she only faking not feeling well? And why?

"But if that's Klara Bellmann's tongue and Rita had it, what about Harald?" Heller asked.

Zaitsev held up two fingers. "This only means there are two murderers. Rita Stein killed the Bellmann girl, that maniac Harald killed the other women."

"What about the human skin? Why was it in Schorrer's room? And the corpse of Irma Braune?"

"Heller, you still don't get it. People like Schorrer are insane. They aren't just crazy, like that Harald, they're worse. With Harald, you know what you get. Never with people like Schorrer. You had the dead bodies taken to him, and he kept the skin. Did you know that in Auschwitz they made lampshades from human skin? Maybe this Braune girl knew about Klara Bellmann."

"And Rita recognized Schorrer as one of her own?" Heller stared at the Russian in disbelief. It just didn't seem plausible.

For once, Zaitsev didn't blame Heller for being skeptical. He even very briefly placed his arm around his shoulder. "Come on, let's see if we can find Rita. Then you can ask her yourself."

It seemed unlikely to Heller that Rita Stein and Dr. Schorrer would hide out in the burned-out cellar where Erika Kaluza died, of all places, but it was his only lead, and they had to start searching somewhere. Zaitsev followed him in silence as they crossed Blasewitzer Allee and turned into fields of rubble. To find the cellar on Reissigerstrasse, they again used Trinity Church to get their bearings. Before they went inside the cellar, they drew their weapons. But the cellar was empty. Nothing pointed to Schorrer or Rita Stein being there. Where should they look now? Maybe the boathouse, where this all began? Heller went back outside. "Let's head toward the Elbe."

"There's no point, not in this darkness," Zaitsev said as he stepped out of the cellar.

"Come on, let's keep looking," Heller insisted. He was uneasy. Every second counted.

"Heller, the whole area is surrounded. Those two can't get away."

"What am I supposed to do? Just go home?"

Zaitsev snorted. "There it is: that vaunted German perseverance. Never giving up. Fighting until the bitter end."

Heller whipped around. "Stop it."

"I can't, Heller. You will all hear this for decades."

"But you can't live like that. You can't go on hating forever."

"Sure I can. When there's nothing else left. And I have nothing left. Not a thing. Understand? Nothing! No people, no place, nowhere to return, no future. Only my hate . . ."

Zaitsev fell silent. Heller couldn't tell what the young Russian was doing. Was he wiping his eyes? Heller went over to him and put a hand on his shoulder.

"I'm sorry."

Zaitsev glanced up, trying to smile. His expression suddenly stiffened. He stared into the darkness over Heller's shoulder. "Move real slow," he whispered.

Heller turned around.

"See that bent steel beam, about twenty yards away? Look to the right of it."

Against the night sky, Heller saw the silhouette of a stooped figure, swaying back and forth and pacing around like a captured animal. Harald.

"We sure could use Ludwig Klepp right now."

"He will never get out of prison," Zaitsev whispered. "And I will nab this one too."

Heller held him by the arm. "Don't kill him."

"Why, because you promised that Nazi wife?" Zaitsev shook free of Heller. The figure noticed him moving and disappeared. Zaitsev sprinted off.

"Don't shoot him, Zaitsev!" Heller said once more but stayed where he was. It made no sense to give chase through all this rubble in the dark. They should've tried to lure Harald in.

Heller heard a rattling sound to his right. He whirled around and drew his pistol, accidentally dropping the little box from his pocket.

"Harald!" he shouted. The mentally disabled young man was creeping over the rubble toward him. Only about ten yards was left between them.

"Oh-oh, ah," Harald grunted.

"Harald, stay calm. Everything's all right. You be a good boy."

Heller heard a dull sound he couldn't identify. Then he saw that Harald was banging his head against a chimney, over and over.

"Stop that!" Heller ordered, and slowly bent down to pick up the box. His fingers felt that same strange powdery sensation as on the attic handrail at the second crime scene. And he recalled those dusty streaks on the broom handle near Klara Bellmann's body. Not dust—talcum powder. Now Harald was bounding down the slope of rubble, bringing rocks and dust with him, and charging fast at Heller with his arms swinging wildly. Right before Harald reached him, Zaitsev suddenly arrived and tackled Harald. Harald bleated like an anxious calf, flailing away, crying, resisting.

"Zaitsev!" shouted Heller. "Alexei, let him go!"

"Help me!" Zaitsev had restrained Harald but couldn't get up without letting go.

"No, Alexei. He's the wrong man. It's not him!"

"Who else can it be?"

"He's not the murderer. He's like a child, has no idea what he's doing. It's just all fear. Don't you see?"

Zaitsev had his hands full keeping control of Harald. "Goddamnit, Heller, who else could it be? Come give me a hand!"

Heller went over to Harald and placed a calming hand on his head. Harald rolled his eyes to look up at him and turned more docile.

"Here, look." Heller pulled out the little box. "You yourself said it had to be someone who knew everything the whole time, who knew what I was doing and how the investigation was coming along. In the locker where I found this, there was a fine layer of dust. At least I thought it was dust. But now I see it was talcum powder—from rubber gloves. I also found it at the crime scene of the second victim. Schorrer was awfully alarmed when he discovered those bites on the third victim, and now it's clear why: those were Harald's bites." He grabbed Harald's mouth and pulled his lips open. His incisors were deformed, one of them all crooked. "Zaitsev, I'm telling you, Rita didn't have anything to do with it. It's Schorrer, and now he's got Rita under his power."

"How exactly do you know this?"

"Schorrer doesn't come from Görlitz—he's from Berlin, like Klara Bellmann. She knew things about him, and that's why he killed her. And then Rita was onto him. She'd gone to Klara Bellmann's relatives and found something there."

"But people saw them sitting together."

"Maybe Schorrer was forcing her, or she was drugged. She's in danger. Let Harald go. Maybe he can lead us to Rita."

Zaitsev shook his head. "He'll just run away."

"Alexei, I'm twice your age. Just trust me for once. Please."

Heller watched Zaitsev struggle with the decision.

"If this is true what you say, then Rita is long gone," Zaitsev said, yet he let go of Harald and stood.

Harald crawled away, but he didn't flee. He cowered in a corner, pulling his knees to his chest.

Heller approached him gently, crouching down beside him. "Harald, did you see the bad man?"

"Oh-oh!"

"Harald, do you remember? A woman? Like Magdalena, but younger?" Heller wondered how long chloroform kept a person drugged. He was certain that Schorrer wanted his victims to be conscious, with their eyes open. It might not be too late.

Harald grunted, covering his face with his hands.

Heller took a deep breath. "Can you see the blood? Do you know where the blood is?"

"Ha-ah, ha-ah." Harald slapped his hands together.

"Harald, you're a good boy. Show it to me. Show me the blood!"

They didn't have far to go. Harald moved fast and knew the way. He took shortcuts over collapsed buildings and through openings and cellars, confidently leading Heller and Zaitsev through the rubble wasteland. Soon they were standing before the destroyed St. Andreas Church on Striesener Strasse. Harald knew the entrance into the catacombs. There lay a handcart, tipped over. Harald giggled and wanted to go down inside. But Zaitsev rushed in front, grabbed him, and held his mouth shut.

"Heller, go! I'll follow!"

Heller, hesitating at first, forced his way through the narrow opening, which had been dug in order to rescue people buried under debris. A path descended deeper and deeper, to a crevice hacked out of the foundation's masonry. Heller wriggled through. It smelled like soot and stone grit. A dim beam of light showed him the way. He reached a vaulted cellar with dozens of columns and walls of roughly hewn fieldstone and sandstone. He ran, ducking, to the nearest column, crouched in its shadow, and looked around. A small light flickered—a kerosene lamp. And then he saw her, Rita Stein, tied to a column. Her head hung down, motionless. She was naked. He moved to the next column and looked around. Where was Schorrer?

"Rita," Heller called to her in a faint whisper. "Rita!"

She didn't move. Her arms had been wrenched back around the column, the ropes throttling her wrists. Seeing her from the side, Heller realized her mouth was gagged. He looked around again and decided to take the chance. He crept up to the column from behind and tried to untie the knots. They were too tight, he couldn't do it, and he didn't have a knife on him. He moved around the column, running the risk of stepping into the light, and to his relief realized that Rita was still alive. She looked up at that moment, seemed to recognize him, and, her face contorted with fear, rolled her eyes to the left.

Heller understood her warning at the last second and dove behind the column. Schorrer reeled past him, his ax barely missing Heller. The force of it threw him off balance, but he didn't fall. Schorrer recovered swiftly and lunged at Heller. Heller raised his gun to shoot, but Schorrer reacted lightning fast and hit Heller's arm with the ax handle. Heller's pistol flew into the shadows, far from his reach. Heller turned and feinted, planting his feet right as the ax blade clanged against the wall behind him. Then Heller dove out of Schorrer's reach. Schorrer spotted the pistol and picked it up.

"Goddamn snoop," Schorrer said.

"Give it up. Help's coming any second."

"Who? That crazy kid?"

"You're the crazy one, Schorrer."

"I'm not crazy at all. I'm a genius. Haven't you noticed what a wonderful thing a human body is? What it can withstand? People think a human always has to die, since we practically collapse from every little boo-boo, yet meanwhile we're being attacked by billions of bacilli day after day. It endures so much—hunger, cold, fire, pain—and your standard human is capable of enduring so much more. Isn't it marvelous beholding the body so clearly, so cleanly, finally liberated from all that bothersome skin? How it twitches and throbs under there, how the lungs rise and fall, the diaphragm quivers, how the heart beats. Ba-bump, ba-bump."

"Is it true what Zaitsev says? Is it true what you did to people in the camps?" Heller asked.

"Of course it's true. Yet not even those running the place could fully comprehend all that I can do, all that I know. There, among all those maniacs wanting to kill for killing's sake, I was like a god in the flesh, a white, radiant god. I paid homage to the human body, to this divine creation. The others were just chasing a dog gone wild, bellowing 'Heil,' trying to make me believe I was the one who was mad. Just like you, Heller. Step into the light. Come and see what I'll do with her. I'll let you take part. All it takes is a little ammonia, some adrenaline for the heart, a little Novocain."

Heller ducked down low inside the shadow of a column. He knew he had to keep Schorrer engaged in conversation, to distract him. "You killed Klara Bellmann because she knew you from Berlin. You were afraid of being found out. Why? Had you murdered others in Berlin? Are you the Berlin Slasher?"

"I don't murder. Understand? And Klara Bellmann was a nuisance. She was sticking her nose in things that didn't concern her. Asking around about me in the personnel department. She even forced her way into my room and stole my files. I simply couldn't allow that."

"You could've just thrown her into the Elbe. Her murder never would've come to light. Why leave her corpse lying there? And now you bring Rita Stein here to torture her instead of running for your life? That's something a person does when they're not in their right mind."

"I'm always in my right mind. Always!"

"You need to stop this, Schorrer."

"Why? I'm a dead man. I will complete the work I've started here. I will create the perfect being, all bones and flesh, the machine without its shell. And if you don't come out of there, I won't wait until she's conscious—I'll start slicing her up right now." Schorrer set the ax down, pulled a scalpel from his breast pocket, and held it to Rita's stomach. Rita's eyes opened wide, wild with panic.

This was the moment. Heller came out from hiding.

He suddenly heard grunting and giggling near him.

"Oh-oh!" echoed through the cellar.

Schorrer whirled around. "Not you again," he screamed. "You idiot!"

Heller tried to grab the ax, but Schorrer seized him by the shoulder and pressed the pistol into his neck. Schorrer shoved him toward the entrance.

Heller broke out in a sweat. He felt cold shivers down his neck, knowing that Schorrer had nothing to lose. What happened to Zaitsev? Was he dead? And Harald? Where was he?

"Where are you, you stupid oaf?" the doctor called out.

"Oh-oh," came a squawk from the darkness.

"Come here, you stupid ape, come here, and I'll teach you to take a bite out of one of my masterpieces."

Schorrer tightened his grip on Heller's shoulder and hauled him through the darkness, between the columns, along the narrow passage.

"Ah, ah," Harald said, suddenly right behind them. Schorrer was furious, but also less sure now. He yanked Heller around and shoved him back into the church's catacombs, facing the light streaming in.

"Is there no shred of decency left in you?" Heller said through gritted teeth.

"Those just might be your last words," Schorrer warned.

Heller had ceased being afraid. "I thought highly of you, Schorrer. I actually let myself believe you were from the old school. But now I see clearly: you're completely insane."

Schorrer clenched his jaw. "No, I'm not, for Christ's sake. That's what no one understands."

They heard more groaning. "Ah, ah, ah."

"You shut your goddamn snout!" Schorrer said, and fired into the darkness.

Two shots rang out in response. Schorrer screamed and dropped to the floor, groaning and grasping his shot-up leg. Zaitsev burst out of the shadows. *"Sobaka!"* he cursed, and kicked Schorrer's gun out of reach.

Heller froze. "You even see what you were shooting at, you moron?"

"Keeping Harald quiet took all my chocolate," Zaitsev said, grinning at Heller. "Now he wants to follow me like a puppy."

Schorrer was trying to crawl away from them.

Heller snapped out of his shock. "We need to help Rita!"

Right then Schorrer pulled out a second gun and aimed it at Rita. Heller lunged and kicked at Schorrer's wrist. Schorrer screamed out, and Heller ripped the gun from his hand. Zaitsev crouched over Schorrer and frisked him for other weapons. He rolled the doctor onto his back, to open his jacket, and discovered a small bottle of colorless liquid, needles, vials, cloths, a second knife, and a wallet.

"See to the woman. I can watch him."

Heller grabbed one of the knives and freed Rita from her restraints. He tore off his jacket and placed it around her shoulders. She tried to remain standing but collapsed, and Heller caught her. He gently lowered her to the floor and began massaging her wrists.

"Do you have anything to drink?" Rita asked in a hoarse voice.

"No, but we'll get something. Rita, I have to ask: What did you get from Klara Bellmann's room at the Schurigs'?"

"Klara, she'd lifted documents from personnel. She knew Schorrer from Berlin and thought it odd he was denying things so adamantly."

"Why didn't you tell me that before, right after Klara was murdered?"

"How could I have known he was the one? What was I supposed to tell you? And how was I to know who you were? I still don't know! Are you a Nazi? Or a Communist now?"

"I'm just Max Heller."

Rita grasped at his shoulder and pulled him close. "Sure, but what side are you on, Max?"

"No side. I'm just me. And I always will be, till the day I die."

Rita looked into his eyes, then she let go of his shoulder and stroked his stubbled face with a gentle touch.

"I'm so tired," she whispered.

Heller looked to Zaitsev. "Let's get her out of here."

The Russian only stared at him.

"What?" Heller said.

Zaitsev smiled, then nodded. "You are just Max Heller. I think I finally understand."

May 25, 1945: Midmorning

"Paper!" demanded the Russian sentry.

"Max Heller. I have an appointment with Major General Medvedev."

The sentry went into the guardhouse and telephoned. "Wait!" he ordered when he came back.

Heller waited. He'd had to wait a whole week for this appointment, so a few more minutes didn't matter. After a while, a soldier appeared and led him into Soviet headquarters. He had to wait again outside the office, and was finally let inside. The staff clerk was waved away by Major General Medvedev.

Medvedev invited Heller to sit across from him with a friendly sweep of his hand. Then he pulled out two small glasses and a bottle of vodka and poured in silence.

"Za zdorov'ye," he said, and tipped back the vodka. Heller did the same. Medvedev poured again, and they repeated the act.

Medvedev cleared his throat. "German soldiers are good soldiers. Good in battle. But not good winner. But you know, I believe, deep down here . . ." He tapped at his chest. "Germans not want to win at all. Rather they complain their fate and go down with large orchestra." The commandant laughed and filled the glasses a third time.

Heller raised a hand. "Not for me, thanks. I came by bike and haven't eaten much."

"Just this one!" declared Medvedev. Heller nodded.

"Well, well . . ." Medvedev gazed at him. "You are stubborn. Three times you ask for appointment."

"I was hoping to conduct proper questioning of Dr. Schorrer. Even though currently there's no proper jurisdiction—"

"We are jurisdiction!" Medvedev pressed a hand to his chest, looking quite content. "We passed a final sentence on Schorrer, for his crimes as concentration camp doctor. The sentence was carried out."

"Now we'll never—" Heller had to hold back a burp. The vodka was giving him trouble. "It's been nearly impossible to get connected to Berlin, even with Zaitsev's help. Yet the way it's looking, Schorrer must have been terrorizing people even before the war—in Berlin, though, admittedly, all the police officers that were investigating back then are dead, and no documents survived. There was talk of three victims, yet also seven. So now we'll never know if these can be attributed to Schorrer or not."

Medvedev gave Heller a thoughtful gaze. "Comrade Zaitsev says you are good man. And you know, Zaitsev hates Germans like only he knows how to hate! Now he is called back to Moscow. But here? Here things must continue. We will establish a new police force, even though many of my superiors do not realize this yet. But this will happen. You should consider whether you are right man for this."

"A German police force?"

"That is correct."

"Under Russian control?"

"Of course under Soviet control!" Medvedev laughed.

"Do I have a choice?"

Medvedev nodded, slightly amused. "Absolutely, yes."

Heller pushed back his chair and stood. "Well, then, I assume you'll be getting in touch when it comes to that."

Medvedev laughed again. "I also assume this. So. I don't wish to keep you. But one moment . . ." He pulled out a worn yellow envelope from a drawer and pushed it across the desktop. "This is for you."

Karin stood outside, bent over the washing tub, as Heller rode up to Frau Marquart's yard on his borrowed bicycle. Karin straightened up in surprise, not expecting him back so soon. She wiped her hands on her apron and walked up to him.

"You've been drinking, haven't you?"

Heller nodded.

"Were they civil to you?"

"They asked me whether I'm the right man for when they form a new police force."

"That was it?"

Heller shook his head. He felt a little giddy.

"But you didn't get any work?"

"Not yet," he said, and took her hand. "Come inside with me."

"But the laundry . . ."

"Come on," he said as he pulled her through the front door and into the kitchen, sat her on a chair, and gave her the yellow envelope.

Karin eyed him, then opened it, her hands shaking now.

> *Dear Mother, dear Father,*
>
> *You're alive! I've just been told the news. I only have a minute to write this. I'm interned in POW Camp #326 in Bryansk. Will be going to Moscow for a training course, volunteered for it myself. Erwin is with the Americans, in a camp near Rheinberg. He's doing well.*
>
> *All my thoughts are with you,*
> *Your Klaus*

Heller was watching his wife, how she read it, how her eyes rushed right back up to the top of the letter to read it all over again, how she held a hand to her mouth and her eyes filled with tears.

"Max! Our boys!" She jumped from the chair, laughing and crying at the same time, and threw herself into his arms.

And there they stood.

ABOUT THE AUTHOR

Photo © 2017 Jens Oellermann

Frank Goldammer was born in Dresden and is an experienced professional painter as well as a novelist. *The Air Raid Killer* is his first crime novel translated from German. He's a single father of twins and lives with his family in his hometown. Visit him at www.frank-goldammer.de.

ABOUT THE TRANSLATOR

Photo © René Chambers

Steve Anderson is a translator, an editor, and a novelist. His latest novel is *Lost Kin* (2016). Anderson was a Fulbright Fellow in Munich, Germany. He lives in Portland, Oregon.

www.stephenfanderson.com

$2_0 \gamma$